THE DAGGERS OF IRE

THE DAGGERS OF IRE

J. C. CERVANTES

HARPER

An Imprint of HarperCollinsPublishers

Library of Congress Control Number: 2023948807
ISBN 978-0-06-331207-4

Typography by Joel Tippie
24 25 26 27 28 LBC 5 4 3 2 1

First Edition

For Alex, Bella, and Jules

PROLOGUE

Like all good stories, this one begins with magic. And a pinch of disaster.

The full moon loomed, a giant fish eye floating in the black summer sky, watching closely as four young and beautiful sisters rushed toward the river for a peaceful midnight swim. But little did they realize, they weren't alone.

Curled up beneath a tree was a young man, fast asleep. The oldest sister was already wading in the cool waters of Río Místico, but the other three inched closer, curious. The second oldest sister smiled slyly and said to her younger siblings, "I dare you to kiss him."

Foolish humans that they were, the sisters leaned in one at a time and pressed their lips against his cheek.

Agitated by the touch, the young man awakened, and a

burst of silver light exploded all around him. As it faded, he roared, "How dare you humans touch me? Do you not know who I am? I am Nocturno, god of night and burden!"

The sisters recoiled in fear, realizing their terrible mistake. For legend said that no human was ever to touch a god without an invitation to do so. A terrible dread consumed them. Soon that same dread permeated the air as if the god had cast it over the whole riverbank.

The eldest sister flew onto the scene just as the god crept closer.

"Now you must die," he said.

Trembling, the sisters huddled together.

With a wave of the god's hand, four daggers shimmered in the air—blades made of dreams and nightmares, of smoke and divine breath, that only they could see. One by one, the daggers flew toward the sisters—and plunged into their hearts.

Yet they didn't die.

The god blinked. He snarled and raged.

"What's happening?" the oldest sister managed.

"The besos," he growled, "they hold a spark of my power—a power that is now swimming inside your blood. Even yours," he said to the oldest sister. "Your bond has both united you and saved you, but not entirely."

The sisters stared, confused but too afraid to speak.

"You see," the god said, "the power you stole from me is now becoming something that has never existed before." He hesitated, then added, *"Magic."*

"Magic already exists," the youngest sister countered.

"None that has been born of a god," he said. "And not with this burden."

"Burden?" the oldest echoed.

The god began to fade. His voice swept across the river. "You shall learn the wickedness of your thievery." And then he vanished altogether.

Shell-shocked, the sisters stared down at the daggers in their chests, hoping they'd disappear as the god had. But they did not.

Many moons passed. And thanks to the daggers that had become a part of them, the sisters' magic grew, as they learned that each daga carried one dominant power: Fire, Water, Earth, and Air, making them powerful brujas.

Over time, they had children and their children had children—all born with magic themselves. The sisters taught them spells and created rules to guard the magic, to keep it in check. With each passing decade the witches' descendants expanded their knowledge and power.

The sisters tried to use their magic wisely, and though each day they felt the god's ominous warning drawing closer, they buried the memory deep.

Still, the daggers held the truth.

Until one stormy night, it is said that the four original witches were enjoying a moonlit dinner when they mysteriously evaporated into thin air, never to be seen again.

And the daggers, you ask?

Those were lost too. And as time passed, the legend around them grew, as they were said to carry the ire of the ancient god, making them the most powerful and dangerous magic in the universe.

For many years that was where the story ended.

Until now.

De la muerte y la suerte no hay nadie quien se escape.
Death and luck do not discriminate.

Chapter One

Esmerelda Santos crept down the shadowy hall.

It was midnight, the hour when a dark and spectral world begins to stir. When the unseen becomes seen.

That made it the perfect time for what Esme had to do.

Gripping a paper sack, she paused outside the door.

The tall grandfather clock at the end of the hall ticked quietly. The house creaked and groaned as old and tired houses do.

She stared at the tiny silver lock on the door, her mouth twisting to the side.

Magicked.

Esme's jaw always tingled whenever there was magic nearby, no matter how small or big. It was a unique talent, for sure, but it would never make up for her own lack of real magic.

Dad must have spelled the lock, but why? Had he found out she'd been sneaking into her mother's dressing room? The one place he said no one could enter?

For once Esme was glad his powers weren't what they used to be.

She closed her hand tightly over the lock until her pulse beat against the silver, the weak spell barely resisting her.

Thrum. Thrum. Thrum.

Each beat was a magic plea to allow her inside.

Click.

Esme's mouth curled into a small smile, her pulse quickening. Was she really going to do this? Break two rules in one night? Sometimes she wished knowing that something was forbidden didn't feel like such an invitation.

With a quick glance over her shoulder, she pushed open the door and closed it behind her with a soft *swish-chk*.

The glow of the large December moon streamed through the window, flecks of dust floating through the stale air.

If Esme was quiet enough, sometimes she thought she could hear her mother's whispers, smell her rose oil. Even feel the vibration of her leftover Earth magic. At those moments her heart felt like a chiseled piece of stone that would never be smooth again.

If only she possessed that kind of magic—or even her dad's Fire magic or her older sister Lennon's Water magic—she'd be the kind of powerful bruja who could pull off this spell, but instead she could only do small things like turn off lights with a whisper or instantly change the color of her hair. Or find her way through weak hechizos like the one on the lock.

Still, if she did every single step of the spell just right, then maybe . . .

She planted herself on the velvet chair at her mother's vanity and clicked on the lamp.

The mirror had been removed by her dad after her mom died two years ago. Lenny had told her it was because ghosts could get trapped in the reflective surfaces they gazed into when they were alive, adding with an ominous whisper, "A fate worse than Oblivion."

Esme couldn't imagine anything worse than a place of utter darkness that sucked a witch's memories out of their heads and the magic out of their souls, a terrible place also known as the Garden of Shadows, or the Place of Halves. Some called Oblivion's existence a mistake, others called it a punishment for witches who used too much magic at once.

With a heavy heart, Esme stared at the half-used jars of cream, the golden brush etched with her mother's initials—*PS* for Patina Santos. She scanned the tubes of lipstick that were lined up neatly, just the way her mom had left them before the accident.

"I miss you," she whispered, tracing her fingers over a bottle of rose oil. "Dad's getting worse, and I don't know what to do, and . . ."

Her dad had changed when Patina died. He had curled up into a ball of grief and wouldn't open up for anyone, not even his own daughters. When he'd finally emerged only a few months ago, he was no longer the dad she used to know. He was different—talking to himself, drifting absently through each day. She and Lenny couldn't let anyone find out, certainly not the Witch Council. What if they thought he was an unfit parent? Or worse, an unfit witch, and they sent him away? What would happen to Esme and Lenny then?

Esme removed the contents of her sack and set them on the vanity:

  ✦ a stout purple candle burned once at a witch's funeral
  ✦ a box of spelled matches
  ✦ a tiny vial of consecrated river water
  ✦ a dead rose from her mother's garden

She took a deep breath, then another. Once she lit the candle, she knew there was no going back. If this even worked, that is.

It *had* to work.

Esme shook out her trembling hands, and before she could talk herself out of it, she struck a match and lit the candle. It sparked, then popped.

As its tall flame burned a deep bluish purple, a distant wind whistled and the scent of rotting wood permeated the air. The room grew alarmingly cold.

With a shiver, Esme touched the dead rose to the candle flame. Ribbons of green smoke curled into the air.

The witch at the botanica had been clear: "Whisper into

the smoke. Do not let your thoughts wander or you risk a disruption of the magic, which could cause terrible consequences."

With single-minded focus, Esme began. "Mom," she whispered, "can you hear me?" A useless question, as this spell was for a one-way message only.

"I—I had to tell you that Dad is getting really bad." The flame wavered, growing bigger. "I think he's not going to get better, and I know I'm not supposed to be doing this, but you told me once that the dead can reach into the real world sometimes, that they can touch a heart, or send a dream message, or . . . I don't know."

The candle blazed brighter. Esme's heart pounded with a hope that felt impossible.

"I was just thinking that if you could help Dad—"

She caught a flutter of movement out of the corner of her eye. *Don't look. Don't get distracted.*

It moved again.

Esme's eyes flicked toward it.

Something was poking out of the drawer. A bit of paper with . . .

Don't look!

Keeping her gaze on the candle, she refocused, but the paper was wiggling out of the drawer like it was alive.

She grabbed hold of the page, which was no bigger than her palm, and spread it out across the desk. Strange symbols were written across it. They looked like they were stretching, struggling as if trying to peel themselves off the page.

A chill snaked through Esme, cold and biting.

The paper shivered.

And then, because she wasn't paying attention to the burning candle, purple wax dripped onto the paper.

Flames erupted.

Esme squealed, dropping the burning paper onto the floor and dousing it with the river water.

In the same instant, the funeral candle hissed. Dark wax began to pool on the vanity, spreading and oozing, spilling onto the ground.

"What the—hey, stop!"

Esme watched in horror as the blackness mutated into a silvery, smoking trail that was now crawling up the walls, spreading like wintry branches.

The room grew icier.

And all Esme could think was *I'm going to be in so much trouble!*

Maybe Lenny could fix this. Esme cursed herself for forgetting her cell phone. She bolted to the door.

But when she tried to open it, it was locked. Panic spread through her as she tugged on the unyielding handle.

Raspy whispers filled the room. *Playing with the dark?*

Esme froze.

Do you want to see the dead? A terrible laugh echoed. *Tsk, tsk, tsk. Not even a full witch.*

"Go away!" Tears flowed down Esme's face as the silver branches slithered toward the window. Faster and faster.

Let me out.

Let me out.

Esme was about to try and stomp the thing to death when the door flew open.

"Lenny!"

"What did you do?" her sister cried, the door magically slamming behind her.

But before Esme could answer, Lenny was casting a spell, her hands dancing in front of her like a cyclone.

Water began to flow down the walls, washing the wax onto the floor, choking its life away.

The drapes flew shut, plunging the room into utter blackness.

Angry whispers rose up. *NOOOOOOOO!*

Esme watched the waxy forms writhe on the floor like dying snakes. "What's happening?" she cried.

Lenny was nearly trancelike in her focus. Her jaw was clenched, her eyes closed, her nostrils flared.

Esme watched and she wished.

Half a minute later, the wicked wax evaporated along with any traces of water.

Chest heaving, Lenny spun to Esme. Her dark eyes burned with anger.

"I . . . I can explain." Esme's chest and throat and head felt as though they were filled with sand.

Not even a full witch.

Lenny shoved a bright red lock from her face, so unlike

Esme's curly ebony hair. "You were doing illegal magic! Were you . . . summoning the dead?"

"Not summoning . . . just—"

Lenny snapped her fingers, and a piece of paper appeared in her hand. She shoved it in Esme's face. "Read this!"

Esme thrust it away. She knew it was the decree that hung in every witch's home and was visible only to those of magical descent.

> *A bruja is a guardian of Original Magic, and as such will never use their powers for personal gain, to inflict deadly harm on another, to summon the dead, or to undermine the all-knowing Council. And under NO circumstances are they to employ dark magic.*

There was also a booklet with loads of fine print that outlined details like *never open the dreamworld to dark spirits because they can pass through, never blend two spells because it always leads to disaster, always report witchly wrongdoings, and above all remember that a break in the rules could create another Oblivion.*

"Lenny, I swear I wasn't summoning the dead."

"But you did!"

"I didn't mean it. I was trying to . . ." Esme fell into the chair. Defeated tears collected in her eyes.

Lenny grunted. "Why don't you ever listen, hermanita? Why can't you follow just one rule?"

Lenny was sixteen, four years older than Esme, but half the time she acted as though she was thirty.

Esme said, "I was trying to send a message to Mom."

A few beats of silence passed between the sisters. Then, in a softer voice, Lenny said, "What was the message?"

Esme looked up at Lenny. "I wanted to tell her about Dad."

"Why would you do that?"

"She told me once that the dead can sometimes help the people they loved."

Lenny's expression wilted as she glanced at the floor and whispered, "Mom can't help Dad."

Frustration spread through Esme like wildfire. "How do you know?"

"Because you misunderstood, Es. The dead can't reach across the threshold."

"I didn't misunderstand! She told me that the dead can touch a heart or send a dream message."

Lenny sighed.

"Then what were those whispers?" Esme asked.

"The leftovers of a restless spirit."

"Leftovers?"

"Like an echo, a memory of someone. Not exactly real."

Except that they had seemed to be talking directly to Esme, which made it feel very real. She wrapped her arms around herself, furious that she had gotten distracted and let the magic be disrupted.

Then she remembered. "I saw something, Len. A piece

of paper poking out of the drawer, and it had weird symbols on it."

"So?"

"So it wasn't here last week!"

Lenny pressed her fingers into her eyes. "Tell me you didn't sneak in here last week."

"And the week before that, but that isn't the point! The point is—"

"Save it. I don't care what the point is."

"Someone's been in this room, Lenny, and it couldn't be Dad, right?" Esme began to pace. "I mean, he never comes in here and . . ."

"Even if he did, why would he leave a spell?" Lenny shook her head. "He hasn't done any real magic since . . ." She didn't need to finish the sentence, *since Mom died*, because the words were too painful, too powerful.

But not nearly as painful as watching their dad spiral deeper and deeper into some kind of black hole.

Lenny drew in a long breath. "Let me see this spell."

Cringing, Esme said, "Uh, I accidentally set it on fire."

A low groan erupted from Lenny's mouth as she dragged her hands down her face. "Listen, I know you want to help, but the anniversary is next week and Dad's not doing so great. You busting his lock and being in here would definitely freak him out even more. He might seal the room forever or maybe even cast a spell to move it to some secret corner of the house that you'd never find."

"He wouldn't," Esme argued, but truth be told, she had no idea what he would or wouldn't do anymore. It was like living with a stranger.

"He's unpredictable," Lenny said. "I mean, yeah, our old dad wouldn't do that, but . . ."

Old dad.

The kind, funny version of Siempre who had dressed up like a clown for birthdays, taught Esme how to play blackjack, packed silly notes in her lunchbox, and could hold his breath for a full two minutes.

"Thanks," Esme said. "For . . . getting rid of that thing."

"That's what older sisters are for."

"Getting rid of leftover spirits?"

Lenny slung her arm around Esme's shoulders. "Fighting monsters. Come on. Let's get out of here before Dad finds us."

They stepped into the dark hall.

Their father stood near the staircase, flicking a lighter open and closed, open and closed. His dark hair hung to his chin. He looked up at them, the glow of the flame catching in his dark eyes.

He was of Fire—a type of magic known for uncontrolled dreams, daring natures, and creative gifts. But too much fire, and the magic could burn you to ash.

Esme stiffened, expecting a lashing, but the only words that came out of his mouth were, "A storm is coming."

Chapter Two

Siempre Santos's black eyes narrowed. A muscle jumped in his chiseled jaw.

Then, as if his fatherly senses had returned, he straightened and asked, "What are you girls doing here?"

"I can explain," Lenny said so quickly her words ran together, sounding more like *ikicksplain*.

"It's my fault," Esme threw in. "Lenny didn't even know I was in there and—"

Siempre held up a hand, silencing her. "You defied me."

Esme shrank under his glare as she felt her sister inching closer to her side.

"She—we—" Lenny floundered, but Esme knew what she wanted to say. *We have a right to be here.* Except the more their dad had vanished on them, the further her usually outspoken sister had retreated into a silent part of herself.

"I just wanted to be close to Mom," Esme finally said. *And I wouldn't have had to do the spell if you would just come back to us.*

Siempre's scowl deepened. "Your mother is gone."

The words infuriated Esme. Her dad wasn't the only one who had lost everything.

"Why does this room have to be locked, anyway?" she asked. "Why does everything in this family have to be a secret?" Secrets that had begun just fifteen hours after Esme was born, when her mother cast a concealment spell over her.

For Esme had not been born a regular witch—she was a Chaos witch. Which meant that she wasn't just of Air or Fire or Water or Earth like most other brujxes, but rather had bits of every element in her blood. Which sounded sort of cool, but not when it made her an outcast.

Considered evil and wild, Chaos not only scared other brujxes—it was illegal. And so Esme's power had to be kept hidden from the Witch Council. If they ever found out, Esme's bruja memory would be drained. And without her memory, she would never have any hope of practicing or controlling magic. Only her family and her best friend, Tiago, knew her secret.

"Secrets offer protection," Siempre said, his eyes glazing over. Esme could see him falling into his dark place, and the very idea of it turned her stomach to acid.

"It's going to be cold tonight," he uttered. "We have to close all the windows, all the doors."

"Dad?" Lenny said gently.

"You'll have to stay inside for a day or two," he said, rubbing his chin. "Until the storm passes."

Esme knew the only storm coming was the one brewing inside her father. Her heart sank.

"But the motorcycle races!" Lenny cried. "They're tomorrow."

For a second she looked as though she might argue that her boyfriend, Efrain, was competing, but thankfully she stopped herself since their father knew nothing about the guy.

Siempre's eyebrows knitted together. "No races," he said. "Too dangerous."

Esme stared at her father. He was wrong to lock the room. Wrong to peel himself away from her and her sister when they needed him most.

"I saw something in there," Esme said defiantly. "A spell with strange symbols."

Siempre's blank expression didn't reveal even a flicker of surprise. "There are many spells in this house," he said. "Inside the walls and under the floorboards. Spells like to hide—they are very good at games."

He wasn't making any sense. Esme knew she should walk away, but she couldn't stop herself from arguing, "Except that it wasn't there before."

The moment the words were out of her mouth, she cringed. Hopefully he didn't register that she had been in that room more than once.

There was a beat of agonizing silence until Lenny jumped

in with, "She means that it was there one second and gone the next."

Siempre just shook his head. "Many things lost, here and gone." He fluttered his fingers like a bird's wings and slammed the door to Patina's room shut.

Lenny took Esme's hand and squeezed it, telling her to let it go. But Esme didn't want to let it go. She wanted to yell at the stranger before her, to order him to give her dad back.

Siempre turned and made his way down the stairs, muttering something about securing all the doors.

Lenny stared down the hall, scowling. Tears pooled in her eyes.

"Len—"

Lenny shook her head. "He really believes a storm is coming. He's going to lock us in. I'm going to miss the races because of you!"

Without another word, she turned and made her way into her bedroom, closing the door in Esme's face.

Esme crept into her own room, defeated.

She collapsed onto the bed and stared up at the ceiling. How had everything gone so bad? If only she hadn't gotten distracted. If only she had focused on the spell.

She sent a quick text to Lenny. I'm sorry. I'll fix it.

But there was no answer. Only a lonely silence that filled up the house.

Again.

Chapter Three

Sisters can hold grudges for forever and a day, but they can also forgive as quickly as a summer storm.

Esme was hoping her escape plan would plant her in the storm category.

But when she told Lenny her idea to sneak out of the house the next day, her rule-following sister balked. "Are you losing it?"

"It's brilliant and you know it."

"What if Dad finds out?" Lenny asked.

"He won't."

"How do you know?"

"Because I believe in fate, and we're meant to be at the races."

"Too risky. He spelled the doors—"

"With weak magic. Besides, I found an open window."

Lenny blew out an exasperated breath. "Why does that not surprise me?"

Seeing that her sister was unmoved, Esme went all in. "What if something happened to Efrain?"

Lenny gasped. "Don't say that!"

"I mean, he could get hurt and . . . I really think you need to be there. Just in case."

That did the trick.

Lenny concocted a sleeping potion made of rosemary, honey, lavender, and sea salt. Esme's job was to drop it into Siempre's evening tea.

She found him reading the paper in the library.

Esme sat across from her dad in a wicker chair, clutching the tiny bag with the potion. "Read anything good?" she asked as cheerfully as possible.

"News is rarely good," he grumbled, keeping his face hidden.

Esme's eyes darted to her dad's black mug. It was half-full. "So I was thinking," she said, scooting her chair closer, her heart stomping anxiously. "How about we all go to the races together?"

The whisper of a page turning. Esme swallowed. *Do it now. While he's distracted.*

She inched even closer and extended her hand, the potion hidden in her palm.

Just as she was about to empty it into her dad's brew, he said, "I saved an article for you."

Esme sprang back.

"About butterflies." He lowered the paper so that only his dark eyes peeked over the edge.

Esme had always been fascinated by the winged creatures, especially the monarchs, which migrated thousands of miles to warmer climates.

"Their internal compass never misguides them on their long journey," her mom used to tell her.

"I'm going to be a butterfly when I grow up," five-year-old Esme had announced.

Her mom had laughed, pulling her into a hug. "Then you'll never get lost."

Except that Esme did feel lost, and she felt alone. She knew that her mom was never coming back, but her dad could. A thick ball of guilt expanded in her stomach. She didn't know it was possible to miss someone who was sitting right in front of her. "Can we go to La Fortuna del Diablo?" she asked again. "Together? The three of us?"

"The races?" Siempre stared at his daughter, and for just a moment, she saw a glimpse of her old dad. His soft, welcoming eyes on the verge of a smile. Then he blinked, and the spell was broken. He raised the paper over his face once more and cleared his throat. "A storm is coming. But the weather section doesn't mention it. How can they not see it coming? How can no one see the truth?"

Esme sank into herself. She felt like a deflating balloon floating aimlessly across the sky. Then, remembering her mission, she leaned across the table, poured some tea into her dad's mug, and emptied the potion inside.

"More tea?" she said, extending the mug.

Without looking, he took it, sipped, then sipped some more. Minutes later he slumped in his chair, and all Esme could think was *I'm a bad daughter*.

An hour later, she and Lenny crept out of the unspelled window.

"How long will he be asleep?" Esme asked guiltily as they shimmied down the vine-choked trellis.

"Oh, for hours," Lenny said. "But I still think this is a bad idea. What if someone sees us and tells him later?"

"We could do a conceal spell, so no one recognizes us."

"Too risky. Don't you remember what happened to Taylor?"

"You mean the horse ears and whiskers?"

"And the tail, Esme. The tail!"

The sisters made their way down the cobblestone road, past sand-colored walls and brightly painted doors with brass knockers shaped like hands and eyeless faces.

Esme understood why tourists liked the place so much.

The high desert town of San Bosco sat on the bank of Río Místico. The river's sparkling purple and green stones were so bright beneath the water they looked as though they'd been dipped in melted crayons. On the other side of town was a thick forest and an arroyo whittled away by rain, wind, and time—so wide it looked as if the earth was yawning.

In the town center, narrow, crooked alleys often led to dark places and dead ends. There was also a certain crackling in the air, an electrical current that buzzed beneath the uneven roads, tickling the bottoms of your feet if you paid attention. A feeling that was both unnameable and totally unexplainable. Artists and poets had tried to capture its essence, but it would always be just out of reach for the non-magical.

As they turned the corner toward the center of town, Esme spied her best friend, Tiago, through the mob up ahead. She'd know his long, lanky form anywhere. They'd been inseparable since birth, and their moms had been best friends for forever.

Well, until forever ran out.

He was leaning against the wall of an antiques store, staring down at his phone. He let out an enormous sneeze, blowing his reddish-brown hair across his face before it settled back near his shoulders.

Esme ran over, nearly sliding into him before socking him in the arm. "Hey! I thought you were too sick to come to the races."

He pushed off the wall. "According to my mom," he groaned. "But I feel fine. Never better." He sniffled, then coughed.

Lenny scrunched up her nose in disgust. "Keep your germs to yourself."

He let out an even bigger sneeze.

"You did that on purpose!" Lenny growled.

"Absolutely did not," he said with a smirk.

Esme bit back the laugh bubbling up her throat. He had *so* done that on purpose.

"I'll meet you on the rooftop," Lenny said impatiently. "I

don't want to get stuck with a bad view."

After Lenny drifted into the crowd, Esme turned to Tiago. "So how'd you get out of the house?"

"I made a deal with my mom."

"Oh yeah?"

"What a joke, right?" he said. "We're on winter break for a whole month, and this dumb cold attacks me."

"A real monster," Esme teased.

"I'm serious, Es."

At the same moment, Tiago's mom, Clara, came out of the shop carrying two big paper sacks. She was a petite, pale woman with thin wrists and wire-rimmed glasses that were always slipping down her nose.

Esme adored her. Not only because Clara had been so close to her own mom, but because she was a memory keeper of sorts, always unfolding new stories about Patina that Esme had never heard.

"Well, hello, Esme!" Clara said with a wide grin.

Esme gave her a quick hug as Tiago took the bags from his mom. "What's in here?" he said. "An elephant skull?"

Clara laughed lightly. "Just a few odds and ends."

"Can we go now?" Tiago said. "The races are gonna start soon."

"Fine, fine," she huffed.

"You guys want to hang with us?" Esme asked.

"We don't want to spread Tiago's cold," Clara said. "So we're going to watch from a distance."

Tiago sniffled, then sneezed again, this time miserably. "I won't breathe on anyone."

"I bet he's not even contagious," Esme argued.

Clara shook her head at Tiago. "A deal is a deal, and we agreed that you could watch the races—"

"From the nosebleeds," he said, rolling his eyes.

Esme knew there would be no changing Clara's mind. She was just like Patina in that way—steadfast and bullheaded. Esme gave Tiago a sympathetic pat on the shoulder, and then she coasted into the crowd.

A minute later, she stood at the edge of the hotel roof, waiting for the cheering to begin.

Soon engines would roar and winds would shift. The black sky and blacker forest would lean close to see who would win the race.

The annual event brought the entire town of San Bosco together, all in the hopes that a lucky (risky) racer would catch the attention of one of the four original witches. For it was said that danger and courage, when mixed just right, could attract one of the long-dead sisters. A feat that would reward someone with a single wish.

But in Esme's twelve years she had never known a soul who had seen or communicated with one of the original witches. Sure, there were rumors of whispering winds and murmuring dreams, but it had been over one hundred years since the brujas had vanished . . . and yet the *what if* of it all hovered over San Bosco like a thick fog.

Of course, most of the town's residents believed the sisters were the stuff of legends, but the brujxes knew the truth.

Witchcraft and magic were as real as the frost moon slung low in the sky.

The town's flat rooftops were overflowing with onlookers, fans, gamblers, all angling for the best views of the winding narrow roads several stories below. Esme spied a few kids from school, too. They were laughing, horsing around, and taking pictures. Esme didn't socialize with them, mostly because they didn't like her or Tiago—or any witch, for that matter. Not because witches weren't cool, but because there was a natural wave of unseen energy that repelled non-witches so that they stayed with their kind. Thankfully, this wave evaporated once a witch reached adulthood, but for now it only reminded Esme that young brujxes weren't trusted to keep magical secrets.

Esme lifted her binoculars, scoping out the treacherous course the racers would take, looping through the town's streets three times, crisscrossing the steep dirt roads into the woodlands and back again.

The bets had been placed, and now, as the aroma of freshly brewed hot cocoa and melted marshmallows wafted through the December air, the crowds waited, each gambler hoping their driver would cross the finish line first.

"Can you see him?" Lenny asked.

"Who?"

"Efrain!"

"Oh, right. Not yet." Esme lowered her binoculars. "Why are you so freaked out anyhow?"

"It's his first race, and even you said he could get hurt. What if . . ."

"Uh, he's a brujo, Lenny. He can cast a spell to make his bones harder in case he falls."

Lowering her voice, Lenny said, "First, that's not a thing. And second, he can't use magic in the race. That wouldn't be fair."

"If it keeps his skull in one piece, who cares about fair?"

Lenny twisted her emerald ring nervously. A gift from their mother, it gave the wearer the power of telepathic dreaming. Lenny never took it off.

Esme glanced over her shoulder at a couple of tourists, easily identified by their puffer coats, craned necks, and oversized cameras. They always visited this time of year, intrigued by the notion of magic and wanting the proof. "And why are you whispering?"

"You know we aren't supposed to talk about magic"— Lenny scowled—"not in front of non-brujxes." Which was about 99 percent of the town's population of five thousand. That left roughly fifty practicing witches in San Bosco, all descendants of the original witches.

Over the years, most had left, gone to live in other places around the world, even though their power was weakened the farther they got from the place where magic itself had been born, the place that actually fed their powers. Esme wasn't sure why they would want to leave their magic behind. Didn't they like being witches? She'd once asked Lenny, who'd said, "Some people just want things other than magia."

It seemed odd to Esme, who had only ever wanted to have magic that didn't need to be a secret, the kind she could control. "Like what?" she'd asked.

"Like to live in a big city or to live by the sea or . . ." Her voice had trailed off, but Esme was already filling in the blanks. *Or to just be normal.*

"I'm so glad Efrain's of Air." Lenny dropped her voice to a whisper now. "If he gets thrown off his bike, he can float to the ground." And not a single non-witch would be able to see it, because their eyes weren't made for that sort of thing.

Sometimes Esme wished she had inherited Efrain's brand of magic. She liked the idea of secrets and storms, of being as light as dust with the ability to be invisible like Tiago, who was also of Air. Well, Tiago was still working on the whole invisibility thing.

Truthfully, Esme loved something about every element. Fire witches could control heat and flames, even conjure fire if they were really good. Earth witches could speak to animals and trees and flowers. They could also make things grow more beautiful than even nature intended. And Water witches had the ability to heal and to command water with a single thought, the way Lenny had last night.

Through the binoculars, Esme peered across the shimmering rooftops. Her gaze landed about four buildings over, on the only vacant rooftop in town: Chaco's place. Chaco was the keeper of San Bosco's magic, sort of. On his roof were what might look to the average person like solar panels, but they actually measured any and all magic in San Bosco and made sure it stayed within acceptable limits. The system had been put into place forever ago, when too much magic was being used all at once and supposedly created havoc—like monsters and a terrible darkness that started to grow and even breathe. Some said it was all that unruly magic that created Oblivion itself. So now it was Chaco's job to compile nightly reports on the town's magic levels for the council.

Just then old hag Malu, head of the council, emerged from the circular staircase that led to the roof, breathless, wiping her sweaty forehead with the back of her hand.

"Buenas noches, Santos girls," she said, weaving through some tourists, who looked annoyed by her intrusion. "Do you have a horse in the race?" She wore a tent dress painted with palm trees, and she was the only one in the vicinity not wearing a coat—typical for a Fire witch, whose blood ran hot.

"Horse?" Esme said, confused.

"Figure of speech," the woman said haughtily as her beady eyes drilled into Esme. "And your father? Where is he?"

Conked out, Esme thought guiltily.

"At home," she said.

"Is he unwell?" Malu asked, eyebrows raised as if she was waiting for some delicious gossip.

"He's fine," Esme threw in. "Just, you know . . . has a cold."

She hated making excuses for her dad. He should be here, cheering and celebrating with everyone else.

"Yes, there's one going around. Maybe I should pay him a visit."

"Or maybe not." Esme clamped her mouth shut. Had she really just said that out loud? One annoying—and terribly inconvenient—side effect of being a Chaos witch was saying things she wasn't supposed to, when she wasn't supposed to. Almost as if the words were bulldozing a path out of her mouth.

Lenny chuckled nervously. "We wouldn't want you to get sick."

Esme pressed her traitorous lips together, hoping Malu would think she'd just been rude or impetuous—or both. She peered through her binoculars again, anything to avoid Malu's judgy gaze. She was sure the woman could see the Chaos magic bubbling right beneath Esme's skin.

At times like these, Esme was grateful for her mother's protection spell, which hid the Chaos inside her. But in placing the spell on her daughter, Patina had also reduced any hope that Esme would ever be a full witch in command of one dominant element—and that meant she would only ever be able to do small, insignificant spells. She'd always just be a "beginner" with a deep secret.

The only silver lining was that witches didn't come into any kind of real magic or power until they turned thirteen, so she still had six months before anyone noticed her lack of a dominant element. All the brujx kids at school talked about it nonstop, excited to begin their lessons. Maybe that was why Esme had always kept a distance from other witch kids. They'd eventually catch on to the fact that she was defective, and she couldn't bear to see the pity in their faces when they found out. Which made her even more grateful for Tiago.

She scanned the forested horizon, hope-hope-hoping that Malu wouldn't actually come by the house and find Siempre knocked out by a sleep spell. Or in one of his half-dazed states. Or worse, what if Malu told him she had seen Esme and Lenny at the race?

Esme was sick of keeping so many secrets. Sometimes she felt like they were choking her.

"How was school this semester?" Malu asked.

"Great!" Lenny chimed.

Esme shrugged. She wasn't a big fan of sitting in a classroom with fluorescent lights while some cranky teacher barked information that she had no interest in memorizing. She'd rather be hiking or climbing trees or butterfly hunting.

With a snort, Malu said, "Well, you won't be able to attend the Summer Academy for Witches unless your grades are good."

"It won't matter," Esme blurted, then cringed. Sometimes she could feel the slipperiness of each letter, each word, that she had no control over. No other magic caused this kind of side effect, which was just another reminder that her Chaos was unnatural, unnecessary, and wholly undesirable.

Thankfully, Malu was too busy blabbing to notice.

"You should follow your sister's example, Esmerelda. Lenny's been such a star at the academy. Her Water prowess is truly impressive."

Esme's blood was simmering, ready to boil. Lenny must have sensed her anger, because she leaped in with, "Esme is going to be awesome!"

Lie.

"And she's showing real promise in Earth magic."

Bold lie.

A flash of green caught Esme's attention, and she swung the binoculars back over to Chaco's roof. Directly above the panels, there was a strange glow. It sort of looked like a ten-foot rope floating in the sky.

"Are you listening?" Malu's voice jerked Esme back to the conversation, and she lowered the binoculars. "Yes, um . . . be like Lenny and like school."

"I didn't say you had to like it," Malu barked. "I said to get good grades."

Esme nodded, but she had no intention of following Malu's orders. She just wanted the woman to leave so she could show Lenny what was going on at Chaco's.

Malu's eyes glittered with annoyance. "Tell your father I expect to see him at the next council meeting." And then she slipped into the crowd.

Esme quickly turned back to the glowing rope. It stretched

upward from Chaco's roof, illuminating the dark sky. "What the . . ."

Lenny snatched the binoculars away. "The race is starting."

"Look! Chaco's roof! There's a green, glowy thing. . . ."

"I don't see anything!"

"How can you not?" Esme reached for the binoculars, but Lenny jerked them up and away. They flew from her hands and smashed onto the cobblestones below.

Lenny gasped. "I'm sorry! I'll buy you new ones."

"I don't want new ones!" Esme shouted. She needed those binoculars *now.*

"Oh, quit acting like a toddler."

"*You're* the one who dropped them!"

A quick glance over to Chaco's confirmed this fact. She could still see the glowing rope, but the details were sketchy. If she could just get closer—

A starter gunshot rang out.

The roar of engines cut across the night. Cheers rose, growing steadily louder.

That was when Esme noticed Lenny's fingers vibrating with barely perceptible magic. "Lenny, don't," she warned.

Rubbing her jaw, she glanced over at Chaco's again. The strange light pulsed against the inky sky. If she got a running start, she could hop a few roofs and get close enough to check things out.

"It's just a tiny spell of protection," Lenny said. "No one will know." Water witches were always looking to heal and protect. "And besides, I'm not breaking the rules."

No, just my binoculars, Esme thought grouchily.

The motorcycles flew closer, rounding the bend like a fleet of demons. Esme and Lenny peered over the rooftop's edge. In the lead were Efrain on his electric-blue bike, and some girl on a tricked-out black motorcycle with oversized wheels and a neon-pink light-up windscreen.

Music blared. The crowd's jubilation swelled.

Esme inched back, away from her sister, who was too captivated by the race to notice her leaving. She slipped through the crowd, making her way to the northwest corner of the roof. Then, with a running start, she leaped the five feet across the gulf to the next building. She sprinted to the next edge, repeating the leaps until she was only a single rooftop away from Chaco's. Squatting low, she peered over the half wall.

Chaco was tugging at his hair, inspecting one of the panels.

The glowing rope was suspended right above him, but he didn't seem to notice.

Esme blinked. She raised her gaze.

That was when she saw that it wasn't a rope at all. It looked jagged, like a shard of glass.

And it was splitting open the sky.

Chapter Four

Darkness floated from the open seam like bits of ash.

Esme leaned closer, watching as the black flecks rose higher and higher.

In the distance, engines zoomed. Tires squealed.

Mesmerized, Esme floated her hand in front of her, reaching for the inky trail, which seemed to be made of a magic she had never felt before. Her jaw didn't tighten or tingle. No, this was more like an uninvited chill, gathering and spreading down her body.

She needed to get closer. But that meant making an impossible leap since Chaco's roof was a good ten feet from here.

Abruptly, the crowd's cheers faded to silence. Everything went terrifyingly still. . . .

And then the crack in the world closed and the darkness

floated up and over the trees, vanishing into the forest.

Esme stood, dumbfounded. Where had the darkness gone? The night air felt suddenly dangerous.

I have to tell Lenny! She ran back to her sister, every footfall echoing in the silence. Just as she returned to Lenny's side, Efrain came back around the loop.

When she saw him, Lenny let out a small cry of relief that Esme felt deep down. Efrain had fallen into third place, and at the last moment another bike zipped past and crossed the finish line ahead of him.

The crowd exploded in celebration.

"I'm sorry he lost," Esme said, "but we need to talk. You won't believe—"

"Sorry?" Lenny smiled. "He's alive!" She picked up Esme and spun her around. "Come on."

"Wait! I saw something over there at Chaco's, and I think"—Esme lowered her voice—"it was like a big crack between this world and . . . there was, like, all this darkness spilling out and it went into the woods."

Esme waited for Lenny to either raise an eyebrow in doubt or gasp in shock. But she did neither of those things. Instead, her expression morphed into the one Esme hated more than any other—a sad pout that screamed *pity.*

"I know what I saw."

Lenny planted a kiss on the side of Esme's head. "Then we can talk about it when we get home."

A few minutes later they made their way to the winner's

circle in the plaza, where the trophy ceremony had already begun. Efrain rushed over and pulled Lenny into his arms. "Almost."

"You did amazing," she told him, pushing a dark strand of hair from his face.

Efrain nodded and glanced around. Then he pulled the girls away from the crowd. "Is your dad okay?"

Lenny went stiff. "What do you mean?"

"I, um, saw something." Efrain hesitated, rubbing the back of his neck.

Lenny tugged on his arm. "Give it up already!"

"I saw your dad early this morning, before the race, I think . . ."

Before the sleep spell, Esme thought.

"He was on Chaco's rooftop," Efrain added, "doing something to the panels."

Esme sucked in a sharp breath. Touching the panels was a high crime, one that would land him in Ocho Manos—an island prison for exiled brujxes, which was supposedly named after the eight monster hands that had built it.

See? I told you something was up at Chaco's! she wanted to shout, but if her dad really had been there, she didn't want to get him in trouble.

Lenny shook her head. "How could you see that from down here?"

"I was directly across from Chaco's rooftop," Efrain said, "checking out the lay of the land before the race, you know,

to make sure I got all the bends and corners right. But, uh . . .
I'm pretty sure one of the panels is broken."

Was that why Chaco had been freaking out earlier? If a
panel was in fact broken, that meant the town's magic surveil-
lance was weak. Was that why there had been a crack in the
sky—and why no one was looking into it?

Lenny shared a worried glance with Esme. Then her face
brightened. "We should be celebrating!"

Efrain laughed, dropping the subject. "Woo-hoo! Fourth-
place winner here, folks."

Through the laughter, Esme's heart settled in her gut like
a heavy stone.

Later that night, Esme was startled awake not by the rain
trickling down her window, but by the whispers.

It had to be Lenny, probably blabbing on the phone with
Efrain. When putting a pillow over her head didn't drown it
out, Esme threw off her blankets and marched across the hall
to her sister's room.

But there was only silence.

Until her father's low voice swept up the staircase. Each
word bright and clear as if searching for her.

"Many moons ago," he said, "magic took its first breath. A
cosmic accident that occurred when four young and beautiful
sisters went for a midnight swim in a nearby river."

The whispers fell away, followed by a strange buzzing that
sounded a whole lot like magic.

Esme should have gone back to bed or crawled under Lenny's cozy comforter like she had so many times before, but she was too curious.

She had just turned to make her way downstairs when Lenny's door opened with a soft *click*.

Esme's eyes went wide. "Do you hear it too?"

Lenny frowned. "Of course I hear it."

"Shh," Esme said, worried they'd disturb something that wasn't meant to be disturbed.

"Don't shush me."

"Can you at least whisper?"

"I am whispering."

She was absolutely not.

Moments later the sisters found themselves outside their father's wood-paneled study.

The mahogany doors were closed, but a wedge of light shone beneath.

"Dad's doing magic," Esme breathed. And not some simple door-lock spell. This felt bigger.

Shaking her head, Lenny gripped Esme's hand. "We shouldn't be here."

Esme shook herself free, listening to the buzz of magic, feeling its vibration in her jaw like a wire tightening. "Don't you want to know what he's doing?" she whispered. What if it had to do with him messing with Chaco's panels?

Lenny blew a bright red curl from her face. "Not really."

"Mentirosa."

"I'm not a liar, and if we get caught . . . I'm going to cast a spell of nightmares on you."

Esme rolled her eyes. As easy as the spell was—especially for Water brujxes, who were deeply connected to the dreamworld—Lenny was unlikely to follow through. Not because it was against any rule, but because she was always launching threats at Esme, though that was all they ever were. Except for that one time she froze Esme's shower water because Esme had swiped her brush again.

"Pretty sure that's deadly harm," Esme reminded her sister, "and against the Witch Decree."

Lenny snorted. "I'll make sure the nightmares don't kill you."

The seconds ticked by, collecting into a pool of minutes.

A thump.

And then the sound of magic was gone.

Lenny pressed a thumb to one of the doors and dragged it slowly down. A streak of shimmering water appeared, sliding gently down the wood, creating a small, transparent opening for them to peer through while remaining unseen. "He's asleep."

Slowly, Lenny inched open the door, cringing when it creaked on its hinges.

Together the sisters tiptoed into the dim room. Their father was slumped in his leather club chair, snoring softly. On the table next to him was an open book.

"It's an old grimorio," Lenny breathed.

Esme traced her fingers over the page. "So?" Brujxes used spell books all the time. But before Lenny could answer, Esme felt a strange magic floating up from the book, not too different from the vibration of magic she'd felt when she saw the sky splitting open. And the paper—it looked familiar.

Lenny slapped her hand away, shooting her a warning look. "It's a grimorio de sombras!"

"A grimoire of shadows," Esme whispered, knowing she had heard the term before, though she didn't remember any details.

"Legend has it that only two ever existed, and one was destroyed decades ago," Lenny said. "The spells inside were the most powerful in the world, and came with a price no matter how benign they seemed. If you could even read them, that is."

Lenny went on to whisper that the books were written in one of many ancient secret languages, created to keep witches safe and to keep their magic secret. Now they were just dead languages that no one spoke anymore, including their dad. So why did he have this—and what was he doing with it?

"How do you know?" Esme asked.

Lenny gave her a guilty look. "I've been studying the languages, trying to understand our magic better."

"You speak this language?"

"I've been dabbling."

"So then dabble."

"There are dozens of them, and I'm only just starting on Brucera."

Esme stared at the open book as a memory surfaced. "Lenny."

"Yeah?"

"This paper . . . it looks like the one I saw in Mom's room." Keeping her place in the book, she flipped through the other pages, but it didn't look like any had been torn out.

"We should go." Lenny's voice quivered.

"Hold on," Esme said, studying the indecipherable language. She touched her fingers to the page. Instantly the words began to bleed down the paper, running together in pools of ink. They twisted and swirled and morphed until words reappeared.

Words that Esme could read.

Heart spell. To render a heart full again.

Esme blinked. "Did . . . you see that?"

"See what?"

Esme blinked and looked again. The words were as plain as day. How could her sister not see them? Then again, how could she not have seen that glowing rope above Chaco's? "The words—they mean to render a heart full again."

"What are you talking about?" Lenny asked. "You can read this?"

"Not exactly. The words kind of translated themselves."

It sounded impossible, but Esme didn't know any other way to describe it. She glanced at her father's sleeping form. *Could this spell be the answer to his emptiness?*

"You think Dad was trying to spell himself?" Lenny asked.

"I don't know."

Lenny nodded toward the grimorio. "Well, ask it."

"Is that a thing?"

"How should I know? But it sounds good," Lenny said eagerly. "If the words made themselves known to you, then maybe they'll tell you something else. Touch them again."

This time Esme let her entire hand linger on the page, pressing her weight into it.

Straightaway, she felt the spell rising up, soaking into her fingertips, warming the cold rush of her blood. Her hand trembled but she couldn't pull away. "What—what's happening?"

"It's trying to get inside you!" Lenny tried to jerk her back, but Esme was pinned in place.

She struggled against the hechizo's power, but it was no use. Lenny chanted her own spell, her voice desperate. A bitter chill swept through the room. And then the magic finally released Esme. She stumbled back, breathless.

Lenny pulled her from the room, away from the forbidden magic.

Back upstairs, the sisters crawled beneath Lenny's sheets, silent except for the sound of their rapid breathing.

Esme hesitated then said, "Do you think there really is a price for anyone who uses the forbidden spells? Like, does something bad happen?"

"No idea, but I'd never risk it." Lenny gripped the frayed comforter. "If the Witch Council found out Dad had that thing . . ." Her voice trailed off.

"Is the spell really inside me?"

Lenny stared at Esme with fear in her eyes. "I—I don't know."

"But you said . . ."

"Maybe it didn't succeed."

But Esme knew the truth she hadn't wanted to see. She could feel the spell's magic racing through her veins.

"I think . . . ," Lenny began. "I heard a story once that if a spell chooses you, then it wants you to use it."

"But I'm not even a full witch."

"Actually, that makes it easier. A full witch would be able to fight the spell."

"So it chose me because I'm *weak*?" Esme said, feeling the weight of her words.

"I didn't say that."

Esme's heart felt like a wild beast thrashing in her chest. "Where do you think he got the grimorio? And why do you think he was at Chaco's?" It was bad enough that he had broken one law, but two in the same day? What was their father up to?

"I have no idea." Lenny turned to face Esme. "But you said you saw something at Chaco's. A crack in the sky with, like, all this darkness spilling out."

Esme felt a spark inside her chest. Like something big was about to happen.

She swallowed.

"Look." Lenny shifted her weight onto a single elbow. "Are you sure you saw it? Like, super sure?"

Esme was about to say she was sure, but Lenny looked so tired and worried. Esme didn't need to add to her sister's troubles. She'd figure it out on her own.

"Well?" Lenny said.

"I'm . . . not sure," Esme lied. "It was probably nothing."

Lenny exhaled. "Well, that's good. I can only take so much mystery for one night." She plopped back onto her pillow. "You can't tell a soul about the grimorio. And don't touch that libro or look at it or even think about it."

"You said the spell wants to be used," Esme argued. "This could be the answer—"

"Don't even think about it! We don't know enough about it. I need to investigate more to be sure. Magic like that can turn dark really fast—didn't you learn anything from last night?"

To render a heart full again.

"You don't get to decide everything all the time," Esme said.

"I'm trying to keep you safe."

"I can take care of myself."

Lenny snorted, a small sound that made Esme feel even smaller. "You . . . you think I can't do the spell," Esme said.

"I think you aren't trained. I think you don't follow rules and"—Lenny's voice rose—"and, yeah, I don't think you're ready to take care of yourself. Not where magic is concerned."

Tears burned Esme's eyes. She was sick of being treated like a baby, of being underestimated.

Lenny sat up. "Be logical, Es. What if I hadn't shown up last night in Mom's room?"

"I'm not useless, and I don't need your help or your dumb protection. I don't need you!"

"Really?" Lenny's cheeks reddened. "It sure seemed like you needed me, because you blew the spell!"

"I wanted to talk to Mom!" Esme shouted. "I was trying to do something for Dad!"

Lenny stiffened, her mouth an angry line. "You're never going to talk to Mom again, and the old Dad is never coming back."

A terrible silence stretched between them. Esme blinked back the tears, struggling against the words forcing their way up her throat. "I hate you, Lenny!" She jumped up and marched to the door, hoping her sister felt terrible—no, worse than terrible. She half expected Lenny to try and stop her, but she just let Esme go.

"The spell chose me," Esme whispered as she left the room, closing the door behind her. She knew her sister hadn't heard her, which was probably for the best.

As Esme fell asleep that night, she felt a mountain of fear growing—but her hope to bring her dad back, to make her family right again, was bigger. And if Lenny was too stubborn to hope along with her, then so be it.

That was her last thought before she fell into a dream.

She was in her science classroom. Her teacher, Ms. Brees, stood near the sink, washing beakers.

"So glad to see you, Esme," she said over her shoulder. "I have your ingredient list right here."

Esme walked over to her teacher, a slight woman with bright freckles. "Ingredients?"

"To render a heart full again." She dried her hands on her apron, and then, from her pocket, she handed Esme a piece of paper with scritch-scratch notes. "It's all there. Quite simple, really."

Esme took the note and read the ingredients she would need.

- ✦ a sinner's tooth
- ✦ the claw of a crow
- ✦ a single strand of hair from a dead thief

"Number three will be a challenge," Ms. Brees said with a sympathetic sigh, "but you've always been bright, so I'm sure you'll work it out. Just be sure to think of the person whose heart you want to make full and follow the instructions exactly."

"Wait," Esme said, "Is this—are you real?"

Ms. Brees frowned. "Real? What does that even mean? I have taken the shape of someone you know to make this easier."

Esme stared, confused. Her mind darted here and there and back again as she tried to make sense of her teacher's words.

"I'm the spell," Ms. Brees said.

The one inside me, Esme thought.

Ms. Brees nodded. "Now back to the instructions."

Esme turned the page over. "There aren't any."

"You're not looking in the right place."

With that, her teacher vanished into a plume of smoke, and all that was left was the piece of paper with the heart spell in her place.

I'm the spell.

Esme picked up the paper, read the instructions, and committed each ingredient to memory just before the page exploded in her hand.

Chapter Five

It was the perfect night to rob a corpse.

The sky was a blanket of endless black, and the air was brisk and biting. It was the kind of night when anything could happen under the bright, golden moon's vigilant watch. And tonight, it looked on as Esme Santos brought a semi-warm meal to her father.

Siempre seemed more lost than ever since the disaster in her mother's room, as if each day was taking more and more of him. Thankfully, Esme had spent the last two days getting hold of the first two items of the spell to make him whole again. She was surprised how easy it had been to get a sinner's tooth. First, because everyone was considered a sinner, and second, because dentists kept teeth just so they could donate them to dental schools. And getting the claw had been as easy as popping into the botanica, a local apothecary shop hidden at the back of an alleyway that was made to look like a dead end to non-brujxes.

She found her dad in the dead rose garden, pale, drawn, with a patchy beard, his eyes so hollow Esme was sure his soul had floated away on a cloud of despair.

Esme hadn't realized a heart could break more than once, but hers did every time her dad wandered to a place she knew she could never follow. Looking at his frail form now, she was sure Efrain had been wrong. No way could her dad have been on Chaco's rooftop meddling with the magic panels. But if the town's magic detection *had* been weakened, no one seemed to know about it, and Esme now had a small window to get the last item for the spell: a strand of hair from a dead thief. Otherwise, performing the spell from the forbidden grimorio might be detected, and she couldn't take that chance.

Siempre hummed a sad tune as he clipped the ghostly blooms. Esme knew what came next—gloomy, dead arrangements all over the house.

"I brought you some dinner," she said brightly, thinking that if he didn't eat more, he might vanish. "Macaroni and cheese." That was all she knew how to make. She set the plate on a stone table.

Her dad looked up, deep wrinkles set around his vacant eyes. "Esmerelda," he said lightly.

"Do you want some iced tea with it?" Esme asked, suddenly nervous about what she had to do.

But if she was successful, they'd be a family again. And then he'd tell her about the book of shadows. About why he had it, who it belonged to, and whether or not he could read it. Lenny would have to eat crow for being such a naysayer and suck up to her little sister until Esme decided to forgive her.

Siempre shook his head, picking at his food. "Soon there will be no more roses to cut," he muttered.

Patina Santos's rose garden had become a place of nothingness, where, no matter the season, the vines were withered and the flowers were so parched they crumbled in your hands like forgotten dreams. The jardín had been dead for two long years, just like Esme's mom. Patina had been of Earth magic, a raw, grounding form of power that had allowed her to feel what trees and flowers and animals felt. Esme was sure that if her mom hadn't died, she eventually would have unspelled Esme's Chaos and taught her how to manage it, but instead all Esme had was the memory of her mom telling her, *One day you will harness all that power. You'll no longer need spells to do magic. Earth, Fire, Water, and Air will all bend to your will.*

One day.

But Esme would give all that up if she could just laugh with her dad again, or go on long drives into the forest just to count the stars and watch the sun set. The two of them used to sit on the hood of the car in the middle of nowhere, and as the sun dipped low, its colors fading, they clapped as if a cosmic curtain had lowered on the biggest miracle in the universe.

He turned his gaze to her, studying her. "Your Chaos is stirring."

Esme wasn't sure if it was the grief talking or if her dad knew something she didn't. And if it *was* just the grief, then why was her heart pounding so hard? "What's that supposed to mean?"

"I mean, I'm your father and I can feel your magic. There." He pointed at her chest and then her hair. "You came into this world with a head full of black locks."

Esme had heard the tale a million times. She had been born with hair blacker than a raven's wings, and the first night when she slept in her mother's arms, shimmering white rose petals had appeared between her newborn locks—a trait inherited from her mom, who had once told her, "The flowers are your connection to Earth magic."

Esme twisted a strand of hair, remembering. After her mom died, the enchanted petals had only reminded her dad of Patina, so Esme had convinced Lenny to spell them away so that they never grew again.

She had planned to convince Lenny to help her because she needed a Water witch to perform the heart spell. Well, after she robbed the corpse tonight for the final item. But now, with things so sour between them, Esme knew she'd have to find another Water witch.

But she'd worry about that later. She could only think about one thing at a time, and right now she needed to meet Tiago outside the Museum of the Macabre.

"Your macaroni is getting cold," she told her dad.

He nodded and took a small bite. "Bueno."

"Things are going to be better soon," Esme said with a

pinch of guilt. *After tonight, everything will be better.*

His gaze met hers. "Yes, things are going to be better than you could imagine," he said in a distant tone.

She so badly wanted to ask him whether he had messed with the magical panels, and about the split in the sky and the darkness that had spilled out. Where had it gone? And why had it appeared in the first place? But she didn't think she'd get a straight answer.

Besides, she was already late for her date with a dead guy.

CHAPTER SIX

The moon watched as Esme raced through the cobblestone streets and across the back roads of San Bosco.

She whizzed over the river's bridge, across the meadow, through tight alleyways that opened to a wide plaza, where shops and restaurants and a church stood dark and empty for the night. The high desert air smelled of mesquite and mystery.

Tiago was already there, waiting beneath the old oak tree.

Esme's mom used to tell her that she and Tiago had a special bond because they had been born under the same waxing moon, just minutes apart.

You two will have a great destiny, she'd said.

Tonight, Esme just wanted that destiny to be getting in and out of the closed museum without being caught.

Tiago stepped from the shadows. "You're late."

"You're early."

"Thieves should always be on time." Tiago's voice had started changing in the last few months, and sometimes it croaked and squeaked.

"Feeling better?" she asked. "You look . . . less sick."

"I'm good as new."

Esme felt suddenly winded and jittery. "Museum is all locked up? No one inside?" She liked how official she sounded, as if she was an experienced thief.

Tiago nodded, his dark eyes glittering in the moonlight. "And you're sure about all this, Es? Like super, super sure?"

"I'm not changing my mind."

Tiago blew out a steady breath. "I know."

"Then why'd you ask?"

"Sometimes people surprise you."

A car rumbled down the road, forcing Esme and Tiago back into the shadows. Once it was gone, she said, "You don't have to do this. I can do it myself."

Even though she didn't feel that brave, she at least wanted to sound like it.

"Except you need a Water brujx and Air brujx for the spell. Besides," he said with a crooked smile, "you seriously think I'm going to pass up breaking into a museum, stealing from a dead guy, and performing a forbidden spell?"

Esme couldn't help it. She laughed. Tiago was a thrill seeker. It was one of the things she loved most about him.

"Just remember, spells have minds of their own," Esme

said, remembering how she had messed up getting a message to her mom the other night.

Tiago rolled his eyes. "Are you seriously going to bring that up?"

It took Esme a second to catch on. "Oh—you mean the spell you botched last month. Actually, I wasn't bringing it up. You did."

Tiago had wanted the ability to talk to animals. The thing was, only Earth witches could communicate with animals, but Tiago was too stubborn to accept this, thinking he could bypass the rules of magic. Instead, he now sometimes involuntarily transformed into them—usually at the worst moments. He couldn't ask his mom for an undoing spell, since he wasn't supposed to be playing with magic. Thankfully, she worked a lot and he hadn't had any episodes in front of her . . . yet. Or maybe he was just too embarrassed about the whole mess. Either way, he'd made Esme swear not to tell anyone. She promised, but figured it was only a matter of time before he— *poof!*—changed into a pig or a goat or something else in the middle of aisle ten at the grocery store and everyone knew anyway.

But now this problem was coming in super handy, because Tiago had turned into a lizard earlier and used the opportunity to check things out at Chaco's, where he'd confirmed that one of the panels was indeed busted. But who knew for how long? Which meant they had to ándale.

"Ready?" Esme asked.

Tiago grinned, then took off toward a hidden door tucked

behind a garbage dumpster.

Esme rushed over, muscling her way in front of him. "Let's hope that old map was right," she said. They had seen it on the wall of the museum when they had cased the place just yesterday.

"Of course, it's right," Tiago said. "Didn't you read the sign next to the map? This is a historic building. That means no one can touch it."

"Ever?"

"How should I know?"

Esme adjusted the utility belt around her waist, which was packed with a screwdriver, a nail file, a tiny hammer, and a pair of scissors. Then she clicked on her flashlight and ducked inside.

The narrow tunnel was damp and chilly, and smelled like vinegar mixed with pee.

Not exactly a promising start, Esme thought.

With her flashlight, she scanned the tunnel, which ran between the old monastery and the museum, a secret passage that had been used by the monks for who knew what purpose. Now it only led to the museum. Regardless, Esme didn't care, because right now this passage was her ticket to a heart spell that was going to make her dad better, happier.

And then she could be too.

Esme had to crouch to avoid hitting her head on the ceiling. As she inched through the tunnel, the space seemed to get smaller and smaller, forcing her and Tiago to crawl the rest of the way.

In another twenty feet she would reach the storeroom of the Museum of the Macabre, where she'd get her hands on the corpse that would probably be on display by tomorrow morning. Señor Aguilar, the museum's director, had been bragging all over town that he had a mummy, reported to be a famous thief in its day. He hadn't put it on display yet, and Esme was pretty sure he was just trying to get people interested so he could raise the price of tickets.

Just then her phone vibrated. She tugged it from her pocket and glanced at the message. It was from Lenny.

Where are you, monstruito?

Esme didn't like the way she had left things with her sister. But she had been right and Lenny had been wrong, and Esme wasn't ready to forgive her just yet. Her plan was to perform the heart spell successfully—then Lenny would have to take back what she'd said about their old dad never returning to them.

Esme was half-tempted to ignore her sister's text entirely, but a piece of her felt guilty for telling Lenny she hated her. Even though it had been true in the moment. But the truth was, she loved her sister even if she sometimes wanted to pitch her off the roof.

In a tunnel with Tiago, Esme typed. What's up?

Her phone vibrated with another message, but Esme didn't get to read it, because Tiago was shoving a bony knuckle into Esme's back. "Want to get a move on? This place reeks, and I'm getting a cramp in my knee."

"Just a sec. It's Lenny." Esme glanced back at the message.

I have something to tell you.

???, Esme sent. Could it be about the grimorio? Or the heart spell, which her sister had promised to investigate? Or maybe she was ready to apologize. Esme sighed. She wished she were good at holding on to her anger, but truthfully, she hated ignoring her sister and just wanted to make up with Lenny. If she was lucky, and her sister felt bad enough, Esme might be able to talk her into acting as the Water witch for the heart spell.

When you get home, Lenny wrote.

Esme pocketed the phone, annoyed that Lenny was being so cryptic, but she couldn't let herself get distracted. She continued to crawl as trickles of water ran down the rock walls, collecting into little pools of darkness. "Hey," Tiago said, "is it me, or does that stuff dripping down the wall smell like pee?"

"Why would a wall be peeing?" Esme said. "It's just gross water."

Tiago grunted. "Maybe from a toilet." He began to hum a haunting tune, the sound echoing across the walls.

"Hey!" Esme whisper-shouted over her shoulder. "Keep it down!"

"Right," Tiago said. "Don't want to wake the dead guy."

"Har. Har. Har."

A minute later they came to a small wooden door, no bigger than a seat cushion, secured with a rusted padlock.

Figuring it would be faster to pick the thing than to search for the right spell to open it, Esme reached for a small tool on her utility belt, but Tiago was already stretching his long arm past her. His fingers touched the lock, and he whisper-chanted some words. Air was the only form of magic Esme couldn't sense, being that it was invisible as a speck of dust. Understandable, since it was made of secrets and stardust and soundless dreams.

But for Esme, the best part of Air magic wasn't the whole invisibility thing. It was the fact that it gave witches the ability to fly! She could only imagine the rush of soaring through the clouds and staring down on a life that might look small but maybe didn't have to be.

The lock trembled once, twice, and then—*click*—it popped open.

Esme's heart galloped across her chest. "We're only inches from the corpse." She took a breath. "And the last thing I need to complete the spell."

"You're sort of dramatic."

"Hey, listen," Esme said, "if I get caught, run, okay? Don't try to be some kind of hero."

Tiago smirked. "You won't get caught. And if you do, no way am I letting you get sent to Ocho Manos without me."

Esme swallowed. "No one is going to jail, Tiago! And even if I did, you have to stay on the outside so you can bust me out."

"Hey, you never know. I mean, it's an island, which means it could actually be a paradise."

"Well, I don't want to find out."

The two climbed across the threshold and into the store-room, just like the map had indicated. The dusty space was small, maybe twenty by twenty, and was filled with bizarro things like skeletons, a pile of crime scene photos, a stuffed two-headed goat, and a life-size clown statue complete with a waistcoat, bow tie, and rainbow suspenders.

Esme swung the flashlight beam around the room in search of the mummified corpse.

There. In the corner, near a shelf of jars—a wooden box with a big black *X* on its side.

As Esme made her way over, thunder rumbled in the distance.

"This place gives me the creeps," Tiago said, rubbing his arms. He stared at the coffin. "We should have brought garlic. Or a wooden stake."

"There aren't any vampires in here."

"And you know this because you've got vampire radar?"

Straightening her shoulders, Esme pushed past him. The coffin cover creaked as she lifted it to peer inside.

"Well?" Tiago said.

"No vamp."

Inside were the mummified remains of someone, its bones draped in stained, gauzy fabric. The skull was cracked above the right eye socket, and stringy white hair grew down its shoulders like cobwebs.

"So that's the dead thief," Tiago said, unimpressed. "Not much left of him."

"I just need a strand of hair, and there's plenty of that." Remembering the spell, Esme thought, *Man, I really hope you were a robber or at least a pickpocket.*

Tiago leaned closer. "Why do mummified corpses always

look terrified? Like all buggy-eyed, with wide mouths like they're screaming?"

"I think he looks mysterious. Otherworldly."

"He just looks dead to me." Tiago grimaced.

"Well, you're not looking at him right." Couldn't Tiago see that these bones had once belonged to an entire person with a beating heart that carried thousands of stories?

"You're such a weirdo." Tiago wandered over to a stack of shelves.

"Don't touch anything," Esme warned.

"Too late," he said, holding up a jar with a tiny animal skull suspended in liquid. "It's official. Señor Aguilar is a whack job."

"Can you just put that down?" Esme groaned.

"Why?" Tiago smiled and tossed the jar into the air before catching it. "You think I'm going to break it?"

"Thieves never touch stuff they aren't there to steal," Esme warned. "Don't you know anything?"

He rolled his eyes and set the jar back in its place. "You're seriously no fun."

Ignoring him, Esme blew out a steady breath and reached for the small scissors that hung from her utility belt. With a sweaty hand, she brought them closer to the mummy, doing her best not to touch the thing. "I really hope you don't mind," she whispered before cutting a single strand of hair, long and wispy. Just as she withdrew her hand and pocketed the goods, a door slammed somewhere in the museum.

She and Tiago jumped, staring at the metal door. Wasn't

the museum supposed to be locked up for the night?

Footsteps thumped across the floor. Then came a voice.

"I knew this was too easy," Tiago said. "Come on!" He was already rushing back to the passageway, and Esme was about to follow when she felt the familiar tingle in her jaw, the one that told her there was magic nearby. But why would she feel that here? Aguilar was no brujo.

She went to the door.

"Esme!" Tiago growled.

But Esme wasn't listening. She was too interested in the magic on the other side of the puerta. Pressing her ear to the cold metal, she barely made out, "Yes, I have it ready for you." That was Señor Aguilar.

There was a pause that told Esme he was likely on the phone.

He let out a low grunt of a laugh and added, "So it has begun." And then, "Finally, the hunt can begin and the witches will pay."

Hunt? And pay for what? Wait a second! How did he even know about witches? Who'd told him? They were a secret guarded by a spell that would instantly drain someone's memory if they ever saw magic or found out about the brujxes. Which meant either he'd found a way around it—or a witch had lifted the spell.

Closing her eyes, Esme pressed her fingers to the metal to get a clearer sense of the magic pulsating in her jaw. It was icy, dark. Her blood went cold, and it felt as if all the oxygen had been sucked out of the room.

The rain fell harder, pounding the roof relentlessly, as though warning Esme to get out now.

Slowly she backed away from the door—right into a table filled with glass jars.

With a gasp, she spun. A few jars were rocking back and forth, and she quickly steadied them—danger averted. Until her elbow knocked into a stack of candles. She watched in horror as they cascaded to the floor.

"Who's there?" Señor Aguilar shouted. Footsteps beat against the stone floors, fast and insistent.

The doorknob began to turn.

Esme thrust out her hands and repeated a simple chant to keep the door closed. At the very least it would buy them time. But Tiago must have been thinking the same thing, because he was casting his own magic—a muy big problem because magic was moody, and giving it two different orders at the same time always spelled disaster.

Which was exactly what happened when the door began to melt as if it was made of wax.

They bolted into the tunnel. Esme's heart plummeted. "My belt!" She must have dropped it. "It's got my name on it."

Tiago turned back to the room. "No!" Esme tried to grab his arm, and she would have succeeded if the air hadn't begun to sizzle and buzz, then—*pop*. Tiago transformed into a rat.

Before she could stop him, he darted back for her belt and, with a powerful kick, he slammed the tunnel door in her face.

CHAPTER SEVEN

Esme wanted to go back for Tiago, but she couldn't risk it. At least as a rat he'd go unnoticed. Well, until the rat was caught carrying a utility belt that identified her as the intruder.

No. Tiago was too fast and too smart.

She rushed away from Aguilar's now booming shouts, hoping Tiago had found his own exit.

When she finally emerged from the passage, the storm thrashed violently around her as lightning shredded the sky.

Esme ran to the oak tree, hiding in the shadows to wait for Tiago. Just then the rain began to glow an eerie bluish green that lit up the night sky.

Trembling, she reached her hand out to touch the glimmering rain. Cool blue drops fell into her palm, and for a nanosecond she thought she heard a whisper.

"Hello?" she said softly.

It had to be the rain lashing the leaves. She glanced around, searching for a source, searching for answers she might never find—not about the rain, not about Aguilar.

His voice echoed across her memory.

Finally, the hunt can begin and the witches will pay.

What was that supposed to mean? Which brujxes was he talking about? And who was going to do the hunting? Aguilar?

"Come on, Tiago," she prayed, pushing away dark thoughts of him being tossed into a cage, or killed, or . . .

There!

Through the glowing rain Esme caught sight of a black rat, carrying her belt in its mouth, scrambling in the opposite direction from where she stood. A moment later Aguilar crawled out of the tunnel and stumbled into a puddle. Cursing, he rose to his feet and shook his fist in the direction Tiago had gone.

Before Aguilar could notice her, Esme took off, racing through the back streets and across the park. Rain streaked down her face, into her shirt.

When she got to the far edge of town, she huddled under a tree, catching her breath, watching as the shimmering rain fell across the agave-studded canyons, thick with junipers and ponderosas.

The storm pulsed with so much magic Esme's jaw felt as though it was being tased. She could feel the power radiating across her bones.

Still panting, she sent Tiago a quick text. Call me asap. Tiago had never stayed in animal form for more than an hour, and she hoped that was the case tonight.

Esme ducked back into the storm and rushed the last two blocks past sand-colored homes with wooden gates and stone walls. Just as she rounded the corner to her crooked street, the rain halted.

A shadow, long and lean, shifted near the jacaranda tree ahead.

Esme stopped. The night felt restless.

Lightning cut the sky in a great flash. Enough to see a figure emerge from behind the tree.

"Lenny?"

Her sister didn't move.

"What are you doing here?" Esme asked.

"Es . . ." Lenny gripped her stomach.

Esme ran to her older sister. Her heart stopped cold in her chest.

There was a dagger plunged into her sister's stomach.

Shock and terror coursed through her in equal measure. And then her Chaos stirred, as if pressing with determination against the spell that had kept it hidden.

"Es . . ."

Esme's knees nearly buckled, until she saw that there wasn't any blood. Only swirls of dark smoke rising from the blade—black, like the smoke that had floated from the magic panels into the sky.

Lenny stumbled forward and collapsed onto the street. The only sound in the entire world was her voice, echoing in Esme's ears: "They . . . they . . . came . . ." Her face contorted in pain.

Just as Esme opened her mouth to scream for help, Lenny flicked her wrist and silenced her with a thread of magic. "Shh!"

Tears sprang to Esme's eyes as she knelt next to her sister, fumbling for her cell phone, wishing she had just stayed home tonight, cursing herself for even *thinking* about performing a forbidden spell.

This was her punishment.

Lenny, with surprisingly strong hands, stopped Esme. "You—you have to listen."

Don't die, Lenny. Don't you dare die on me!

Lenny pointed to the dagger, drawing Esme's gaze. "Ire," she whispered with a pained grimace. "Do you . . . remember?"

Ire. That single word was enough to remind Esme of the four legendary dagas that had pierced the hearts of the original witches. But how was that possible? And how was one of them buried in her sister's stomach now?

Esme's Chaos spread through her so forcefully, her legs went wobbly. Dizziness gripped her, and she felt herself falling over before she forced herself upright. She opened her mouth to speak, but the silence spell prevented her from uttering a single word.

Lenny winced, struggling to speak. "Ire has come for . . ."

Her eyes rolled back, and then, with a grunt, she roused herself once more, enough to say, "It's come for us all. You . . . must find . . . the . . ."

Just then the spell of silence faded, and Esme cried, "What do you mean, 'come for us all'? Where's Dad? He can help." The words sounded promising, but Esme felt a sharp twist in her gut as her sister said, "Gone. All gone."

Finally, the hunt can begin and the witches will pay.

Tears flowed freely down Esme's cheeks now.

Lenny spoke in a long, shuddering whisper, "Find . . . original witch." She clenched her jaw. "The Legend of Ire . . . get the . . ."

"What are you talking about?" Esme cried. "Who cares about how magic was born!"

Her sister's body trembled as she placed something into Esme's hand. It was her emerald ring, the one that allowed her to dream telepathically. For a split second, Esme wondered if that was what the spell recipe dream had been—a telepathic message. But from who?

Esme shook her head vigorously. She couldn't—wouldn't—take Lenny's most prized possession.

Her sister reached out to smooth Esme's hair back, her mouth moving with the words of a spell Esme wished she could understand.

"How am I supposed to find an original witch?" Esme cried. "They're all gone."

Her sister's hand fell away. As it did, Esme felt a tickling across her scalp, like tiny drops of water. Or petals sprouting. "My room . . ." Lenny grimaced. "Under . . ."

Lenny's body shimmered and began to fade.

"NO!" Esme cried.

Quickly, she reached for the dagger. She wouldn't let it take Lenny. Not now. Not ever. But when she tried to take hold of it, her hand passed right through.

A dark trail of smoke swirled around her arm as the blade vanished . . . along with her sister.

And a white rose petal fell from Esme's hair.

Chapter Eight

Esme's legs pounded the pavement, her lungs screaming, her heart aching, and her mind storming.

But she didn't stop until she got home, ran through the foyer and up the wooden stairs. Even though Lenny had said everyone was gone, Esme still hoped. "Dad?"

There was only silence.

She ran into her sister's room.

"Under the what?" she whispered, as tears rolled down her face.

Dropping onto all fours to peer under the dresser, Esme caught a whiff of the clean citrus scent of her sister, and her heart busted open all over again. Sadly, there was nothing under the dresser except for a silver scrunchy, a half pack of gum, and a cherry lip balm.

Next, Esme rushed to the bed and lifted the pink ruffle skirt. Finding her way past dust balls the size of cherry tomatoes, she felt a shoebox pushed up against the wall. A wave of dizziness clutched her as she belly-crawled through the dust, grabbed hold of the box, and pulled it free. With a dull throb in her chest, she threw off the lid, expecting something more than the yellowed, wadded sheet of paper that lay there.

Blinking back fresh tears, she unfolded the page, which was filled with unreadable handwritten symbols and codes. Esme strained her eyes staring at the encoded magic, wishing she could make sense of it, wishing she understood what this had to do with her sister's request.

Find an original witch.

Esme looked down at the ring, a row of tiny emeralds with a single black diamond in the center. Placing it on her finger, she recalled all the stories Lenny had told her about its magic.

"I can dream of anything I want," Lenny had said. "I can communicate with anyone too."

"Even a ghost?" Esme asked.

"Not yet, but maybe someday."

And that *someday* was the greatest promise between them, because if Lenny could learn to talk to ghosts, then she might be able to talk to their mom.

Once again a terrible guilt gripped Esme for the way she had left things with her sister the night before—storming from her room, telling her she didn't need her.

The paper warmed in Esme's hand, a dreamy mist filling

her head. It felt so familiar. . . . And then she remembered—this paper looked like the same kind from one of her dad's notebooks. But the loopy handwriting was unfamiliar.

She pressed her fingers into the words, hoping they would reveal themselves like the spell the other night. But all she felt was a tingle in her jaw, telling her that whoever wrote this message had used magic to disguise their handwriting too, but why?

The silence of the house was all around her, heavy and ominous.

Then came the footsteps. Quiet at first, then louder as they climbed the creaking stairs.

Esme's heart lurched violently. She jumped up. Grabbing hold of an iron candlestick from the nightstand, she searched her memory for a protection spell, but her mind was too jumbled—besides, protection spells only worked when you knew what you were up against. Even then, she'd only ever used one on a bumblebee that wouldn't leave her alone.

Whoever it is, she thought resolutely, *they aren't getting out of here without a busted jaw or a black eye.*

In trembling silence, she inched toward the half-closed door, her makeshift weapon poised. She peered through the opening. A long shadow crept up the hallway wall, growing bigger as it drew closer and closer.

A dreadful thought zoomed across Esme's mind: *What if I'm not strong enough to knock this shadow out?*

What if—

Her terror turned to desperation.

Then, out of the corner of her eye, she spied a bouquet of dead roses on the hall table.

She leaped across the hall, grabbed a bloom, and crushed the petals in her hand. Then she whispered, "Petrified bones cold as death, weak as dust."

And just as the perpetrator rounded the corner, Esme threw the crushed rose petals into his face.

He collapsed to the floor, going instantly rigid with the exception of a flailing arm—and his mouth, which was cursing up a storm.

"Tiago!" she cried.

"What's wrong with you!" he cried, his neck straining so hard his veins were popping out.

"I thought you were a killer or . . ."

His face twisted into an expression of frozen shock. Tiago lay there, lifeless as a dead bug. "My mom is gone and she . . . ," he managed through gritted teeth, "left a spelled note. Telling me that the witch hunter was in San Bosco."

"I heard Aguilar say that the hunt can begin. He must be the hunter!"

"Then he succeeded, because my mom's note also said all the witches have vanished."

Ire has come for us all.

"Vanished." Esme swallowed. Her voice quivered. "But not . . . *dead.*"

Tiago took a shaky breath. "She also said . . . Oblivion."

Esme's skin prickled. Her blood went cold. "Tiago," she whispered. "Witches who linger there too long will lose their minds. They'll become like zombies!"

Tiago's paralyzed stare did nothing to hide the terror in his eyes. "First things first. Can you undo this spell?"

"Uh . . . I don't know how."

A low groan came from Tiago's lips.

"Look, it's not my fault," Esme insisted. "You shouldn't go around skulking in the dark."

"I was worried that maybe the witch hunter was *here at your house*," he said. "I had to be careful."

"Oh." Esme sniffed. "Well, that makes sense. Do you need to blink? You look like you need to. Or are you crying? It's okay if you are."

"Esme . . . just go find a living rose and say 'reverse.' Or is it 'recoil'?"

"That's too common for something this big! Besides, we don't have any living roses." Not anymore.

Even paralyzed, Tiago looked as though he might pop a blood vessel. "Just spell the flower. Use your magic."

Esme nodded, but she had never done a return from the dead spell. Except that one time when she'd brought back a spider that she had accidentally squashed—but that had been total luck. Plus, she'd had Lenny's help. Tiago and Esme were only six months away from turning thirteen and attending the Summer Academy for Witches. Couldn't all this have happened *after* that? Maybe then they'd have a fighting chance.

"If only we had an Earth witch. And a Water one too."

Tiago grunted. "Well, you've got both magics. . . ."

But Esme was already shaking her head. It didn't work like that. Even though she had each element in her blood, she was Chaos—uncontrollable energy, wild in nature and so unpredictable. But this was an emergency.

"Es, you have to try."

Tiago was right.

"Okay. Okay." Esme grabbed another dead rose from the vase and whispered into its crumbling petals, "Beauty lives." But the rose stayed deader than dead.

"You're too freaked out," Tiago groaned. "Magic hates anxiety."

"Then you do it." Esme placed the flower in front of his mouth.

He grunted. Then, to the rose, he whispered, "Bloom big, bloom full. Live. *Live.*"

Nothing happened.

"Maybe we should do it together," Esme suggested.

"Good idea, but we have to be super confident. Magic likes that sort of thing. Ready?"

Esme twisted Lenny's ring and nodded. Together, they whispered the words.

The flower vibrated, then shimmered, its petals unfolding slowly. "It's working!" Esme cried, then threw the flower at Tiago with a simple "Reverse."

His whole body went rigid, and his eyes popped with a

look of utter agony. He threw his head back, then curled into himself.

"Tiago?"

With a pained grimace, he unfolded himself, wiped a bead of sweat from his brow, and slowly sat up.

"Are you okay?" Esme said, gripping his arm and helping him to his feet.

"Not any worse than coming back from rat-dom," he said with a forced chuckle. "Okay, maybe a little more painful, but . . ."

"And speaking of rats, you could have told me you were going to go all rogue at the museum," Esme said, her voice on the edge of a shiver.

Tiago glanced around. "Mm-hmm," he said, turning his attention back to her. "So . . . tell me everything, and don't leave anything out."

Esme quickly told him about the night's horrid events.

When she got to the Dagger of Ire part of the story, Tiago's eyes went wide as an October moon. "So that's how the witch hunter was able to beat all the brujxes."

"And the storm was so glowy . . . what do you think it means?"

"Glowy?"

"Yeah, like shimmering with dark magic. It felt like some kind of warning. But from who?"

"I didn't see anything."

Esme pursed her lips. There was no way she had imagined

that. But how was it possible that Tiago had missed it? It reminded her that Lenny hadn't seen the glowing rope over Chaco's either. "Maybe you were too hyped on adrenaline."

"Or maybe only Chaos witches can see—" He stuttered to a stop. "Esme!"

"Yeah?"

"That's why the panel was broken. Whoever did this wanted to weaken San Bosco's magic detection system, so no one would see this coming. What if we're the last ones? The last brujxes they need to catch?"

A cold ball of fear tightened in Esme's stomach. Her dad had been seen messing with the panels. Maybe he was trying to fix them, or maybe . . .

"The night of the races," she said, "there was a split in the sky and this creepy darkness floated out and into the woods."

Tiago's face went blank. "Why didn't you tell me?"

"It didn't seem important until tonight."

"Right," Tiago huffed, "sky opening. Darkness spilling out. No big deal."

"Well, I'm telling you now!"

"It has to be related. I mean, think about the timing of it."

Esme nodded. Tiago was right—whatever that blackness was, it had started all of this.

Tiago said, "Why do you think Lenny unspelled your hair? Like, how can your flowers help?"

Esme shrugged, wishing magic didn't have to be so mysterious and perplexing. "She gave me her ring."

Tiago said nothing at first and then, "Her dream one?"

Esme nodded. She flashed the paper in front of his face. "And she told me to find this, but I can't read it."

Tiago studied the sheet. Then, rubbing his chin, he said, "This isn't like any encryption I've ever seen."

"Well, we have to figure it out! I think it has to do with the Legend of Ire. Do you think . . . ," Esme began.

"What?"

"Well, remember how the legend says that whoever possesses one blade will have tremendous power, but whoever possesses all four will rule the universe?"

Tiago was already nodding. "So you think whoever is behind this wants all the blades so they can be a god?"

"It's one theory." Esme's mind was spinning with so many pieces to the puzzle, she felt suddenly dizzy. "Maybe we should go back to the beginning."

"Beginning of what?" Tiago asked.

"I think this paper is from one of my dad's notebooks, but the writing isn't his or Lenny's. Or if it is, then they disguised it with a spell."

"So let's go check out your dad's study. See if we can find one of the notebooks."

Esme pocketed the note and raced downstairs. Her footsteps echoed loudly against the hard floors as she rushed into her dad's study. Tiago was right behind her.

But none of Siempre's notebooks looked to have had a page torn from them. "Uggh!" Esme grunted in frustration.

"Hey," Tiago said, glancing around. "Show me that forbidden grimorio."

"Why?"

"Maybe there's a spell in it to help us."

"Tiago, I'm pretty sure there isn't a 'break your families out of Oblivion' spell."

He sighed dramatically. "Just show it to me."

Esme glanced around, but the book wasn't where she had seen it last.

Within seconds, she was rummaging through antique oak drawers, searching under the loose floorboards and any other hiding spot she could think of.

"I've got a better idea," Tiago said. "How about a locator spell?"

Esme shook her head. "The last time I tried one of those, I vanished the keys I was looking for."

"How do you vanish something that's already lost?"

"Well, I found the key ring, but the llaves were missing, so . . ."

Esme felt a warning prickle down her spine. She glanced at the enormous painting of Gisele, one of the original witches—a queen of beauty with long, silvery hair that glistened even on the canvas. Her sisters' images graced other areas of the house, but behind Gisele—an Air witch and the reina of secrecy—was where Esme's dad kept a magicked cubby, the perfect place to hide something.

In a heated rush, Esme tugged on the frame, which opened

on a hinge. But behind it there was only a blank wall. She pressed her hands into the wall's surface, repeating a simple reveal spell. A small, weathered door appeared, shimmering with a blue aura.

Time seemed to stop, and for a heartbeat Esme stared at the glittering door.

"Way to go, Santos," Tiago said from behind her.

His eyes flicked to the door. "It's spelled."

"And you're better at locks than I am."

"I said I've been practicing. I never said I was a master. I mean, I'm the guy who randomly turns into animals, remember?"

That was the nature of spells—some were easy, others were hard, and a vast majority were entirely maddening and complicated.

Esme leveled a pleading gaze at him. "You opened the lock at the museum. Please, try."

He blew out a long breath and grunted, "Yeah, okay . . ." He strode over, staring at the door as if it was made of pure poison. Esme's heart did a little flip as he raised his hands and pushed them against the wood, chanting under his breath. The air sparked with his magic—tiny bolts of electricity snapped, then vanished.

The door trembled and groaned; then a deep, almost robotic voice warned, "Curses upon your head."

Esme and Tiago jumped back. "That's not real, right?" Tiago frowned. "What he said about curses?"

"It's just a threat." Her dad wouldn't actually curse someone.

She grabbed Tiago's hand and dragged him back to the door. "Hey!" he cried, tugging free. "Didn't you hear the door? Or the word 'curse'?"

"I'm pretty sure some voice can't curse anyone."

"That doesn't sound like you're *extremely* sure."

"The grimorio might be able to help us like you said," Esme argued. "Do you want to find our families or not?"

Tiago gave her an incredulous look, then drew in a long breath, set both hands on the door, and whispered a chant just like he had back at the museum. His entire demeanor was one of single-minded concentration. The door trembled violently, but Tiago never released his grip. He just kept chanting.

The aura and the door began to fade.

No! Esme pressed her hands on top of his, focusing her own frequency of magic into the effort. She could feel her Chaos stirring and stirring, like a hurricane gathering speed and force.

Focus. Focus. Focus.

The air vibrated; a tremor shook the floor. Esme held her breath for one-two-three seconds . . . and the door popped open.

With a gasp, she peered inside. But there was nothing more than an empty chamber.

Chapter Nine

The disappointment was like a punch in the gut.

"Now what?" Tiago said. His voice was urgent, on the verge of panic.

"I . . . I . . . It has to be here!" Desperation flared in Esme's chest.

"We can search the whole house," Tiago said, not so reassuringly. "I'm of Air. I'm halfway decent at finding lost things."

"There isn't time. What if the hunter comes back for us?"

Esme stared at the note. The harder she willed it to reveal the message, the more her head throbbed with the effort.

She paced, trying to get rid of her jangly nerves. "We have to figure out what this message says. Something tells me it has to do with the Legend of Ire and maybe even finding one of the original witches like Lenny said."

"And then we'll get our families back?"

The question felt too big to answer. But she had to hope—and she knew hope needed space to breathe. Esme nodded.

Tiago gave her a worried look. "But neither one of us can read it. And according to my mom, all the witches are gone, so there's no one to help us."

"I'm afraid that is correct," drawled a cold, familiar voice.

Esme spun to find Señor Aguilar blocking the doorway, grinning like a cat with an overfed belly. "And now you two little brujxes will face your destinies."

Esme backed away, right into Tiago's chest. His heart was pounding, matching the wildness of her own. He gripped her hand tightly. "Where did you take our families?!" Esme demanded.

Señor Aguilar threw back his head with a laugh. His fake hair flopped back awkwardly. "You are too late. All the most powerful witches have been seized."

"But why?" Esme cried.

"Because he's a sicko," Tiago growled. Then to Aguilar, "You're the witch hunter!"

Aguilar's dark eyes glittered. "Wouldn't you like to know."

Something didn't compute. Why would someone non-magical be put in charge of rounding up witches?

Stroking his chin, Aguilar mused, "I do wonder why you two nothings weren't swept up by the magic with everyone else."

So Aguilar didn't have all the answers either. But someone

did, someone with the real power to seize the witches, and that meant that Aguilar was just a middleman doing someone else's bidding. Unless he really had found one of the Daggers of Ire.

But the daggers were supposed to be useless in non-witch hands.

The terrible truth crashed into Esme with full force: Only a witch could have pulled this off. A brujx hunting its own.

Her stomach roiled at the thought.

"You are mere whelps with no true power," Aguilar went on. "And last I heard," he said to Tiago, "you're nothing but a weaselly little rodent."

Esme fumed. "And you're nothing but a bully with a bad wig!"

Aguilar's eyes brightened with anger. Then his face fell into a fake pout. "Oh no, did I hurt the little rat boy's feelings?"

"Don't listen to him!" Esme growled.

But it was too late. The air around Tiago rippled and swelled and pulsed with heat, then—*poof!*—he morphed into a raccoon. With Aguilar distracted by the enraged animal racing toward him, Esme looked for something heavy to clock him with.

Aguilar screamed.

She spun to find Tiago's fangs gripping the man's ankle— and no matter how hard Aguilar shook his leg, Tiago wasn't letting go. If it wasn't so terrifying, Esme might have laughed.

With a howl, Aguilar grabbed Tiago and yanked him off his leg, clutching him by his skinny throat. "You filthy animal!"

Tiago's tail swished wildly; his eyes rolled to the back of his head.

"No!" Esme screamed.

She lunged, a blur of magic fueled by pure anger. Aguilar twisted, jumped, spun out of Esme's way as her Chaos erupted into a violent windstorm, blowing through the room, pushing him back with a force Esme had never manifested before. And one she didn't know how long she could hold.

The winds howled viciously as Aguilar dropped Tiago and reached for the toupee that had flown off his shiny bald head. "You little brat!"

Claws out, Tiago circled back to bite Aguilar's other ankle. "OWWWWW!"

"Run!" Esme screamed to Tiago as she bolted past their hobbling enemy, trying to maintain control of the storm long enough to slam the study doors and run out of the house into the shadows.

Tiago was right behind her. They sprinted through the park, across the Río Místico bridge, and into the woods. Only then did they stop. Esme wheezed, collapsing against a tree. Her heart thudded so loudly she was sure Aguilar would trace them.

Tiago's small raccoon eyes blinked, staring up at her.

"Are you okay?" Esme asked.

Tiago blinked again.

"Where did that storm come from?" Esme wondered, exhaling a long breath.

Tiago scurried over and planted himself next to her. He squeaked repeatedly—his version of screaming.

She patted his head. "I don't speak raccoon, Tiago."

Tail thrashing, he squeaked again.

An icy knot settled in Esme's stomach as she processed what had just happened. "Aguilar isn't alone in all this. He's not even a witch, which means someone powerful is helping him—and I think that someone is a brujx."

Tiago stood on his hind legs. His little ears perked with interest.

"And what if it was the same brujx who summoned that darkness from the sky?"

With a sigh, Esme tugged the encrypted spell from her pants pocket, staring at it so hard her vision blurred. "Do you remember the spell we used in fifth grade to show us the answers for that history test?" she said, more to herself, since Tiago couldn't answer. "Maybe we could try something like that. Give me your paw."

Tiago snorted and turned up his chin.

"Tiago! It'll give us a bigger frequency if we combine our magic."

With a sniff, he cruised over and held up a tiny paw. "Thanks," Esme said, pressing it to the page with her hand. "Okay, now imagine the symbols and words becoming readable."

She closed her eyes and brought an image of what she desired into her field of consciousness, then whispered, "All truths will set you free."

She opened one eye and peered down at the page. Not a single letter or symbol had changed. "It must be infused with some serious power," she muttered. If someone wanted to keep whatever was on this page a secret, of course they'd bind it with magic.

Tiago let out a series of squeaks, which Esme interpreted as I *could have told you that!*

Not one to be defeated easily, she tried again. She went still, breathing, thinking, thinking, breathing. *Who can help us if all the witches are gone? Who . . .*

Then, like soda fizz, an idea bubbled to the top of her mind.

"I have an idea. It might be totally out there."

Tiago's tiny nose twitched as he sniffed the air. Then, in a puff of dust, he transformed back into his human form. With a groan, he got to his feet and said, "Please, no more woo-woo ideas."

"You haven't even heard it yet."

"Yeah, but I know that look."

"We have to go see Chaco."

Chaco wasn't a full witch—or even a half or a quarter witch. More like someone with a speck of magic in his sangre, watered down over the generations. Which was what made him the perfect person to watch over the panels. It also meant he probably hadn't been hunted down.

Tiago grabbed hold of her arm, stopping her mid-stride. "What?" she asked.

"What was that storm you made back at your house?"

Esme blinked. "I didn't do it."

Tiago's gaze held hers. Unblinking, he released his hold on her. "Yeah. You did."

Fear expanded in her chest. Hearing the words fall from Tiago's mouth made her realize he was right. She had created that storm, one born of fear and rage and confusion.

Lenny hadn't just unspelled Esme's hair. She had unspelled her Chaos.

Chapter Ten

A few minutes later they arrived at the keeper's house. It was nearly midnight, and Esme hoped Chaco was still awake.

After several knocks, the door swung open and Chaco tugged them inside.

"All is amiss," he said with wild eyes, and even wilder white hair poking out in all directions. "The panels . . . the detection . . . so much darkness. Were you followed?"

Esme shook her head. "I don't think so."

Huffing, Chaco spun on his heel and rushed across a jungle-like courtyard into his bright yellow kitchen, where copper pots hung from the ceiling. A gray cat leaped off the counter and slinked under a chair with a hiss.

Esme quickly explained the night's events, and Chaco covered his face with his hands. "It's my fault. I should have reported the broken panel immediately, but how could I? I thought I could fix it before anyone knew."

"It's okay," Esme said, patting the man's skinny arm.

Chaco began to pace. "The night before the races, the panels went berserk, sparking and flashing—even moaning. There was a terrible swirl of dark mist."

"Very dark," Esme said. "And it floated into the sky."

Chaco snapped his surprised gaze to her. "Floated?"

She explained what she had seen, and with each word the man's eyes grew wider.

"Ay!" he exclaimed. "It makes sense. A panel was broken, so this entity could come into our world and do these bad things."

Esme nodded, but then a question popped into her mind that she wasn't sure she wanted to know the answer to. "But where is it now?"

Chaco stared up at the ceiling. "No idea. But if it was powerful enough to break the sky . . ." He threw his hands up. "This is dreadful. Horrific. Grim!"

Tiago said, "Right. But, uh . . . we need your help now."

"Help? Me? I can't help you." The man's face fell. "I can't even fix what's broken. Did you not hear the grim part?"

Esme produced the cryptic note. "Can you read this?"

Chaco took a quick glance, then shook his head miserably.

Esme leaned against the green tiled counter, trying to stay calm but feeling like the entire world was on fire. "Then we need to find someone who can."

Chaco sighed. "Impossible."

"It's our only choice," Tiago said.

Esme took a deep breath. "Lenny left this for a reason. It's the key to understanding what's happened, I just know it."

"Do you think she wrote it?" Chaco asked.

"I have no idea," Esme said. "The handwriting's been disguised."

Chaco frowned. "Why would she do that?"

Esme shrugged, but it didn't matter because she knew in her heart that her sister would never have told her to find something unless it was important.

Without another word Chaco hurried from the room, then came back with a magnifying glass. He peered at the message. "Well, well, well."

"What?" Esme cried.

"Look for yourself." He handed over the glass. And as Esme took it, he said, "It appears that someone traced each symbol, each letter."

Chaco was right—someone had carefully gone over every detail with another pen, one that wasn't the exact black ink as the original.

"I bet that's how Lenny read it," Tiago said. "Maybe with a spelled pen or . . ."

It was a good guess, but they couldn't be sure—and Esme wasn't about to tell them that Lenny had been dabbling in ancient languages that might or might not be illegal. Still, her sister must have been desperately curious if she'd touched the grimorio again, especially after she'd made such a big deal about telling Esme to forget it even existed.

"We think it's the answer to saving our families," Esme said. "You've been around forever. . . . I mean, you must know something, some way—"

Chaco tightened his hands into fists and then shook them out nervously, still pacing. "Oh, Dios mío . . . you will never survive."

Esme swallowed. "Survive what?"

Chaco looked up; his gaze met theirs. "You need a true Air or Water witch to break that code."

"I'm of Air," Tiago asserted.

"No," the man said. "You are too young. You have not come into your full powers, haven't even begun your training. I suppose a Fire witch could work too," he mused.

"But there aren't any witches around!" Esme hollered. How utterly wrong and unfair it was for the witches to be stolen, their fates left in the hands of two untrained witches.

The memory of Lenny's words stabbed Esme's heart. *I don't think you're ready to take care of yourself. Not where magic is concerned.*

Chaco frowned. He paced. The kitchen clock ticked slowly, as if each second was made up of two or three. "There is one place. . . ." He hesitated.

Tick. Tick.

And in between, the realization crashed over Esme like a tidal wave.

"Ocho Manos," she breathed.

At this Tiago went still. "We are *not* going to a forbidden island where the most dangerous witches in the world are locked up. Why would you even think that?"

"Tiago, we have to—they might be the only witches who can help us, who haven't been taken." A terrible thought occurred to her. "Unless they've been taken too!"

Chaco snorted. "Impossible. Too much security. Too much power. Too much darkness."

"Sounds like just the place I want to go!" Tiago snarked.

With a huff, Esme said, "I thought for sure you'd be down for something dangerous."

"Dangerous, yes. Dying? Not so much." Tiago dragged a hand down his face. "I heard about a man who delivered supplies there and came back with missing limbs, Es. *Missing!*"

"That's just a myth."

"Yeah, well, some myths are truth disguised."

"He has a point," Chaco put in.

"Fine!" Esme growled. "Do you have a better idea? Because in case you haven't noticed, we can't stay in San Bosco. Not with Aguilar out for our blood." She didn't finish her thought—*and not with the witch hunter in possession of one of the Daggers of Ire.* Why was Aguilar doing the witch hunter's bidding, anyway? What was he getting out of it—and why couldn't the hunter do it themself? Then she wondered which sister the hunter had stolen the blade from. Gisele, who was of Air? Lucinda, of Water? Triana, of Earth? Or the Fire witch, Escarlata? And more importantly, who was the witch hunter? Was it someone they knew? Or was it a stranger? Had they slipped into San Bosco through the crack in the sky?

Tiago rubbed his throat. "I hope I gave him rabies."

Esme said, "The only problem is getting to the island. I mean, I don't even know where it is."

"Plus, there's a magical boundary that keeps it hidden," Chaco said. "You need a spell." And for the first time, the man smiled.

Esme narrowed her eyes, studying him, the way his head was tilted to the right and his eyes sparkled.

"What do you know?" she asked.

"I am not worthless!" Chaco practically sang, pumping his fists into the air. He turned to Tiago gleefully. "Your mom. She came here many moons ago, shortly after you were born, and she told me that someday you would show up on my doorstep."

Esme turned to Tiago. "She must have seen the future in some lake or river or . . ."

"Yes, Agua witches are quite good at that," Chaco said. "Too bad none of them saw *this* coming."

Lenny had once told Esme that seeing the future was only as good as knowing what to look for.

Tiago scowled. "What else did she say?"

"That you would need something that was forbidden," Chaco said, "and then she paid me to hide it." He cleared his throat. "I mean, she *asked* me."

Tiago's dark eyes grew wide. "What are you talking about?"

"A transporter spell," Chaco said, tugging a cookbook from the shelf and flipping through its pages until a small piece of yellowed paper fell out. He handed it to Tiago. "It's meant to break through magical boundaries, but can be used one time only." He pushed his shoulders back. "It's forbidden," he repeated. "Banned. Prohibited." He said the words as if he was relishing being an outlaw, or at least an accessory to an almost-crime.

This particular spell gave a lot of power to one witch, and like every other hechizo, too much power made it illegal.

Tiago twisted his mouth to the side, staring at the paper, while Esme peered over his shoulder. "Why wouldn't she have just told me herself?" he asked. "Or put it in the note she left me?"

"Maybe there wasn't time to write it all out," Esme guessed.

Chaco said, "Futures are wiggly things, child. If she had told you, it might change your choices, and your choices affect your future."

Tiago wore a deep frown. "I could botch the spell—which, let's face it, that's super likely—and then we could end up somewhere else entirely."

"She wouldn't have gone to all this trouble if she didn't believe you could do it," Esme said encouragingly.

Chaco pressed his lips together firmly. "Perhaps this is why she never told you. She didn't want to give fear time to grow."

"You have to try!" Esme said. "This is the answer. We locate the island, go there, find a witch nice enough to decode this for us, and *boom*—we're in business!"

Tiago deadpanned, "Ocho Manos doesn't have nice witches."

Chaco said, "And you can't exactly knock on the door."

"We'll figure it out," Esme said, heart beating with a hope so fragile she was sure it would vanish in the next breath.

Clutching the spell, Tiago nodded. "Okay." He cast a worried stare at Chaco. "How long do they have?"

Esme understood what he was really asking. How long until Oblivion turned their families' minds to mush?

Until their minds are lost.

Chills swept over Esme as she waited for Chaco's reply. The man scrubbed a hand over his head. "I can only surmise based on hearsay, but . . ."

Esme felt like she was going to explode. "Just say it!"

"Four and three-quarters days."

"Wow," Tiago muttered. "That's super specific."

Chaco offered a timorous smile. "I do like precision. And now I must reveal another terrible bit of truth. Unless of course you would rather not know."

"There's more?" Tiago squeaked.

"Well, perhaps it won't matter to you in light of your families potentially being turned into zombies," Chaos said.

"Just say it," Esme groaned.

"If you can't save the witches, then . . ." Chaco shook his head dramatically, followed by an enormous sigh. "San Bosco will suffer too."

"What do you mean?" Esme's voice quivered.

"Witch magic keeps this place going," Chaco said with another shake of his head, this time with even more dramatic flair. Esme was sure he was trying out for some reality TV show. "Without it, the river will dry up, the earth will rot, the people will leave, and the town will fade away into nothingness. It will become a ghost town."

Esme stared in shock.

"So you're saying that the fate of the whole world is on our shoulders?" Tiago said.

Chaco smirked. "No, just San Bosco."

"How come I've never heard of this?" Esme asked.

"I believe it's one of the first courses at the academy," Chaco said, "or maybe the second."

Esme had enough worries on her heart without the possibility that her town—her home—could die.

Chaco said, "Now, before you leave on this terrible"—he cleared his throat—"I mean adventurous and very brave journey, you must leave your cell phones here."

"Why?" Esme asked, feeling sicker by the moment.

"Too easy to track you."

Reluctantly they handed over their phones.

For the first time, Tiago studied the spell. "Seriously?"

"What's wrong now?" Esme asked.

Tiago exhaled. "I'm going to need rotten water, sacred dirt, and a sad memory."

Esme had had her fill of sad memories, but there was no other choice—not for her anyway. She knew exactly where they could find all three.

And it would not be pleasant.

Chapter Eleven

El Paraíso was definitely not a paradise. Darkness consumed every inch of the witch graveyard.

It was set in the wooded hills, enclosed by a stone wall with wrought-iron fencing. Some called the old cemetery *the place of sombras* because, even during the day, the sun couldn't break through the trees to touch the dead.

At the far end stood a stone church, its walls and roof crumbling, its marble angels choked by hungry vines.

Weeds and dead leaves blanketed the moist earth, obscuring the path.

"This place is so creepy," Tiago groaned.

Esme for once agreed. She wasn't usually one to shy away from "creepy," thinking there was always something interesting to learn from the uncanny. But tonight, stalking through the darkness, carrying the memory of loss and terror, she felt the eeriness like bony fingers raking through her hair.

She and Tiago were only twelve years old, hadn't even started any formal training, and now they were supposed to save their families from Oblivion with a mysterious witch hunter on the loose? *And* their town might wither away without magic? How was any of this fair? The seriousness of the situation felt like a ton of rocks sitting on Esme's chest.

Shoving her dark thoughts aside, she managed to conjure a tiny orb of light that floated above her as she high-stepped through the weeds toward a grave with a small headstone. She felt a sudden chill. "Here's some rotten water," Esme said, lifting a vase of dried-up daisies from the grave.

Tiago shook his head and lowered his voice to a whisper. "I'm not stealing from the dead!"

"Uh, we already did," she said.

"That was a mummy, and he wasn't in a grave."

Esme held the vase up to her nose and took a whiff. "Ick! You're not stealing," she said, holding the vessel out to him. "You're doing this guy a favor. This water stinks!"

Tiago groaned, swiping the vase. "If some ghost rises up and steals *me*, I'm going to haunt you forever."

"Fine." Esme pushed a long strand of hair over her shoulder. "And you said you needed sacred dirt." She reached down, scooped up some moist dirt, and extended her open hand to Tiago, who looked away, then removed the dead daisies from their container and set them back on the grave. "Sorry," he whispered to the headstone, "but I really need this water."

Then he sprinkled the dirt in the vase, swirling it with a twist of his wrist.

"Now what?" Esme asked.

"We really are cursed," Tiago groaned.

Another breeze touched Esme's face, lifting her dark hair. But it was no ordinary wind; it carried a shiver of magic and a chorus of whispers. *"All. Is. Lost."*

Esme's heart hammered like a fist.

"What's wrong?" Tiago whispered.

Esme felt a sudden dread that turned her stomach. "Didn't you hear that? A voice—it said, 'All is lost.'"

"Nope." Tiago's solemn face tightened. "And that's pretty rude. We haven't even started yet."

"I think it's a warning. Maybe we shouldn't be here."

"Too late for that." Tiago glanced over his shoulder, then back to Esme. "We need to hustle."

Esme waited, but Tiago just stood there staring at her. "Okay?"

"So we need a sad memory."

Esme looked around at the cemetery, filled with sorrow and regret and lost dreams. "Well, it's not like we can just pluck one from a grave."

"Right. But I think it, uh, needs to be . . ." He blew out a long breath. "What I mean is that I tried thinking of one, but all of mine are sort of"—he shrugged—"not super sad, and I think for this to work it needs to be kind of miserable."

"How about a sad movie memory?"

He shook his head. "I think it has to be real. So, uh . . ."

There was that look again.

Esme caught on. "You want *my* sad memory?"

Scrunching up his face, he said, "Sorry, but yeah."

Esme didn't feel like digging up something awful—but if they wanted to save their families, she had no choice.

"Fine. I'll do it." She twisted her mouth, thinking. Feeling.

Her chest tightened as a memory surfaced. It was the night after her mom's funeral. Esme had been in bed when she awoke to voices.

She had crept downstairs to find her dad in his study, talking to someone who wasn't there.

"Death has a terrible sense of timing," he'd said angrily. "It's a particular brand of cruel."

And then he had paused, listening to the silence before adding, "Do people really think it's arbitrary? An accident? A rudderless boat wandering the endless sea? No," he said, "death is a well-aimed bullet, the sharp edge of a knife. Death is always the hit man."

Now Esme pressed the heels of her hands into her eyes to stop the tears. The memory was a fearful, messy thing that reminded her of when her dad had started to spiral.

"Hey," Tiago said, touching her arm. "The whispers are wrong, okay?"

"That's not it. I—I have a sad memory for you," she said, stepping away from his touch.

With a nod, Tiago said, "Yeah, okay. Just whisper into the vase and . . . add a tear. I mean"—he handed her the vessel—"if you can."

Esme let out a sigh. That would be the easiest task of this whole horrid night. She walked a few paces away and spoke the entire memory into the bottle as a single tear rolled down her cheek and into the potion. Then she returned it to her friend.

Tiago covered the contents with his hand, as if the magic could escape if he wasn't careful. He looked at Esme. "We're going to crush this, okay?"

"Saving our families? Or the town? Or . . ."

"All of it." He rolled his neck from side to side, then backed up. "I'm going to need some space."

As Tiago chanted his spell, Esme could still see her dad in the study that night, his defeated posture, his angry expression. What had he meant, that death is a well-aimed bullet, the sharp edge of a knife? Was it simply the beginning of his midnight ramblings, or was there something more?

Death is always the hit man, she thought. The idea of it sent her heart fluttering nervously. There was no room for mistakes. They *had* to succeed or risk losing their families forever. And the only home they'd ever known.

The air went cold. Tiago gripped Esme's hand.

As they watched, the trees and the headstones and the weeds and the dark all began to pixelate and then fade.

Esme held her breath. Could the spell actually be working? When it came to magic, she knew the margin between success and failure was sometimes tiny. She tightened her grip on Tiago's hand.

In the next blink, the graveyard vanished.

Chapter Twelve

Esme wasn't sure which came first, the numbing or the shock.

She felt as though she was floating, but when she opened her eyes, she gasped at the realization that they had gone from night to day in a blink. Her feet were firmly planted on a narrow ledge that butted up against a near-vertical rock face. The air was biting cold and far beneath them was a churning sea. Tiago stood next to her; he had that look he always got when the world closed in around him—open mouth, fallen expression, faraway eyes.

A thick and freezing fog wrapped its arms around them.

"Did we make it?" Esme managed through chattering teeth. She tried not to flinch, because there was so little space that one wrong move would send her plummeting into the dark waters.

Tiago glanced up. "This is bad. Real bad."

"Define 'bad.'"

"This is just some rock in the middle of the ocean. It's for sure not an island."

Esme clung to the rock wall, taking deep breaths. "Maybe you said the wrong words, or maybe the memory wasn't sad enough, or . . ."

With a grunt, Tiago ran a hand through his long hair. "I think it's way worse than that. I think—I think I know what I did wrong."

"Wrong as in you can fix it, right?"

"I think so?"

Esme gave a resolute nod. "Good. Okay." She looked over at Tiago. "Go ahead."

"We have to drink the potion."

Esme gagged dramatically. "I'm sure you're joking," she said.

"I'm not. I thought we could bypass the spell's instructions, but, uh, looks like we only made it partway, so bottoms up."

"You want me to drink dirty, rancid water that's most likely mixed with bone dust—and that will probably kill me before I even get to the island?"

"Yeah. That's exactly what I want you to do. Well, not the getting killed part, which is absolutely not going to happen. Or we could hang out on this perch forever and die of dehydration or starvation and have our eyes picked out by vultures."

"I don't see any vultures."

"No dead bodies yet."

"You're really gross, you know that?"

"Just keeping it real."

Esme steeled her nerves. "How much do we have to drink?" she asked, already feeling sick.

"A sip, maybe?"

"Tiago!"

"I told you I'm not great at spells. I'm not even a full witch! But *you* wanted me to try, remember?"

"So this is my fault?"

Tiago stared down at the vase still in his hand. The water had become a greenish brown color. "This is the witch hunter's fault," he whispered.

If only they knew who the witch hunter was. A faceless, nameless person who had managed to get their hands on one of the Daggers of Ire.

"Fine," Esme said. "I'll do it."

"Want me to go first?"

Esme shook her head.

"Oh, and make sure you don't throw it all up."

"How bad can it be?" She took the bottle, plugged her nose, and tipped the container back just enough to allow the dark water to slide past her lips. She gagged.

"Hold it down!" Tiago commanded. "Think of ice cream, or chocolate, or . . ."

With a grimace, she forced herself to swallow. Then, gagging again, she spit into the ocean and passed the potion back to Tiago.

He took a swig, then rolled his eyes and muttered, "So dramatic. It's not even bad."

"If you like the taste of death," Esme groaned, wiping her mouth.

Tiago snickered, then began to chant under his breath, whispering words that ran together, making it impossible to hear exactly what he was saying.

"Why are we still standing here?" Esme asked.

"Magic takes a minute. Jeez."

The fog grew darker, great rumbles of thunder rolling in the distance. Esme could feel the magic rising in the air. There was a shift in the atmosphere, and then great sheets of glowing blue rain fell from the sky.

"Do you see that?" Esme choked out. "The rain is glowing like—"

Tiago didn't answer, only glared at the island defiantly as he shouted over the storm, "A little rain isn't going to keep us out!"

Esme clenched her fists. Tiago was right. They couldn't turn back now. They had nothing to go back to, not when their families were gone. Not when their town was dying. Not when they were being hunted.

Her stomach clenched just as a woman's voice broke through the storm, so clear it was as if the voice was in every drop of rain.

"*You will die here.*"

Esme shook her head. It was the same voice from the graveyard. "Who are you?"

"What?" Tiago shot her a look of confusion. So he *couldn't* hear the voice.

"Leave now or lose your life."

It had to be a trick. Some kind of weird last line of defense to keep people out of Ocho Manos.

Ignoring the warning, Esme looked at Tiago. "I feel sick."

"Then it's working."

"But we're not any closer to the island."

"It's the storm. It's like it's trying to keep us out."

"You're the spell caster of Air," she shouted. "*You* get to decide if we get past the storm. And you better do it fast because I think I'm going to throw up."

Tiago turned his face up to the storm, and then, in the greatest show of confidence Esme had ever seen, he smiled. Smiled!

Next, he grabbed Esme's hand and shouted, "Let us through!"

The storm paused, but only a little—as though it was deciding whether these two brujxes were worth the trouble.

"I am of Air," Tiago hollered, tossing the vase into the sea. "Of secrets and storms. And I demand that you open the . . . gates, doors, whatever, and let us in."

In the next breath, the tempest ceased, only to be replaced by an eerie quiet. Just when Esme started to think they had failed again, the cliff began to move, driving them forward across the sea. As it did, the thick sheet of fog parted like a stage curtain, revealing a rocky island several miles long, with dark formations jutting out of the earth, jagged and fang-like. A sense of foreboding flooded Esme's heart.

The smell hit her next—the foulest odor she had ever inhaled, like rotting fish on hot summer pavement sprinkled with sewer. She swallowed the bile rising in her throat, vowing to never drink a nasty potion ever again. "Is that it?"

"That island is, like, monstrous."

He was right. It *was* monstrous-looking—gray, and bleak, and absent of any color.

Was this what San Bosco would look like if the witches didn't come home?

A black cloud hovered over the craggy land, clinging to the gloomy formations that Esme now saw made up a wall covered with black moss and soot, so tall it was impossible to see what lay beyond.

The cliff came to an abrupt halt, hanging over the shore, where shallow, inky waves rolled in and out around six feet below.

"I guess this is our stop," Tiago said, hopping down onto the black sand beach. "Can you believe I actually got us here?" He was beaming—maybe the only sign of hope or joy in this whole dismal place.

Esme leaped onto the beach. "You didn't even turn into an animal," she teased, patting him on the back.

Tiago glanced around. "And now we're here. With a bunch of dangerous witches behind that wall." He said it as if he was eager to meet them.

Esme felt suddenly empty—as if the island had scooped out her insides, and all she could feel was the darkness. Or was it loneliness? Fury? Or something else she couldn't name?

"This place is supercharged with magic," she whispered, staring up at the massive wall. Her jaw tightened and tingled, and she worked it back and forth gently. "Very dark magic. It's everywhere." Was that why the rain had glowed? To warn her and Tiago to stay put and not come any closer?

But what did it matter? No warning would keep her from her family, from saving them and the other witches.

She scanned the wall, her eyes landing on a section of it that was carved to look like eight stacked hands with interlocking fingers. She pressed her hands into the wall, tracing them across the surface as she searched for an opening. "I think these hands maybe open."

Tiago stared. "And how are we supposed to open some giant stone hands?"

"Only with blood," came a voice behind them.

Esme spun to find a gaunt woman, taller than tall, standing at least ten feet. She blurred in and out around the edges; her vein-riddled skin was nearly translucent like a jellyfish, and she grinned widely, showing a mouthful of very yellow, very crooked teeth. Her long, pointed fingernails were dark purple, and she wore a belt made of keys that hung low around her tattered gray dress.

Tiago laughed nervously. "Ha . . . blood. Funny."

Esme squeezed his hand to tell him to stop talking.

"We don't need to give any blood," he went on. "Just did that last week, actually." *Stop. Talking.* "No, uh, we were hoping you'd know how to get inside the prison and—"

"Prison?" The woman howled with bone-grating laughter. "This is no prison, child. A misconception every magical soul makes. Let me guess, you think that this is the island of Ocho Manos. That it was built using the bones of eight magical hands and is where wicked witches are locked away for terrible crimes of magic."

"Bones?" Tiago said.

"Well, that part is true," the woman said. "And some of us *are* rather wicked." She laughed bitterly. "But not all of us are witches."

Esme swallowed hard. *Of course* this was a prison. Didn't this giant witch see the gates made of eight hands? She shot a glance at Tiago. Had he gotten the destination wrong again? "If it's not a prison, then what is it?" she asked.

The woman sneered. "Why should I tell you? You're just weak little nothings who somehow managed to break through the magical barrier and are likely feeling very full of yourselves right now. But believe me, I can taste your magic and it is pathetic at best."

Esme wanted to shrink into herself, to look anywhere other than at this scary lady. But she wasn't about to give up just because this giant was throwing insults at them. "We only need someone to help us decode a message," she said.

"And what are you willing to give in return?" the woman

said, staring at Tiago. "A soul? Your magic? Both of your ears?"

Tiago reached up and tugged his right ear. "Uh . . ."

Quickly, Esme covered Lenny's ring with her other hand. She'd never give it up. The woman shifted her narrowed gaze to Esme, studying her for so long Esme's cheeks went hot. "Your hair, child . . . it's so shiny. And so magical."

Esme's pulse hammered away.

Adjusting her belt, the witch said, "I will take your hair in return for allowing you entrance, but you'll get nothing more from me. If you want a decoder, that is your problem. Is it a deal?"

Tiago frowned. "How much hair are we talking?"

The witch produced a pair of rusty scissors from her belt. "Six itty-bitty inches."

Esme ran a hand over her curls. She felt a warmth radiate across her palm. Was it just her imagination? Six inches would bring her hair right to her chin. That wasn't so bad—and it would grow back. A small sacrifice.

"It's a deal," Esme said quickly. "But before you cut, I have to know—if this isn't a prison, then what is it?"

The woman clutched the scissors and drew closer, her size shrinking with every step until she was nearly Esme's height. Then, leaning so close Esme felt the cool blade of the shears against her neck, the woman whispered, "A banished realm where forbidden magic runs wild."

And then the giant sliced through Esme's hair.

Chapter Thirteen

Esme bit her bottom lip and stared at the locks of hair in the woman's gnarled hand. They looked ordinary, lifeless. Hardly worth entrance to the island.

A banished realm where forbidden magic runs wild.

That was what the woman had said. Not a prison at all. Could that possibly be true?

But before Esme could ask, the giant smiled and rose a few feet into the air. There she hovered, her tattered dress blowing in the breeze as she glared at Esme and Tiago, said, "Goodbye, little fools," and shot up into the sky in a blaze of silver. The sound of her clanking keys echoed across the shore.

"Whoa!" Tiago's eyes shifted frantically. "Did she just fly?"

All Esme could do was stare at the gloomy sky, wondering where the giant had zipped off to. She ran a hand over her newly short hair. A silky rose petal fell to the black sand.

"What do you think she's going to do with your hair?" Tiago asked.

"Maybe she needs some Earth or Chaos magic for a spell," she guessed.

A chilly breeze blew across the shore. Tiago froze. "Esme?"

She followed his gaze to the gates. Their stony fingers were still closed. *Closed.* Anger spiked within her. "She tricked us!"

Tiago shrugged. "She did say she was wicked."

Esme clomped through the sand toward the stone hands, Tiago right behind her. She threw her hands against the gates, grunting and pushing as if she had the strength to split granite. As if she had the magic.

Tiago said, "If I could control this annoying spell, I could become a lizard and climb up, but then some seagull would probably eat me."

"Do seagulls eat lizards?"

"Don't wanna find out."

"You're of Air," Esme argued, trying to puff up his confidence.

"Yeah, but not properly trained."

Esme hated being reminded that so many fates were in their untrained, unqualified hands. "You've got the magic of secrets in your blood, Tiago. You got us this far, and this place—"

"It's not a secret," a voice said.

Esme yelped in alarm. She scanned the wall but couldn't locate the voice. "Who said that?" she demanded.

A figure emerged from the stone, masked by a cloud of mist. In the time it took Esme to jump back, the mist cleared, and she found herself staring at a ginger-colored fox. His dark, expressive eyes had specks of gold and amber in them, making them look as though they were made of flames. He stood on two legs, bringing him to nearly Esme's height, and he was dressed in a long gray coat. A puff of black fur on top of his head converged into a stripe down the bridge of his nose.

"Did you . . . just talk?" she asked.

The fox tilted his head. "You look surprised."

"That's because animals don't talk," Tiago put in.

"Or wear long coats," Esme blurted. She sighed, wishing her Chaos would go to sleep or at the very least not force words out of her mouth before she had time to properly inspect them.

"Every living thing communicates," the fox insisted, smoothing a well-groomed paw over his coat. "You just don't have the right kind of brain to understand what's being said."

That was a really good point. "Who are you?" Esme asked.

"I'm the guardian of the gates."

Tiago stood taller, nodding as if he was on official witch business. "I'm Tiago, and this is Esme."

The fox said nothing. He didn't even so much as blink. It was then, in the shadow of the gates, that Esme's jaw stiffened as she sensed his magic—something old and dark and mysterious, like the waves rolling in and out at their feet.

"Do you have a name?" Esme said. Her dad had once told her that two things hold a person together—their name and their memories.

The fox narrowed his eyes. "Names are far too limiting. They try to define you. I'm just me."

"Everyone has a name," Tiago insisted.

"We could call you Fox," Esme said, but it was really more of a question.

"If you must call me something," the creature sighed, preening, "call me Fetch. As in Fetching, Handsome."

Tiago started to laugh until Esme shot him a glare.

"Okay, Fetch," she said. He *was* sort of handsome. "That giant lady tricked us. We really need to get inside, and since you're the guardian, you must have the keys."

He snorted. "There are no keys. But there is a spell. And of course I know it. What kind of guardian would I be if I didn't?"

"You seem sort of young to be a guardian," Tiago said.

Tiago was right. Even though Fetch dressed like an old guy *and* talked like one, his voice was youthful-sounding. Esme studied him, and for the first time she noticed the details of his coat—wool, brass buttons, invisible hem. A finely tailored garment that looked as though it had been made by a skilled hand.

"What does age have to do with anything?" Fetch argued. "Skill is all that matters."

"So you *can* let us in," Esme said.

"Why do you want to go in there, anyway?" the fox asked. "It's a death wish."

"We're looking for answers," Tiago said.

Esme nodded. "And the only place we can find them is in there."

The fox's nostrils flared and his whiskers twitched. "You will not find answers here, only sorrow and danger. The last person who broke through the barrier and found their way through these gates is now a stone statue in the square, forever hosting annoying little birds, who peck away at it all day long."

"Why did they become a statue?" Esme asked, horrified.

Fetch turned his gaze to Tiago. "Is she always like this?"

Tiago shrugged. "She asks a lot of questions."

Esme's chest tightened. She tugged the coded message from her pocket. "We have to find a witch who can tell us what this means."

"And then we'll be gone," Tiago added.

Fetch glanced at the page. "Looks like Brucera. It's one of the oldest and most complicated witch languages."

And Lenny was trying to learn it, Esme remembered.

"'One of'?" Tiago asked. "How many are there?"

"Aren't you a witch?"

"Yeah, well, we haven't learned that yet, okay?"

"There are many," Fetch said, "but only two are in use anymore. The others have died out."

"Do you know Brucera?" Esme held her breath.

"Only know of it. Can't read it." The fox looked up. "Why would you come all this way for something that is sure to end in utter failure?"

Esme inched closer. "Because if we don't try, our families and our town will be lost forever." She felt a burning in her throat that radiated across her chest, stirring her Chaos.

"And the witch hunter will win."

Fetch raised a bushy eyebrow. She expected him to ask about the hunter, or about their lost families, but he only said, "How is that my problem?"

"It isn't," Esme admitted. "But . . ." She could feel herself shrinking under the fox's gaze. *Act like you belong here. Stand up straight!* "You look sweet."

"I am a fox. Sly and conniving," he insisted. "I am *not* sweet."

Tiago said, "If you didn't want to help, you could have stayed hidden in the gates."

Fetch's mouth lifted at the corners. "And then what?"

Esme wasn't following. "What do you mean?"

"*If* you decode the message," Fetch said slowly, "and if you somehow manage to go undetected by the creatures of this realm, then what?"

Tiago said, "Then we follow the message and—"

"We find an original witch," Esme blurted.

Fetch went still. His furry brows came together in an almost frown, though it was hard to tell with the black tuft of hair. His mouth opened as if he might say something, but instead he began to pace across the sand, his white-and-orange tail swishing through the vent in his coat.

Esme met Tiago's uncertain gaze. His eyes were one of her first memories, blue and bright as they lay on a patch of shady grass while their mothers' voices spoke somewhere far above them.

You two will have a great destiny.

Was this what Esme's mom had been referring to? This terrible, impossible ordeal?

Fetch's voice pulled Esme back to the moment. "You said an original witch?"

"Yes."

"As in one of the four original witches."

"Exactly," Esme said.

The fox hesitated. He opened and closed his paws, showing off his claws. "Are you *sure* you mean an original witch, or . . ."

"I'm positive!" Esme was growing impatient.

"Very well," the fox said. "I will open the gates."

Esme wasn't sure what changed his mind, only that he seemed uncertain, resigned.

"Why now?" Tiago wore a look of deep suspicion.

Fetch's ears flicked, pointing straight up. "Do you want me to open the gates or not?"

"Yes!" Esme hollered.

With a grunt, Fetch said, "First you must know the three great risks of entering. And then you can decide if it's still worth it."

"It will be," Tiago said with a certainty Esme wished she also possessed. What if the journey *wasn't* worth it? What if Fetch was right and this all ended in utter failure? They'd never see their families again. San Bosco would be a ghost town at best, and a shriveled-up, forgotten nothing at worst. The idea of it nearly broke Esme—not just her heart but her very spirit, the part of her that was tied to her family in more powerful ways than even magic. She couldn't bear the idea of never being with them again. Of not getting to tell Lenny she was sorry for the awful thing she had said.

I hate you.

She wouldn't consider failure. Ever.

Shoving the worry out of her mind, Esme nodded her agreement. She didn't care what the risks were. She had to make this right.

"One," Fetch said, "no one here likes strangers—everyone will be able to smell the outsider in you, and many will try to kill you or eat you or carve away pieces of you to sell."

Eat? Sell?

Esme clenched her fists at her sides, forcing herself to look confident. Tiago leaned closer. "Did he just say carve?"

"Two," Fetch went on, "some creatures look friendly and some not so much, but don't let appearances fool you. Sometimes the most harmless-looking ones are the most lethal. And vice versa. Ready?"

"Wait!" Esme cried. "You never told us number three."

"Oh, right." Fetch circled her and Tiago like a hunter studying its prey. "There are thieves behind those stone hands—wretched thieves who want your witch magic and will do anything to get it."

Tiago lifted his chin. "Why would a bunch of witches want our not-even-full magic? Don't they already have enough?"

Fetch shook his head. "Not all magic makes you a witch,

and not all witches make magic." He unfolded his paw. A silver pocket watch appeared, and he began to fiddle with a sapphire dial. "Have you made your choice?"

Esme's Chaos pressed against her ribs as if to say *Run and never look back*. She turned her gaze to Tiago's, seeing the answer there. "Yes," he said.

"Very well." The creature leaped onto the stone gates, hopping from finger to finger, then back and across in a kind of pattern as his coat fluttered in the sea winds.

What the heck was he doing?

Then a loud crack reverberated across the shore, and the stone fingers unclasped.

Fetch had opened the gates.

Chapter Fourteen

As the trio stepped across the threshold, the gates closed behind them with a whisper.

Esme found herself on the edge of a precipice, staring at a dreary town at least a hundred feet below.

The buildings were old, drab, square things with gray roofs and gray chimneys and gray doors. There were no cars, no people, no sounds whatsoever.

A place for ghosts, she thought. *Like San Bosco.*

No! She couldn't think that.

But the worry had already crept in, and now all Esme could see in her mind's eye was a dead town with dead dreams and dead magic.

The roads here were narrow like San Bosco's—but unlike San Bosco's, they weren't crooked or winding or interesting at all. They were perfectly straight, as though they'd been drawn with a ruler.

On one side of the town was a world of grasslands with no horizon in sight. And on the other, a dark forest with shadows that pulsed at the edges.

And the air—the air smelled of vanilla and rose and freshly ground pepper.

Tiago spoke first. "It's so depressing. It looks like—"

"A bruise," Esme blurted, feeling the pointed jab of each word. Then, realizing it was rude to tell someone their home looked like a bruise, she amended, "I mean, it's sort of . . . unique."

Fetch blinked against the cold. "Things look different from up high. Down there is a whole other world you can't see from here."

A fierce and biting wind swept across the cliff. The gates behind them rattled.

Fetch froze, his ears pricking up. Everything in his guarded stance screamed *trouble*.

"Who opened MY GATES?" a voice bellowed, so loud the ground shook.

What? Esme scowled at the fox. He had told them that *he* was the guardian! Fetch brought a paw to his mouth, gesturing for her and Tiago to be quiet. But Esme didn't want to be quiet. She wanted to scream. To demand answers. Didn't he know her whole world was going to explode if she didn't get this right? That she would blame herself forever?

And forever was such a long time.

Fetch cleared his throat and said loudly to the wall behind them, "You were asleep and there was a delivery."

"A delivery of what?"

Fetch faltered. His eyes darted back and forth, landing on Esme's bobbed hair. Slowly his furry white mouth fanned into a grin. "Enchanted witch hair."

So the fox had seen the exchange with the giant.

There was a grumble from the wall. Or maybe two. "Then why are you standing here instead of making the delivery? Worthless, lazy nothing of a fox. I knew I shouldn't have hired you!"

For the first time, Fetch's shoulders shrank beneath his fine coat and his sparkling eyes dulled. Esme felt a lightning rod of fury burn through her, and as mad as she was that Fetch had lied to her, she still wanted to shake her fist at the voice for being so cruel. Instead she gave the wall a swift kick.

Then three things happened at once.

Esme released a painful howl.

Fetch shouted, "No!"

And enormous wings burst from the wall—black and slick, half-feathered, half-skeletal. Reaching. Searching—

Esme sprang back.

Time slowed, as if her feet knew what was coming before she did—and she tumbled over the cliff's edge.

"Esme!" Tiago screamed.

Then, of all the stupid things, he leaped after her, and all she could think was *We failed before we even began.*

As Esme pinwheeled through the air, a strange rippling sound filled the sky, and Fetch was sailing toward them, fanning out his coat like a mighty matador. In a graceful twist, he wrapped it around her and Tiago and swept them away, his voice softly muttering words that Esme heard loud and clear: "You two are likely not worth the trouble."

Esme felt nothing but warmth, as if she was in a cocoon of safety, and for a blink or two there were no forbidden realms, no whispering winds, no stolen families. There was only the safety of a fox's magical coat.

And then there wasn't.

A light flashed, and they found themselves in a small, windowless stone room with a dirt floor and a shimmering domed ceiling that looked as though it was made of rose quartz. The chamber opened onto a tiny kitchen and two narrow tunnels tall enough for an upright bear to walk through. The only light came from a floor lamp that stood near a leather wingback chair stacked with books. A tattered rug was spread out beneath a velvet sofa and an overturned basket that served as a table.

"Welcome to my home," Fetch said, looking suddenly nervous as he shuffled his feet and tapped his legs with both front paws. "Hungry?" He strode into the kitchen. "Thirsty?"

Tiago swayed, then leaned against a wall to regain his balance.

"Sometimes travel by coat can give you motion sickness," Fetch said over his shoulder. "It could also be that we are a mile underground."

Regaining some composure, Tiago said, "I need a coat like that. How does it work? Is it spelled or—?"

Esme erupted at the memory of his foolishness. "How could you just jump off the cliff like that?"

"You're the one who jumped first."

"I fell!"

"Fell. Jumped. Same result." Tiago shrugged so casually she wanted to sock him. "Besides, I'm of Air."

"That doesn't mean you can fly!"

"But maybe someday." He turned back to the fox, who was still bustling around the kitchen. "So can you fly with that thing or, like, float or—oh, and how did we end up here so fast?"

All good questions, Esme thought, but her anger was swallowing all logic. She whirled to Fetch, who was now holding a tray out. "Peanut butter and jelly?" he said with a wary smile.

Come to think of it, Esme *was* hungry, but . . .

"And YOU," she growled, "you're not the guardian of the gates!"

The fox set the tray on the basket-table, moved his books to the floor, and dropped into his leather chair with an *oof.* "I believe it's customary to say thank you when someone saves your life."

He was right—he *had* saved them. But before she could

thank him, Fetch turned to Tiago, who was now on the sofa stuffing his face with a sandwich. "The coat is not spelled. I cannot fly. More like glide for a few minutes. But this"—he ran a paw over the chest of his coat—"it will always bring me home."

Tiago studied the garment with an intensity that told Esme he was trying to memorize every seam and button.

"Those wings," Esme said with a shuddering memory. "What were they?" She might have been a brujx, but she had only read about fantastical creatures, never seen one in the flesh.

"They could belong to any number of monsters," Fetch said, "but given the black feathers and the exposed skeleton, I think maybe they belong to a dragón de huesos."

"A bone dragon?" Esme echoed as she sat next to Tiago. "Like the ones from fairy tales that feed on magical bones to consume someone's power? Seriously?"

Fetch shrugged. "Just answering your questions. Whether you believe me or not is your problem."

"He's telling the truth," Tiago said, offering her a sandwich.

Taking it, Esme stared at her friend. It wasn't uncommon for Air witches to be able to detect lies, but Tiago had never been able to do it before.

"How do you know?" Esme asked before biting into the gooey sandwich.

"It's weird," Tiago said, "but since we got here it's like the truth is a snake I can feel slithering through me. It's kinda gross."

Fetch added, "This island was built on magic, with magic, for magic. It's like a vortex of energy that seeks likeness, and it will enhance the most natural elements of your powers."

Esme thought she understood. "So there's Air magic here, and that's what's boosting Tiago's powers?"

"Something like that."

"Still doesn't make me a full witch, right?" Tiago asked.

"No idea," Fetch said.

Tiago rolled his shoulders back. Esme pressed her lips together, trying to puzzle it all out. Would Ocho Manos affect *her* magic? Did Chaos magic even exist here?

"But you didn't know Fetch was lying about being the guardian?"

Tiago shrugged. "I never said it was an exact science."

Esme had so many questions, about Fetch and the gates and that giant lady and the bone dragon, but the question that burned in her heart was *why*. She glanced at the book spines on the floor—all fairy tales. "Why did you open the gates for us?" she asked, polishing off the sandwich and reaching for another. "Why did you save us and bring us here?"

Fetch fanned open a book, keeping his eyes on the pages as if he couldn't be bothered with her interrogation. "Why not?"

"Because no one does anything without a reason," Tiago said. "You could have told us that you just work for the actual guardian. Do you have any milk?"

"No."

Fetch got to his feet. His shaggy tail swung back and forth

as he paced. "If everything goes exactly right, you will have something I want. And when that happens, you can pay me back for my trouble."

And it was a lot of trouble, Esme thought, which meant he must want something big. "Like what?" she asked.

"You'll know when it happens."

"That's not really an answer," Tiago said.

"It's the best one I have," Fetch said.

What could she possibly have that he would need? Fetch had been interested the moment Esme mentioned an original witch. But he had also seemed unsure, as though he was weighing the risks and rewards. Esme didn't care about the why. There was only one question that mattered to her. "Does that mean you're going to help us?"

The fox's nose twitched and he sniffed the air. "Why do I smell . . . a rat? No, a squirrel. Wait, that's not it either. Why can't I put my finger on it?"

Tiago's eyes roved the ceiling innocently. "What's it like living underground?"

"It's you!" Fetch inched closer. "*You're* the . . . animal."

Esme cringed, about to tell Tiago to ignore the fox, not to give in to the power of suggestion. Before she could, her best friend groaned—and, *poof,* transformed into a tiny possum with floppy ears.

Fetch blinked. "Does he do that all the time?"

Esme stood, scooped Tiago up, and placed him in the palm of her hand. "It's just a spell gone bad."

"Meaning he's not very skilled at witchery."

Tiago squeaked and kicked his little legs.

"He got us here!" Esme protested. "He is good. He just needs some practice. And what do you know about being a witch, anyway?"

"Only that I'm not one," Fetch said as he studied Tiago, who was now baring his sharp little teeth. "And I wouldn't want to be."

Esme's Chaos stirred to life as words flooded out of her mouth like slippery fish. "If you're not a witch," she sputtered helplessly, "what are you? Is this place really a banished realm where forbidden magic runs wild? How do you have an enchanted coat? How—"

Fetch held up his large paws. "I already told you that not all magic makes you a witch and not all witches make magic. And yes to the banished and forbidden and wild."

"Wild like how?" Esme asked.

The possum leaped from Esme's arms, swinging his tail wildly as he hopped onto the stack of books and squealed.

"Council?" Fetch stared at Tiago. "Why would we have a council?"

Esme gasped. "You can understand him?"

"Of course."

Esme suddenly remembered what he had told her about how every living thing communicates. *You just don't have the right kind of brain to understand what's being said.*

"So if you don't have a council," Esme said, "then, like,

who makes the rules or . . ."

"We have reinas."

Tiago squeaked again.

"Queens?" Esme said. Fetch had to be pulling her leg.

"One for each season," Fetch said. "Laws are different for each. Winter is the harshest, and spring is sort of all over the place."

"If you have laws, then how can the magic here be wild?"

"I never said *magic* follows the laws—only those who live here do. For example, we can't plot against any of the queens, or kill any of their armies, and if we're called to serve, we have to say yes," Fetch said. "Oh, and each winter solstice the winter queen has a big party where she chooses a few magical creatures to give up their magic. It's supposed to be some great honor, but I think it's sick, because no way could you survive here without it."

Esme's heart wedged in her throat. "Why would she want their magic?"

Tiago flicked his tail about wildly as Fetch said, "To keep in the vaults in case she ever needs it."

"What would she need it for?"

The fox shrugged. "You don't have to worry about it. We're in autumn now."

"What's autumn's queen like?" Esme asked.

"Absent" was all Fetch said before he drew his furry mouth into a tight line and clapped his paws together. "It's already seven o'clock here. You should get some rest."

Tiago snarled and whipped his tail furiously.

"How can we rest when we have to find a witch to read the message?" Esme howled. Never mind the fact that she really wanted to know more about the reinas, especially the absent autumn queen and this vault of stolen magic.

"Because the House of Hands and Teeth, the place where you might find your witch, doesn't open until the devouring hour, which is in exactly five hours. Enough time for you to get some sleep."

It was Esme's turn to lean against the wall, to catch her breath and her balance. "The devouring hour?" she whispered. "That doesn't sound so good."

Tiago's tail thrashed back and forth as he danced on his tiny paws excitedly.

"Actually, it's not really a house," Fetch went on. "More like a market that sells darkness and enchantments and all sorts of curiosities." He shook his furry head. "See what I mean about names?"

No. Esme did not see. "What sorts of curiosities?"

Tiago stood on his hind legs as if wanting to know the answer too.

Fetch merely said, "It's something you have to see with your own eyes—well, as long as they don't get gouged out."

And then he led them down one of the narrow tunnels to their rooms to rest.

Chapter Fifteen

Esme lay on the straw mattress, staring up at the ceiling of the closet-sized bedroom. Tiago had transformed back into his human self the moment he saw his own bed, and now he was on the other side of the wall, snoring away.

With an envious grunt, she rolled onto her side, wishing sleep would come to her as easily as it did to her friend.

But there were too many thoughts storming through her mind about Oblivion's ticking clock, and its dark promise to empty out her family's and the other witches' brains. If that happened, they'd also lose touch with their magic. She thought about the cryptic note Lenny had left. When—if—she found an original witch, then what? Would one of the sisters be able to free her family from their in-between prison?

Finally, her thoughts turned to the witch hunter.

Who could be so vicious? She knew every witch in San Bosco and there was no way any of them would do something like this. But the bigger question was *why*? Esme couldn't find even a crumb of a reason.

She stared at the ring on her finger. Lenny had never told her how the magic worked. She'd kept her world of sueños to herself, telling Esme that if she lifted the veil for anyone, then the magic would be weakened. But she must have given her magic to Esme for a reason.

Folding her arms across her chest, Esme closed her eyes. She wrapped a hand around the ring.

Talk to me, Lenny. Please.

Somehow, a few minutes later, she dozed off.

Esme stood on a stone bridge.

A dark and menacing forest encircled her. Something about it felt unnerving, dangerous.

Then a woman's voice echoed through the woods, soft and lyrical. "Borrowed magic is always a bad idea."

"Who are you?" Esme called.

"Look for Ozzie."

Ozzie?

"Ozzie will give but will also take."

Esme was tired of cryptic messages and strangers telling her what to do. She just wanted her sister. "Lenny," she called out. "Can you hear me? Are you there? I'm coming for you. Just hold on!"

There was an agonizing moment of utter silence. A flock of

black birds broke through the trees. *Caw. Caw. Caw.*

And then she saw her. Lenny stood at the forest's edge, a barely-there ghost.

"Lenny!"

Her sister's eyes were dull, her face hollow. "Find . . . original witch."

"I'm trying!" Esme's voice cracked. "And I'm sorry. I was so wrong. I don't hate you and I DO need you!" she cried.

Lenny stepped closer. She was so thin, so pale. "It's cold here, Es. And dark. Please . . . hurry."

Hot tears rolled down Esme's cheeks. "Just hold on!" She reached for her sister—

Only to be startled awake by a paw on her shoulder. "It's time," Fetch said.

"Lenny!" Esme cried, momentarily confused about where she was. And then it all came back to her. "My sister," she blurted. "She was in my dream. . . ." Lenny had looked so awful, so weak. The memory of it turned Esme cold all over.

Tiago stood in the doorway, leaning against the frame and yawning. How could he be so calm when they were about to go to a dark market that might devour them or steal their magic or turn them into stone statues?

His eyes fell to the emerald ring before rising to meet Esme's gaze. His expression was sending her a message that looked a whole lot like, *Don't say another word about the magic.*

She sat up, several petals falling from her hair onto the pillow.

Fetch stared with wide, curious eyes. "That's why the giant

wanted your hair. She needed your Earth magic."

"So she took some of Esme's magic?" Tiago asked the fox.

"Seems that way."

"But for what?" Esme asked. *Just wait until that giant finds out my magic isn't worth anything.*

"No idea, and I'm not about to ask her," Fetch said. "We should go."

Esme stood. Remembering her dream, she asked the fox, "Do you know anyone named Ozzie?"

Fetch shook his head.

"We'll find them at the House of Hands and Teeth," she said, then started. Where had that come from? She hadn't thought the words before she spoke them.

"Wait," Tiago said, looking confused. "Who's Ozzie?"

As Fetch led the way out of the room, Esme leaned closer to her friend and whispered, "My dream. She told me to find someone by that name."

"Lenny?"

"No, the voice."

"The same one from the graveyard?"

"I . . . I'm not sure, but we have to hurry."

Fetch called over his shoulder, "Better get a move on if you want to be there at opening time."

The trio made their way down a descending corridor lit by tiny shimmering rocks embedded in the walls.

Down, down, down they went.

"What happens if we're late?" Tiago asked.

"The duendes get really mad."

Esme frowned. "Duendes, as in little tricksters who live in the forest and torment humans?"

Fetch barked out a laugh. "Uh, more like murderous elves."

"Perfect," Tiago muttered. But there was an eagerness in his steps, as if he couldn't wait to get to the House of Hands and Teeth.

The air grew cooler, and strange sounds echoed, rustling and crunching and slithering that conjured up images of dead leaves and skeletal wings.

Which only reminded Esme of the bone dragon that had tried to kill her. She hadn't slowed long enough to consider the fact that dragons were real, along with murderous elves. That Ocho Manos really existed but wasn't a prison like she'd been told—it was *a banished realm where forbidden magic runs wild.*

Esme didn't know why, but she loved the sound of that. She had never lived in a world where magic could roam uninhibited. It was too dangerous, too unpredictable. Just like her Chaos.

She imagined a place where she wouldn't have to hide who she really was. Where she didn't have to be afraid of some council telling her who she shouldn't or couldn't be. Maybe in a place that was wild and free, she and her magic could be too.

They took a right into a small chamber, its low entrance forcing Esme to stoop as she entered. Her eyes fixed on the back wall, where uneven shelves were lined with what looked like endless spools of thread.

Magic hummed all around. But this magic wasn't of Earth,

or Air, or Fire, or Water. It was something she had never felt before.

"Stand back," Fetch said as he walked over to the wall and removed a spool of silver. An indecipherable whisper floated up and away.

He tossed the spool into the air, where it rotated and whirled, the thread unraveling at lightning speed. The air grew suddenly warm. Esme's scalp prickled.

The thread zipped across the chamber, a streak of bright light that slammed into the far wall with such brilliant ferocity it was as if stars had collided. Esme squeezed her eyes closed, and when she opened them, she saw a row of three silver doors. Each had a different knob—crystal, metal, and wooden.

Tiago smiled. "Whoa!" His adrenaline-junkie heart was probably electrified, but as much as Esme was in awe of this place, *her* heart ached for her sister and her dad. What if the last time she'd seen them *was* the last time? She didn't want to remember the blade in her sister's stomach, or her dad sitting in Patina's garden, so lost and confused.

"Your thread," Esme said, "it's . . ."

Fetch smiled. "Amazing, I know."

"How does it work?" Tiago asked, his eyes roving hungrily across the shelves.

Could Fetch create *anything* with the thread? Or were there limitations, rules? There had to be. Even the most powerful magic had restrictions.

Unless you lived in a realm where it ran wild, Esme supposed.

Fetch's tail swished. "I can create and open doors."

"To anywhere?" Tiago asked.

"Not exactly. I have to have been wherever I'm going."

"So all this thread is to make doors?" Esme asked. There had to be more to the magic than that.

"Each spool is different," Fetch said. "My grandfather left them to me, but he never got a chance to show me everything before . . ." He swallowed and took a long breath. "Before he died, so I'm still figuring things out. It's pretty complicated."

"I'm sorry," Esme said. "Do you have other family?"

"Not anymore," Fetch muttered, smoothing down the black patch of fur on his head. "Now, let's get down to why we're here. You can't go to the House of Hands and Teeth with no protection." He went over to the door with the crystal knob.

No family at all? The cruelty of it sent a pang through Esme's heart.

Tiago said, "Any zombies or ghouls or other monsters behind the door that we should know about?"

Fetch shook his head, and just as Esme was about to breathe a sigh of relief, the fox added, "At least not behind *these* doors."

Well, that wasn't exactly reassuring. "What's behind them?"

"Magical portals," Tiago guessed.

Fetch smirked. "This one," he said pointing to the door with the crystal knob, "is a closet."

Tiago grinned and whispered to Esme. "I bet he's got

magical weapons, or potions, or poisons in there."

Fetch opened the door.

Inside the closet hung a row of gray coats, perfectly spaced.

"Sorry," Esme said to Tiago. "No weapons."

"They could be in the pockets!"

Esme chuckled as Fetch reached in and grabbed two trench coats, longer and thinner than Fetch's. "These will mask your magic so no one will smell that you don't belong here and be tempted to devour you." He was grinning as he said this.

"So no trick pockets," Tiago said. "Or poisoned buttons, or other stuff?"

"What is it with you and poison?" Esme asked.

Fetch held the coats out so Esme could choose. She took the lighter of the two. The color reminded her of a winter dusk.

Tiago took the other coat and shrugged it on. The garment shimmered and sparkled, shifting from gray to a cool blue like his eyes. "Whoa! How'd you do that?"

Fetch rubbed his furry chin. "The coat chooses a color that represents you or some part of you. Not sure why, though. I didn't make them like that."

"*You* made these?" Esme asked incredulously.

"I'm a tailor," Fetch said. "I can weave magic . . . sometimes." He paused, as if he was suddenly aware he had said too much.

A pained expression passed over his face, one that hinted at a story Esme suddenly wanted to hear. "Sometimes?" she asked.

"No time," he said. "Put on your coat."

Tiago gave Esme a look as she pulled on the trench. Just like Tiago's, it shimmered and sparked. The gray tones faded until all that was left was a magnificent winter white.

Instantly, Esme felt a bloom emerge between two strands of hair. She reached up and traced a finger over its velvety petals as it fell into her palm. "White for the flowers," she said, as if it wasn't obvious.

The fox checked his pocket watch, then stuffed it into his breast pocket. "It's time."

"Hold up," Tiago said. "If I turn into an animal, what happens to the coat?"

"Whatever happens to your regular clothes when you change into an animal," Esme said.

"Except *those* aren't enchanted," Tiago muttered.

Fetch went to the door with the plain wooden knob. "Ready?"

"I knew one was a portal!" Tiago said.

"Why three doors if you only use two?" Esme asked.

Fetch smirked. "One is a false door. I just like odd numbers." He turned the knob.

Esme took Tiago's hand. "We stick together no matter what."

"Well, unless some carnivorous witch decides to eat me." Tiago grinned. "In that case, you should definitely run."

And just as Esme opened her mouth to say *never*, Fetch opened the door.

Chapter Sixteen

On the other side, there was only darkness and a rusty ladder.

Fetch climbed up the narrow passage first, followed by Esme, and Tiago in the rear.

"This place smells like dead people," Tiago announced. "Like that mummy dude from the museum."

Sneaking into the museum felt so long ago now, though it had been only yesterday. Still, Esme had to be sure of her timeline. Fetch had said the House of Hands and Teeth opened at midnight, so they had been gone from San Bosco for . . .

Esme said, "Fetch, we left our home at night, but when we got here it was already daytime."

"Your time isn't the same as our time here," Fetch said. "This is a different realm and crossing over to it means you likely lost a good eight hours. Maybe more."

"Eight?!" Tiago shouted.

Esme did a quick calculation in her head. "That means we're now down to four days and a handful of hours before our families are goners."

"So does that mean time is passing faster in Oblivion?" Tiago asked. Esme thought it was an excellent question even if it did make her heart sink.

"Yeah," she said. "How can we even be sure how much time we have?"

Fetch said, "It's only when you cross over from your world to another realm. But any more realm jumping shouldn't affect anything."

Realm jumping?

Fetch fiddled with his pocket watch, then said to Esme, "I've set a timer to help you keep track."

A timer, each tick a reminder to Esme that her family was in danger.

What if she didn't get to them in time? What if she couldn't find an original witch?

What if she wasn't strong enough? And for once, she let herself imagine what might be happening to San Bosco. Was Chaco just being dramatic or was the town actually dying?

Fetch's sigh carried several rungs down to Esme. "Keep up, would you?"

"How far do we have to climb?" she asked.

"Eighty-six more rungs."

"My arms will fall off by then," Tiago groaned.

"We can get you new ones at the House of Hands and Teeth," Fetch said.

Esme paused. "That's a joke, right?"

"I never joke about limbs," Fetch said, then began to whistle.

As Esme climbed, the encrypted note fluttered out of her pocket. In a fit of panic, she spun, nearly falling off the ladder. Thankfully, Tiago had caught the note.

"How about I hold on to this for now?" he said.

"You better not lose it."

"Esme," Tiago said with a hint of exasperation. "I'll just put it in the pocket of this nifty magic coat. Hey, Fetch. How about some thread to sew up my pocket?"

The fox just sighed and kept climbing.

A few minutes and many rungs later, the fox halted. Esme heard the sound of groaning metal, and then glorious light spilled into the dark. Fetch had opened a round hatch and was poking his head through, scoping things out.

Esme tried to force her hammering heart to chill, but her heart wasn't interested. It just wanted to gallop far, far away.

"Coast is clear." Fetch hopped up and out. "Hurry."

Esme scurried up the remaining rungs and surfaced into what looked like a small supply closet, its shelves packed with black candles of all sizes: pillar, tea, votive, as well as dozens in glass containers. There were even some that were shaped like heads, with baby faces, clown faces, and skulls.

Those must be really creepy to watch melt, Esme thought.

Tiago stepped into the room and pushed his hair away from his face. "What's up with all the candles? Is that a baby head?"

"They're magic," Fetch said. "The taper ones are memory candles and can help you remember things you've forgotten. I'm not sure what the baby ones do, but the skulls are all-you-can-eat candles."

Tiago scrunched up his face. "Who'd want to eat a candle?"

"You've got it all wrong." Fetch smirked. "If you burn it, your stomach expands so you can eat to your heart's content. As in you never get full or sick or gain weight."

"Have you tried it?" Esme asked.

"It was awesome," Fetch said. Tiago eagerly reached for a skull, but the fox shoved his hand away. "I wouldn't do that."

"Why not?"

"Anyone who steals from the Hands and Teeth—"

"Loses an arm?" Esme half teased.

"Exactly," Fetch deadpanned.

Tiago recoiled. "Why are we in this candle closet, anyway?"

"We can't just walk into the House of Hands and Teeth at the devouring hour," Fetch declared. "This is a much safer entrance. Keeps us on the down-low."

"You mean you don't have the golden ticket to get in?" Tiago asked.

"Why would I need a ticket when I have this secret entrance?"

"So you've done this before," Esme said.

"I told you I'm sly and cunning." Fetch grinned as though

he was enjoying the prospect of total peril on the other side of the door. "I can find my way into anywhere. Plus, I make deliveries here a few times a year, so I've found out a few things about this place."

"Like what?" Esme asked.

"Like you could lose a limb or your magic or your life," Tiago said, staring down the door like a challenge.

Esme glanced at Fetch for his confirmation, although she knew it was true. The fox had already said as much. But deep down she hoped he'd bust up laughing, telling them this was all a joke.

Fetch adjusted his coat and stepped toward the exit. "Once we go through that door, follow my lead. Keep the chatter to a minimum. And if someone talks to you, ignore them. Pretend you don't see them."

"Ignore, pretend," Esme repeated, bobbing her head up and down anxiously.

Tiago folded his arms stiffly across his chest. "Look, I can do the whole pretending and ignoring stuff, but I for sure don't want to get eaten or dismembered or anything like that, so you're *positive* these coats will mask our magic?"

Fetch cracked the door a sliver and peered out. "No such thing as positive." Then he slipped through the door.

Esme didn't bother looking over her shoulder at Tiago, who she knew was making a face. She was too fixated on the fact that they were most definitely not in a house.

It was a dock.

Well, technically it was a thicket of trees that overlooked a crowded marina no more than thirty yards away.

The night air was biting, filled with the scents of salt and rusted steel. Fist-sized flames illuminated the area, floating above like fiery specters. The water rippled and swelled, shifting from black to orange to green to silver.

"Whoa," Esme breathed.

"It looks pretty," Fetch said, "but that water's like acid, so don't go near it."

"What's the point of water if you can't dive in?" Tiago asked.

"This channel carries dead magic," Fetch said.

Tiago frowned. "Dead?"

"When someone here dies," Fetch explained, "their ashes get tossed into the water, along with their unspent magic."

Esme shuddered. "Humans poison water too," she said. "Just not with magic."

People swept across the dock so quickly, Esme was sure they had wings on their shoes. Most were adults, but there were a few kids too, and they were all dressed in drab colors—grays, browns, and deep, deep blues that were almost black. All wore loose-fitting clothing—tunics, wide-legged pants, long dresses. And they all wore the same solemn expression.

It was the people's stares that got Esme. They looked lost, desperate, grim—the kind of stare her father wore so often. "Who are those people?" she whispered.

Keeping to the shadows, Fetch said, "Some are Maldicioneros. You definitely want to stay away from them—they're always in foul moods."

Esme knew that the word "maldición" meant *curse*, but she'd never heard of a Maldicionero. "So they cast curses?"

"It's what they live for," Fetch said, scanning the crowd. "And let's see. . . ." He pointed. "That woman—kinda translucent, pale? She's an Espíritu. But the rest of them? They're like you. Looking for answers, futures, power, revenge, love . . ." His voice trailed off. "Things aren't as different here as you'd expect."

Esme wasn't so sure about that. After all, this was a place ruled by queens, where fairy-tale creatures lived.

"They look so . . . normal," Tiago put in.

"Normal how?" Fetch challenged. "What did you expect, fairies and dragons and vampires and ghouls?"

"Kinda," Esme admitted. "You *did* mention duendes—and there's also the bone dragon." *And you're a talking fox with magical thread.*

Fetch's whiskers twitched with annoyance. "I never said that *those* creatures weren't real, but you should know that the stories written about them aren't, and the way they're described isn't exactly accurate. At least not here." He hesitated before adding, "For example, did you know that fairy wings hold the power to instantly transport you anywhere you want to go?"

Esme exhaled sharply. "That's amazing."

"Except that that kind of thievery carries a terrible curse."

Fetch shook his head. "Definitely not worth it."

A furry white creature with scaly green wings zoomed overhead. Esme and Tiago ducked. "What the heck's that?" Tiago asked.

"A messenger dragon," Fetch said with a pinch of pride in his voice. "Their job is to deliver the mail. Pretty harmless unless you try to steal their food—then they'll claw out your insides with a single talon."

Queens. Dragons. Duendes. Esme wanted to know more. By the look of curiosity on Tiago's face, she knew he was dying to ask more questions too, but they had to stay focused.

"Come on," Fetch said. He led them in the direction of the crowd, which didn't seem to notice or care about their presence. Indistinguishable voices carried across the night air as they walked down a promenade, over a stone bridge, and into a compact village filled with small storefronts and vendors calling out to passersby.

"Look into the fires for your future."

"Keys to open any lock, anywhere, anytime. Buy one, get one free!"

"Aguas especiales to ward off evil spirits, nightmares, and dark destinies."

Esme leaned closer to Tiago. "Dark destinies?"

"I'd like to get my hands on one of those magical keys."

The stores all looked the same—no signs, no window displays, only strange symbols painted on the closed wooden doors.

Catching up with Fetch, Esme asked him about the symbols.

"Old languages no longer spoken," he said, his gaze fixed straight ahead.

"But they're all the exact same," Tiago said.

Fetch sighed. "Your eyes aren't trained to see the truth. But keep quiet. Stop looking so stunned like a tourist and walk faster!"

Except that she *was* a tourist in a very strange land. Esme set her face and mimicked Fetch's gait—confident, like she belonged here. Tiago did the same, although reluctantly, as if he would much rather storm into every building to check things out.

As they marched down the road, navigating the now-thick crowd, Esme's jaw locked tight—a heavy energy spread through her, moving down her neck and spine and legs. But it was too much, too . . . everywhere.

Her Chaos simmered, coming closer to a boil with each step. Feeling dizzy and disoriented, she slowed her pace. If she could just sit down or drink some water . . .

The mob closed in around her. In an instant Tiago and Fetch were gone from her sight. She spun to locate them when a man in a top hat and a red tailcoat stepped in front of her. His sagging gray skin and dark, glittering eyes made her recoil.

Esme's heart pounded violently.

"Are you going in the right direction?" the man hummed. "Ask the fingers."

He held out a small black bowl filled with what looked like finger bones.

"I—no, thanks," she said, trying to sidestep him. The air was like a furnace turned on high. When had it gotten so hot?

"The fingers say you are not on the right path," he said. "You must turn around. Go back. There is too much danger here."

The preoccupied mob shifted around her and the man with the finger bones. She so desperately wanted to get away from him. She maneuvered around him quickly, but just as she did, he shot his hand out and grabbed hold of her arm.

She whirled to face him, ready to unload her Chaos if need be, then stopped herself. No, she couldn't do that—she couldn't draw any attention to her magic and risk not finding the witch to read the note. Or worse, risk getting carved into itty-bitty bits.

The man smiled, revealing a row of crooked gray teeth. "You will die here," he breathed—but it wasn't his voice that came out.

Esme's blood froze.

She knew that voice. It belonged to the woman, the same voice that had been carried on the storm right before Esme and Tiago had found their way onto the island.

With a sharp twist, Esme broke free and bolted through the crowd, the woman's laughter echoing behind her. Esme ran, weaving and ducking, too afraid to look over her shoulder, too afraid to see that creep chasing after her.

Her head pounded. Her limbs ached. Her Chaos felt like it was fire, burning through her, looking for a way out.

Black dots danced in her tear-blurred vision.

She knew she couldn't hold back her magic—it was going to explode, and when it did, she couldn't be near all these people.

There!

Up ahead, she spied a narrow alleyway tucked between two dark buildings.

She dashed into it, then down a flight of chiseled stairs, until she reached a dead end.

She pressed her back against a wall covered in vines, gripping one so tightly its thorns cut into her palm. Blood dripped down her wrist. She tried one last time to control the Chaos, to tamp it down, but it only grew in its rage. Her body shook with it, as if a hurricane was whipping through her.

Fast. Fast. Faster.

And then she let it go.

CHAPTER SEVENTEEN

There was a thunderous explosion of light.

Wind raged through the alley, spinning wildly, bouncing off the walls.

"A witch who cannot control her magic," came the woman's voice, so close it was as if she was just a few inches away.

"Who are you?" Esme shouted into the squall, which swirled and danced before sputtering out.

The woman was silent.

Esme's magic churned in her chest, pressing against her bones, racing through her blood, and yet she could do nothing to control it, to make it yield. To call on it for help.

The woman was right. Esme was a witch who couldn't manage her own power.

"You are nothing," the woman growled, "nothing but a girl

with too much hope. And don't you know that hope is the great executioner?"

Esme had had just about enough of disembodied voices and mysterious messages. "Yeah, well, you're a coward who won't show her face!"

And then the answer to Esme's question, *who are you*, plowed into her heart like a high-speed train. She didn't know if it was the way her magic was rising or just an undeniable hunch. She blurted, "You're the witch hunter." She stared into the darkness, fury burning through her. That was when she saw the outline of a figure, standing several feet away, barely there, like a wisp of cloud.

Esme whispered a simple reveal spell, one that would make the invisible visible, but she must have said it wrong, because no one appeared.

With a laugh, the woman said, "Is that all you have? A witch of Chaos and you cannot complete even simple spells?" She clucked her tongue.

How did the witch hunter know that Esme was of Chaos?

Her mother's words drifted through her memory: *One day you will harness all that power. You'll no longer need spells to do magic. And Earth, Fire, Water, and Air will all bend to your will.*

If only that day were today, Esme thought. She wanted so badly to yell, *You took my family and I want them back!* But where would that get her? No, she had to play her cards right, try to get some useful information.

"I know you're a bruja, too," Esme ground out. "But why are you hunting other witches?" What did they have to do with the daggers and the power they held? It didn't make sense.

The woman was silent.

"Just—just tell me what you want!"

Maybe that was the wrong question, because just then a dim light illuminated the space and a billowing black mist flooded the stairway. It pressed into the alley tentatively, slowly, as though it was searching. Just like the darkness that had erupted from the sky the night of the motorcycle races.

"I'm not afraid of you," Esme lied, trying to choke the spike of panic rising faster and faster within her.

The darkness crept closer, like a crouched animal ready to pounce.

Esme started to run, trying to sidestep the darkness, but it lunged for her. It swirled up her legs and feet, coiling around her body and freezing her in place.

She struggled against its power, a magic so thick and heavy she could barely breathe.

"Perhaps you'd like to join me," the woman purred.

"NEVER!"

"Oh, come now. I could give you the answers to every question, every secret. And with me you'd never have to hide your true nature."

Esme braced herself as the darkness climbed up her torso, and all she could think of was her sister, and those terrible words Esme had spilled—*I hate you!* Something twisted in her gut like the edge of a knife.

At once there was a blur of movement, and Fetch was there, wrapping her in his coat. His fur was soft and warm, and for a single breath she felt safe as everything fell silent. Even his heartbeat. Almost as if the fox's chest was empty. She blinked, listening harder, but the only sound in the whole world was her own heart thudding against her ribs.

Then he released her. The dark mist had vanished along with the voice, but Esme could still feel the cold stab of fear.

Hope is the great executioner.

"There was a woman—the witch hunter," Esme stammered. She looked into Fetch's eyes. "But she's also a brujx."

"What have you done?"

"Done?" Confused, Esme stepped back.

Fetch narrowed his eyes. The weight of his stare was enough to make her want to melt into the ground. "The flowers in your hair . . . I thought you were of Earth."

Esme swallowed, realizing there was no point in lying. "I'm of Chaos."

"Why didn't you tell me?"

"What does it matter?"

"Because Chaos cannot be trusted. Chaos is dangerous and unpredictable and . . ." A low growl erupted from his throat, and he bared sharp teeth. For the first time, he seemed more animal than human. He looked over his shoulder, then back to her. "Your flowers . . . they hide the truth. They make people think you're of Earth."

Esme nodded numbly.

Fetch studied her for a moment too long, and just when she thought he was going to launch into a thousand questions, he said, "We found Ozzie. Tiago's waiting there. Come on."

Then he wrapped her in his coat again and with a *swoosh* they floated, dreamlike, toward Ozzie.

Chapter Eighteen

They landed in a small, windowless shop that smelled of smoke and moss.

The place reminded Esme of the botanica back home. Rustic pine shelves hovered in midair, each lined with jars containing herbs, incense, honey, and brightly colored liquids. At the center of the room was a beat-up silver cauldron as big as a washing machine.

Esme's jaw went tight. There was magic here, witch magic. But there was also something else . . . a spell was in progress, something old and—

Tiago emerged from behind a curtain, followed by a girl who looked no older than ten. She had dark, stringy hair and a smooth bronze complexion peppered with freckles, and she wore a loose-fitting red dress that reached the floor. As scrawny and young as she was, she looked oddly fierce. Powerful.

"Oh," the girl said softly when she saw Esme and Fetch. "You're back. And she's here. Well."

Tiago rushed over to Esme. "What happened? Where'd you go?" His gaze fell to her hand. "You're bleeding!"

"It's fine," Esme said, cupping her palm with her other hand.

"I'm Ozzie. Of Fire." The girl came over and took a quick look at the injury. "Just a thorn. You'll live."

"Can we get on with this?" Fetch groaned.

Ozzie's smile was on the verge of a sneer. She looked at Esme. "You're here for my exceptional services."

Esme did her best to shake off the unexpected surprise that Ozzie was a young girl. "Yes. Can you read Brucera?"

Tiago held up the note. "I showed it to her but no dice. Or at least not yet."

"Apparently," Fetch said, "the message is spelled for your eyes only, which means we had to wait for you."

"Yeah," said Tiago. "It can't be decoded unless you're here, so . . ."

"Classic Water witch move to cryptasize a note," Ozzie said with an appreciative grin. "So secretive and stealthy."

Esme was pretty sure "cryptasize" wasn't a word, but more importantly, "How did you know this was spelled by a Water witch?" Had Tiago told her about Lenny's magic?

Ozzie's expression tightened. "The Water magic is all over the page. I'd have to be dead asleep not to see it. Do you doubt my powers?"

Esme quickly shook her head, but a pathetic, truthful "yes" popped out of her mouth. *Ugh!* Why did her Chaos have to make things so difficult?

Thankfully, Ozzie didn't seem to hear. She held out a scrawny hand. "First, the payment."

Esme's face grew hot. "I, uh . . . don't have any money," she said, wondering how much a simple translation could possibly cost.

Ozzie smirked. "Look around. My tinctures and esencias and spells and curses are all very costly, never mind my time and talent."

The girl snapped her fingers, and a floating shelf lowered itself so she could reach a jar of pink liquid along with a bottle of honey. She began to pour them into the cauldron, which smoked and bubbled. Esme sensed that the container held the spell she had felt moments ago, the one that wasn't complete. *Something old*, she repeated silently, trying to put her finger on the other parts of the hechizo as she worked her jaw back and forth to loosen it.

"And I do not work for free," Ozzie went on, interrupting Esme's thoughts. "So either give me something astounding or go away. I have other customers who *do* pay."

Ozzie will give but will also take.

That was what the woman from Esme's dream had said. But who *was* the dream lady and why was she trying to help? All Esme knew for sure was that the dream voice wasn't the same as the one from the graveyard and alleyway.

Esme began to peel off the magical coat Fetch had given

her, thinking it was plenty astounding.

"I don't want that," Ozzie said, wrinkling her nose. Then to Fetch, "Didn't you tell her the policy?"

Tiago knitted his eyebrows into a tight frown. "What policy?"

With a heavy exhale, the fox said, "The merchants here will only take a trade. Something of absolutely equal value."

Seconds ticked by and all Esme could think to say was "Why didn't you tell us before?"

Fetch met Esme's stunned gaze. There was an answer there, but he didn't voice it because Ozzie said, "The fox's coats are not of equal value. That would be like trading a bar of gold for a stack of hay."

"I wouldn't go that far." Fetch scowled. "These coats are hand-sewn with magical threads."

Ozzie muttered under her breath, something that sounded like *cursed* or *worst*, but Esme couldn't be sure which. She was too fixated on where Ozzie's eyes had landed.

Lenny's dream ring.

"No." Esme was already shaking her head. "This—it's the only way I can talk to my sister." A painful longing filled her heart. Lenny had always made Esme feel safe. If only she were here to help her now. To tell her what to do.

Ozzie shrugged indifferently. "That's the price. Take it or leave it."

"Esme," Tiago said, "it's a dead end unless we find out what the message says."

She knew he was right. Still, she felt suddenly empty, like the last thread that tied her to her sister was being cut. She just prayed that whatever the message was, it was worth it.

Esme removed the magic ring from her finger.

Smiling greedily, Ozzie snatched it. "It's a deal."

Tiago handed over the note.

There, in the Fire witch's shop with the cauldron and potions and esencias watching, Ozzie studied the paper and whispered across its surface. Esme held her breath.

The page floated into the air above the silver cauldron. A small purple flame erupted, then another and another, until they encircled the note.

Tiago leaned closer. "I thought she was just going to read it."

"The more you talk," Ozzie said with a huff, "the longer this will take."

Fetch stepped back, away from the cauldron. But his gold-flecked eyes never strayed from the magic fluttering above them.

That was when the memory of him wrapping Esme in his coat, of her head pressed against his chest, surfaced, forcing her to reexamine something she badly wanted to ignore. The fox didn't have a heartbeat.

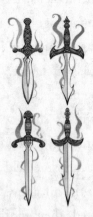

Chapter Nineteen

The realization crashed into Esme just as the page folded itself into a paper bird. It fluttered about the room, then settled into her hands, still as a rock.

Carefully she unfolded its wings, peeling back the layers to reveal words she could read. She blinked. Read them again.

This was wrong. All wrong.

"What does it say?" Tiago asked.

Esme read the text aloud. "'The Legend of Ire is the greatest of lies. Easy to speak and harder to keep. If it is the truth you seek, you will not find it here or there or anywhere. For the truth can only be found inside the deception.'"

Tiago grabbed the note and scanned it with wild eyes as Esme blinked in stunned silence, hoping the words would scramble and change into something that made sense. But nothing changed. She looked up at Ozzie. "But . . . this was supposed to tell us how to find an original witch!"

Ozzie's deep-set eyes brightened and she began to laugh. "An original witch. Impossible."

"This can't be right!" Esme shouted. "You did something with the real message, with my sister's magic!"

Ozzie's face reddened with anger. "How dare you!"

"It's a riddle," Tiago said distractedly. "'Easy to speak and harder to keep.'"

"Our business is concluded." Fetch gave a quick bow and said, "We'll be going now."

"No one is going anywhere!" the witch snarled. "I gave you what you came here for. How dare you accuse me of wrong-doing?"

The flame over the cauldron expanded, stretching itself into a ribbon of heat that swirled around Ozzie, engulfing her entirely.

Tiago's mouth fell open. "This is so not good."

The flame vanished, and before them stood a very old woman with long, very dry orange hair. Her eyes narrowed, glittering black and gold. "I know every language ever spoken. There is no mistake. And for your tremendous insult, I banish you to the Tower of Shadows!" She trembled with rage.

"Shadows?" Esme squeaked.

Ozzie's mouth fanned into a wicked smile. She spoke slowly, as if she wanted each word to count. "A place that grows your darkest emotions. Shame? Hate? Despair? Delicious!" she cooed.

"Doesn't sound delicious at all," Tiago grumbled.

"One night in the tower and you'll become a shadow," Ozzie said almost gleefully. "Wicked and lost. A winning combination."

Esme cringed as Ozzie sniffed once, twice. "Air magic and . . ." Her eyes zeroed in on Esme. "Do I smell Earth magic? Hmm . . . no, that feels off. I cannot quite put a finger on your magic. Why is that? And do not tell me these second-rate coats can guard the truth."

Fetch cleared his throat, laughed nervously. "Ozzie," he said, "I'm sure we can come to an understanding. They're new here and don't know the protocol. Maybe you could overlook this small infraction."

"Exactly!" Tiago offered his most winning smile.

"NO!" Ozzie roared.

"I'm really sorry," Esme pleaded. Everyone knew that Fire witches had the worst tempers, but they also felt the deepest. Maybe she could appeal to the brujx's heart. "I'm just super upset because my family is gone. This was our only clue to find them, and it doesn't even mean anything, so I lost my cool. But, look, you have the dream ring, so it's all good."

Ozzie's expression remained fixed. "You have insulted me, and for that there is no apology big enough, no amount of groveling that will save you."

Esme stared, dumbfounded, worried she'd blurt another insult.

"But I am a fair witch," Ozzie said with a smirk. "So I will give you a choice. You can save yourself or one of your friends from the Tower of Shadows, but only one." She paused theatrically.

"And what happens to the one that doesn't go to the tower?" Esme asked.

"Pick Fetch," Tiago threw out.

"No!" Esme gaped at her best friend, stunned. If they made it out of here alive, she was going to wring his scrawny little neck for being so foolish, so loyal.

So Tiago.

Ozzie grinned at Esme, ignoring Tiago's outburst. "Like I said, I am a fair witch."

"So you'll set us all free?" Tiago said.

Ozzie scowled at him. "Why would I ever do something so foolish?"

"It's not foolish," Esme blurted, trying to think of a way out of this mess.

Fetch made a move to open his coat, and Ozzie barked out a laugh. "Your magic will not work here, you fool. These walls are protected with the greatest of defensive powers."

The witch's face brightened as if she had just thought of a vicious way to torment them. "I've changed my mind," she said. "I shall set *one* of you free. One can stay here with me so I can use their magic to my benefit. And only one will go to the tower. See how generous I am?"

She clapped her hands. "But I get ahead of myself. I offered you a choice, Esme."

Esme's heart had already made the decision. "I have a better idea. Take me. You can use my magic. Let Tiago and Fetch go. And *no one* has to go to the tower."

"I'll give you *all* my threads." Fetch spoke evenly, but his tone was pleading. "Her magic isn't worth what I'm offering."

Ozzie glared at the fox. "And what good have those threads done you? Or your plight?"

Plight? What was the witch talking about? Esme shook her head—it didn't matter. She couldn't let Fetch give up the threads his grandfather had given to him. With her head held high, she stepped closer to Ozzie. "I'm of Chaos."

"She's lying!" Tiago cried.

But Ozzie paid him no attention. "Chaos," she whispered, looking suddenly entranced. An icy knot of dread expanded in Esme's chest as Ozzie came closer, sniffing her. "I will be lauded as a hero. And while that was not the deal, yes, I will take your offer. Your worthless friends may go."

"I'm not leaving," Tiago asserted.

"Of course you are." Ozzie cackled with glee as Fetch and Tiago began to move jerkily toward the front door, as if an invisible hand was shoving them.

"Esme!" Tiago shouted angrily.

The fox's gaze met Esme's. He tapped his coat, and she nodded in understanding. The coat would always take him home. Fetch would whisk Tiago to his den. They'd be safe.

The two were hefted off their feet and thrown through the door. It slammed behind them with a terrible finality.

Ozzie wiped her hands together as if she had tossed Tiago and Fetch out herself. "Now, if you'll excuse me, I must go and prepare your cell. The last prisoner left it quite a bloody mess."

Esme's insides twisted. No way was she going to spend even a second in a bloody cell. Not when so many witches were counting on her. She turned her attention to the cauldron. Something was different about the magic inside. She inched closer and as she did, her jaw went painfully rigid, as if it had turned to stone. The last time she'd felt something this powerful was when Lenny had crafted an itching curse that she planned to use on a mean teacher at school, but then, not wanting to risk the council's wrath, she destroyed it.

Esme stared at the cauldron. The magic bubbling inside was more than a regular spell. It had to be a maldición, a curse.

Before she thought too deeply about it, she ran forward and knocked it on its side, spilling a tar-like ooze all over the floor, though she was careful not to allow it to touch her.

Ozzie screamed.

The curse sizzled.

Taking her chance, Esme bolted toward the front door, but it vanished before her eyes. She spun around. There was no escape, no exit at all.

Only a freed curse and the rage of a Fire witch who looked as though she could burn down the world.

Chapter Twenty

If magic is unpredictable, then curses are downright rebellious.

And now this one was free, zipping around Ozzie in a stream of silver light.

Ozzie shrieked, collapsing to the ground, where she writhed and choked, her eyes bulging out of her head. Her tongue reached out of her mouth, growing longer and longer until it whipped about like an octopus arm.

Esme jumped up, skipping over the errant tongue.

Ozzie threw her head back in agony, her growing tongue wrapping around her dizzyingly fast.

Esme screamed, the sound of it splitting the air. She had to find a way out of here!

"Help me," came a tiny voice.

Esme froze, then glanced at the spiraled tongue. She dared an inch and another to get a better look. There in the center was Ozzie. Well, a much smaller Ozzie, about the size of a soda can.

"You want me to help *you*?" Esme snarled. "After you threw out my friends and stole my ring and tried to—"

"Oh, get over yourself," Ozzie hissed. "You otherworlders are so high-and-mighty."

"At least we have manners," Esme argued.

"You're the one who spilled my curse!"

"Only because you were going to send me to the Tower of Shadows."

"Well," Ozzie said with a small huff, "it seems things have changed. Now, if you'll restore me to my original state, we can forget all this happened and you can go on your merry little way."

"And what do I get out of it?" Esme asked, unsure how she was supposed to help the witch trapped by her own tongue.

The tiny brujx stared up with defiant eyes. "I will tell you how to get out of here."

"I want my ring back."

"Can't do that."

"Why?"

Ozzie held up her ringless fingers. "My tongue swallowed it!"

"Then tell your tongue to give it back."

"That's not how it works, child. Now, you can either help

me or you can spend forever trapped here with me."

Esme glanced around. The front door had vanished and there were no other doors, no exits in sight. If she was going to get out of here, she was going to have to play the witch's game. "What was the curse, anyway? To get shrunken by a tongue?"

Ozzie grumbled incoherently, then said with a resigned sigh, "To get shrunken by the lies you've told, and the only way back is to answer three questions truthfully."

Esme eyed her suspiciously. "Then why do you need me?"

"You spilled the curse, so you must ask the questions."

Sounded fair enough, but there had to be a catch. There always was where magic was concerned. "How do I know you won't grow again and send me to the Tower of Shadows?" Esme asked.

Ozzie closed her eyes and shook her head sadly. "If I tell you one lie, then I am doomed to this state forever, so ask me if I am going to hurt you. But be clear, because wanting to hurt you isn't the same thing as doing it. Go ahead. That can be your first question."

"Are you going to hurt me?"

"No."

Esme let out a long breath. "Okay. Do you know what the riddle means?"

"I do not."

Esme paced restlessly. She had to make the last question count. But before she could formulate anything sound, her Chaos magic sent her mouth into overdrive and out spilled,

"What did you mean about Fetch's plight?"

Ozzie smiled a vicious little smile. "I meant that he is not who he says he is."

"Wait! That isn't an answer."

"Perhaps you should learn to ask better questions."

Fuming, Esme imagined kicking tiny Ozzie across the room, but that would get her nowhere except feeling guilty later. Plus, the witch was growing, foot by foot, like a stretchy doll.

At the same instant, a gaping hole appeared in the ceiling and a bitter wind swept through the shop, hoisting Esme off her feet. "Hey!" She clawed at the air uselessly.

Glaring, Ozzie planted her hands on her hips. "I promised to tell you how to get out of here, but I never promised that it would be a fun ride. Enjoy the Forest of the Fatales," she commanded just as the freezing gale swept Esme into the blackness.

Darkness engulfed Esme.

Stay calm, she told herself. *Calm. Calm. Calm.*

Her best efforts only made her heart pound more violently.

Then, just as suddenly as the darkness had come, the air grew icier and she once again felt the ground beneath her feet, soft and yielding.

Esme knew she was no longer in the shop. She was outside, somewhere.

The Forest of the Fatales.

But what were Fatales? Didn't sound like anything good.

Esme's Chaos leaped in her chest, hot and painful.

The darkness broke apart slowly, like the shifting of a kaleidoscope.

A yellowish moon hung low in the sky, casting a soft glow over a forest of awkwardly bent trees, leaning this way and that. Their smooth branches and trunks were bone white.

A ripple of fear tore through Esme. Her imagination conjured images of monsters with massive teeth and claws.

Bracing herself, she took a deep breath and looked around for the ferocious beasts. But all she saw was Ozzie, still small, still mad, still scowling.

"What are you doing here?" Esme managed, oddly relieved to have company, even if that company was a wicked miniature Fire witch. "And why are you small again?"

"I forgot about a ridiculous rule, the fine print of breaking this atrocious curse. I told you I would help you get out of my shop, but apparently I have to do more than that," she huffed. "I have to help you reach a destination of your choice."

"Oh," Esme said, surprised. A destination of her choice? Where was that? "Can you take me to an original witch?"

"Hmph. If I knew where that was, I'd sell the information to the highest bidder."

Esme clenched and unclenched her fists. She had no idea where to go. She couldn't go to Oblivion without help and she couldn't go home. "Take me to my friends." It seemed like the most reasonable request, since she'd need their strength and support and brainpower.

The tiny witch snorted, then that terrible smile crept across her face again. "At least I can choose the path. Whether you make it or not isn't my concern."

Esme crouched to meet Ozzie's miniature glare, thinking she might be able to use the Fire witch. After all, someone with Ozzie's powers could probably burn down the whole forest with a single breath. "I think you might be cursed forever unless you do it right this time." Esme had no idea if that were true, but right now she had the upper hand and was absolutely going to use it.

"CHILD! Miscreant! Pathetic little nothing of a witch," Ozzie hollered so loud her face reddened. "I know the rules of my own curse!"

"Okay, okay," Esme said, trying to calm the feisty little brujx.

"The forest responds to quick movements," Ozzie said. "It will confuse you, trap you. And then *it* will kill you."

Frustration mounted inside Esme, threatening to erupt like hot lava. "You just said the forest will kill me."

"One can only hope."

Esme stomped her foot dangerously close to the witch, who shrank back.

"You have a terrible temper for someone so young," Ozzie said. She gestured toward a path with a barely-there nod. "If you make it out of here, there's a boat waiting at the costa norte. Your friends will be there."

"How do you know where they are?"

"Because I can smell them."

Esme stared at the witch doubtfully.

"Fine," Ozzie grumbled. "I sent a spy to follow them. We have a telepathic connection, so I have instructed the spy to alert your little friends where to find you. Satisfied?"

"How can I go through the forest? You said no movements, or it would trap me and kill me."

"I said no *sudden* movements," Ozzie said. "Just walk with purpose, slowly, steadily. And follow the path."

"Hold up," Esme said. "I asked for you to take me to my friends, not tell me where to find them, and I'm pretty sure your curse is very specific—I mean, most curses are—so I'd like you to show me the way," she said, quite proud of her quick thinking.

"I cannot."

"But . . ."

"I am prohibited from entering this forest any farther, but you are correct. Curses are quite peculiar and precise, and while I cannot take you to your friends myself, I can offer you this." She tugged something out of her pocket. It was a glass orb with a tiny flame flickering inside. As she handed it over, the orb expanded to the size of a golf ball.

The globe was oddly cool to the touch.

"What is it?" Esme asked.

"It will glow green if you are headed in the right direction."

"So it's like GPS."

"It is also a magnificent weapon," Ozzie said. "Do you have good aim?"

"Uh . . . I think so? Do you always carry weapons in your pocket?"

Ozzie stared up at her. "What else is a pocket for? Now, listen up because I hate repeating myself: If any monster bothers you, you'll have to get close enough to shove this in their mouth."

Esme felt shaky all over just thinking about it. "What will it do to them?"

"It will blow them to smithereens."

Great. Now Esme had more than monsters to worry about. She had to worry about their blood and guts all over her.

Clutching the fire orb, she began to make her way down the path, hoping it guided her back to her friends.

Ozzie's voice rang out. "Oh, I feel the curse lifting already!"

Esme looked back, but the Fire witch was already gone, leaving Esme in a forest of monsters all alone.

CHAPTER TWENTY-ONE

With Ozzie's fire orb in her hand, Esme journeyed through the woods. The path was narrow and eerily quiet; even her footsteps made no sound against the soft dirt.

Slowly she turned the riddle over in her mind.

The Legend of Ire is the greatest of lies. Easy to speak and harder to keep. If it is the truth you seek, you will not find it here or there or anywhere. For the truth can only be found inside the deception.

The Legend of Ire was a lie? Did that mean all of it or just part of it?

Something darted through the trees.

Esme looked up.

It's just a shadow, she told herself.

The forest was still, as if each tree was watching her,

waiting, hoping for the sudden movements that Ozzie had warned her about.

Slowly, carefully, she plodded up a twisty hill, watching the glow of the orb and forcing her thoughts back to the riddle. She didn't see how it could possibly lead her to an original witch.

Esme remembered the text message Lenny had sent just last night, before their lives exploded: *I have something to tell you. When you get home.*

But she'd never gotten the chance.

Esme's heart felt like it was on life support, like it might never beat right again unless she saved her sister, her dad. They had to be a family again. No matter what it took.

"The truth can only be found inside the deception," she whispered, puzzling over the words.

The air grew even colder, carrying the scent of salt. Esme wound around a narrow bend, finding herself at a small inlet. Tiny crabs crawled across the glittering black sand beach, vanishing beneath bits of scattered driftwood.

Beyond, dark waves rolled in and out, splashing against a rowboat that was waiting just as Ozzie had promised. But no Tiago or Fetch. Had the witch lied?

Rubbing the chill from her arms, Esme stared across the inky sea. The rhythm of each breaker reminded her of the seconds ticking past for her family and the other witches trapped in Oblivion. Soon their minds, their memories, and their magic would be lost forever. And if Fetch was right, she'd already lost too many hours and was now down to only three-ish days to find and rescue them.

For the first time, Esme felt the terrible weight of hopelessness on her shoulders. She had been so focused on reading the cryptic message, trusting that it would tell her how to find an original witch, that she hadn't considered it might be a dead end, that she might find herself standing in front of a yawning black sea with no idea what to do next.

If only she hadn't had to give up Lenny's ring, then maybe she could have talked to her sister again in her dreams. She hoped Lenny had heard the message that Esme was coming.

I'm going to save you. I'm going to make this right.

"Esme!"

She whirled to see Tiago racing down a path different from the one she had taken. He barreled into her, wrapping his arms around her and squeezing like a human vise.

"Glad to see you too!" Her words came out in a whoosh as her arms flew around his waist.

"Fetch told me about the alley," he said, releasing her. "Was it the same voice as the dream telling you to find that awful Ozzie?"

Esme shook her head. She looked over Tiago's shoulder. Fetch strolled toward her, the hem of his coat fluttering in the soft breeze. With a glare, she blew past Tiago, forgetting Ozzie's warning about sudden movements. But technically, she wasn't in the forest, so she was safe. Right? "Who are you really?" she shouted at Fetch. "And what do you want?"

Fetch's furry brows came together softly, framing his gold-flecked eyes in a way that made her feel sort of sorry for yelling. "I'll tell you everything, but first we have to get out of here." He glanced around. The tree limbs at the edge of the beach seemed to shiver, as though they were awakening from a long sleep. Or was it just the breeze? "Where did the boat come from?"

"I think Ozzie put it there," Esme guessed.

Fetch's tail swished restlessly. "Why would she do that?"

"Something to do with a curse," Esme said. "I'll explain later."

The fox seemed to understand. "We need to slip onto the boat nice and easy."

"There aren't any oars," Tiago observed.

"You don't need them." Fetch's whiskers twitched. "If I'm right and that boat is what I think it is, once the vessel is in the water, it will take you wherever you want to go. Well, as long as you give it a command. Otherwise, it sort of has a mind of its own and will take off like a wild horse."

"So an enchanted boat," Tiago said, grinning.

"Exactly." Fetch began to make his way to the rowboat. "Follow me."

Esme was tired of people telling her what to do, and she was especially sick of cryptic messages and unanswered questions. She gripped Fetch's arm, stopping him in his tracks. "I'm not going anywhere with you until you tell us exactly who you are and why you helped us."

All the bravado seemed to go out of the fox. He stepped away, blinking, holding up his furry paws defensively. The black mass of hair on his head fell forward, nearly covering his eyes. "I told you that you might have something that I would want. This is it," he said. "I want to come with you. To leave this realm."

Esme glowered at Fetch, remembering Ozzie's words. *He is not who he says he is.*

"And where exactly are we going?" Tiago asked. "All we have is a riddle and now two people who want to murder us. Aguilar *and* Ozzie."

"Don't forget the witch hunter."

Tiago's face bloomed with what looked like a grande revelation.

"What?" Esme sucked in a sharp breath. "Do you have an idea?"

"Nah. I just remembered that they say you're not a big shot until someone wants to murder you."

"Yeah," Esme said disappointedly, "big shots who still have no idea how to find an original witch."

"I know how to find one," the fox said.

"WHAT!" Tiago shouted as a sudden anger burned in Esme's chest. "And you didn't tell us?"

"You didn't ask," Fetch said evenly. "And you were so extra set on finding a witch to read that Brucera message of yours. Besides, I thought Ozzie would be able to read it—I mean, definitively. But we can't forget, riddles are solvable if you know how to look at them. Can we please go now?"

The fox was right. But would they figure the riddle out in time to save their families and the other witches trapped in Oblivion?

"You still haven't told us *why* you want to come with us," Esme said. "And how do you know where to find an original witch?"

"I know this realm better than anyone," the fox said with a confidence that didn't quite match the way his ears drooped against his head.

"Are you seriously saying they're *here*?" Tiago scoffed.

"Not here," Fetch said, waving his hand to indicate the woods only a few feet away. "This realm sits on top of—"

"Portals," Esme interjected, remembering what she had been told about Ocho Manos. But could it actually be true? "They lead to . . ." She felt suddenly woozy. "Dark and dangerous realms—"

"Alternate dimensions." Tiago's eyes were ablaze with excitement, as though he could hardly wait to jump headfirst into one of these unknown worlds.

Fetch nodded. "You'll find an original witch in one of those realms, and I—I want to go there because I need one of them to help me and I don't care which one it is."

"Help with what?" Esme asked.

The fox's gaze dropped to the sand. "I'm cursed."

"Oof," Tiago said. "Wasn't expecting that."

"I was cursed into this." His shoulders fell, and he sighed. "I'm not really a fox."

"Wasn't expecting that either," Tiago muttered.

Esme's heart seemed to lean closer to Fetch. "Then what are you?" she asked.

"Human like you," he said. "Well, not exactly like you, because I'm not a witch. I'm a Zindero, a weaver. I weave magic with threads." He opened his coat to reveal dozens of pockets.

"Jeez, how many pockets do you have inside that thing?" Tiago asked, looking closer.

"Hundreds," Fetch said, beaming, "but you'd never know it, right? Anyhow, all my enchanted spools are now inside my coat."

Esme's Chaos stirred. She bit her lip, but the words came anyway. "How can you be human," she blurted, "when you don't have a heartbeat?"

Tiago's mouth fell open. "Say what? How do you know?" he asked Esme. "And how did I *not* know?!"

Fetch said, "I was warned that if I ever tried to break the curse, my heart would stop. And I can't say much more than that, so please don't inquire about the who and the why and—"

"If that's true, then how are you still alive?" Esme asked. It was a terrible question to ask and probably worse to answer.

Fetch stiffened. "It's exponentially more agonizing to have to wait for your death than for it to happen quickly. I guess that's part of the punishment. The waiting."

Esme felt nauseous. "Do you know how long you have?"

He glanced at his pocket watch. "Precisely twenty-six hours

from now. Unless I can find an original witch to break this curse."

"That's only, like, a day and some change!" Tiago said.

"Are you sure about that?" Esme asked Fetch, hoping he was wrong. Hoping he had more time.

"I was given a very clear warning," Fetch said, "and you don't forget something like that. Ever."

How could he be so cavalier? So calm?

He glanced back at his watch. "And speaking of a ticking bomb, you have seventy-eight hours, give or take."

The thought of it made Esme sick with worry and doubt, but this was no longer just about her and Tiago's families, or the town of San Bosco. This was now also about the cursed fox.

"Hold on," she said. "How did you try to break the curse?"

The fox hesitated, then said simply, "By agreeing to help you."

Chapter Twenty-Two

His words took all the wind out of Esme.

"Come again?" Tiago said.

"When you told me you were looking for an original witch," Fetch said, "I knew it was my only shot to break the curse, and I guess my intentions were pretty loud."

Esme frowned. "You could have just told us."

With a smirk, Fetch said, "I didn't know you. Would *you* have trusted you if you were me?"

"A thousand percent," Tiago said. "But respect, man. Making a choice you know could end you? Brutal."

Esme thrust out her hand, palm down. "No more lies."

Tiago placed his hand on top of hers, and Fetch added his paw to the pile. "No more lies."

"Okay, then," Esme said, satisfied. "What do you need us for? Why not go to one of those dimensions alone?"

"Only a brujx has the power to find an original witch."

Which meant that Esme's hunch was right. "So the witch hunter, the one who got their hands on a Dagger of Ire, *is* a witch," she muttered.

Tiago blew out a long breath that sounded like a whistle. "And that means they're from San Bosco—so we probably know them, right?"

"I hope not." The idea of a brujx hunting their own was like a fist to the heart.

"We should go," Fetch said.

"Wait," Esme said, her curiosity turning like a tornado. "Who would curse you like this?"

"And like why?" Tiago threw in. "You must've really pissed someone off."

"Something like that," Fetch said, scanning the forest. "But right now, we need to get to that boat."

"And then what?" Esme needed a plan, a course of action beyond figuring out the riddle. She desperately needed to feel like she was moving toward her family, toward saving the witches, faster than the seconds were ticking by.

A horrible sound filled the air, like a knife scraping glass.

Esme whirled.

In the blackness of the woods, something began to take shape. Three forms, floating like ghosts.

Tiago said, "What the—"

No, Esme realized as they floated to the forest's edge, not ghosts.

Semitransparent women with bloodred eyes, hollowed

cheeks, and mouths so cavernous, an entire human body could fit inside.

"Don't move," Fetch whispered shakily. "Just take it nice and easy to the boat."

"You said not to move!" Tiago said.

"Fatales," Esme whispered.

"Let me guess," Tiago muttered. "They're fatal?"

A tight ball of fear coiled in Esme's stomach.

"Nice and slow," Fetch warned as the trio crept backward. "Or they'll notice us."

"Looks like they already have!" Esme said, wishing she could look away from the winged wraithlike Fatales with their tattered gowns and vacant stares. Her jaw tensed painfully, as if someone was screwing it shut, and no matter how much she tried to work it loose, the dark magic tightened the screws.

A few more feet, Esme chanted silently. Her heart pounded. A few—*thump*—more—*thump*—feet.

She stumbled into a piece of driftwood. Tiago's arm shot out to catch her.

There was an instant, a brief moment of total silence, of *maybe it's going to be okay*—

Then the Fatales flew at them.

SCREEEEE!

The unworldly shriek was so piercing, so excruciating, Esme thought her head would explode as she fell to her knees, covering her ears.

A thick tunnel of fog wrapped around her. She could no

longer see or hear her friends. The only thing in her line of sight was a single monstruo winging toward her, its foaming mouth wide with hunger.

Warm blood seeped from Esme's ears as her pulse thrashed, her head throbbing with agony. She threw out her arms, hoping her Chaos magic would explode out of her and incinerate this beast, but there was . . . nothing.

The Fatal advanced.

Closer and closer. The creature's tattered gown rippled around her skeletal body.

Esme got to her feet and stumble-ran through the thick sand, trying to stay upright.

In a flash, the thing was on her, knocking her to the ground. With a deadly snarl, the beast pressed her bony arms into the earth, locking Esme in place.

She lay there helplessly, staring into the eyes of death.

The Fatal's mouth curved into a chilling grin, exposing sharp gray teeth.

"Get off me!" Esme growled.

The beast licked her slimy lips. She began to open her mouth again, slowly, tauntingly.

Esme's heart thundered with a terrifying echo. *Defeat. Defeat. Defeat.*

No! She wouldn't die. Not tonight! Not before she saved her family. Not before she made things right with Lenny.

With a snarl, she jabbed the Fatal in the throat. But her fist went right through the monster, as if she was made of the dark mist still surrounding them.

The Fatal hissed.

Her mouth fell open as if there was no end to her gape—distant, terrified screams echoed from the monster's lungs. *Her victims*, Esme thought in horror.

Frantically, she shifted to the left, to the right, but the mist, the bony arms—there was nowhere to run, nowhere far enough to escape the Fatal's killing shriek.

"Please," Esme cried.

The monster unleashed a gust of rancid, ancient-smelling breath.

She glared at Esme with enraged eyes. Then, in a moment of absolute fury, the Fatal drove a claw into Esme's ribs, but . . . there was no pain. Esme dared a glance—the monster's hand was nothing more than a ribbon of mist.

Esme blinked, frozen with terror.

The beast glared at her ghostly claw still buried in Esme's side. She threw her head back, opened her mouth, and screamed.

The Fatal shattered like glass.

Bits of dark ash floated into the sky. The fog parted.

Heart pounding, Esme couldn't stop to question—she leaped to her feet, desperate to find her friends.

She spotted Tiago a good thirty yards away, but even from here Esme could see the blood leaking from his ears, and a monster floating in circles around him, mocking him. He swayed, jabbing his fists pathetically into the air.

"Fight *me*!" Esme screamed at the creature.

The Fatal's head jerked up. Her wicked eyes met Esme's.

Esme's body flared with a heat she had never felt, as if she was made of thunder and lightning. She took off running toward Tiago and threw herself between the monster and her best friend. He was trying to push past her, but she shoved him back protectively.

A cold darkness gathered. Winds charged the shore.

Teeth bared, the Fatal flew at Esme.

Remembering the orb Ozzie had given her, Esme wrenched it out of her pocket and lunged, driving the weapon right into the monster's mouth. The Fatal wailed, smashing into a million bits just like the one before.

Chest heaving, Esme spun back to her friend, but all she found was a baby otter lying lifelessly on the sand.

"Tiago!" she cried, dropping to her knees next to him. He was out cold, but he was breathing. Gently, she lifted his small form into her arms, eyes darting around for Fetch.

There!

He was halfway to the forest's edge, squat-walking across the sand like a duck. What was he doing? And where was the third Fatal?

"Fetch!" Esme yelled. He didn't turn.

Wait. Fetch wasn't just duck-walking, he was unrolling a spool of thread, laying it on the ground with care and precision.

Tiago stirred. With huge, round otter eyes, he stared up

at Esme. Then, with a twist, he rolled softly out of her arms. Right before he landed on the sand, he shifted back into human form.

"Tiago!" Instant tears of relief streaked down her face. "Are you okay?"

"I'm made of steel," he muttered, pulling himself up with a groan. "Was I really just an otter? 'Cause it would really suck to die as one."

She wanted to hug him, to kiss those skinny cheeks of his, but the trees began to shudder, and Esme knew it was only a matter of minutes, maybe seconds, before more Fatales arrived.

Quickly, she and Tiago got to the sandbar, jumped inside the boat, and waited for Fetch.

A horrific crash sounded in the forest. The waves grew restless, doubling their size and power. Crashing, reaching toward the boat, carrying it out to sea.

"WAIT!" Esme yelled. But the vessel kept on going. So much for following orders!

She spun back to shore.

Fetch was racing toward her, his face determined. A new army of ten or more ravenous monsters emerged from the dark forest, gaining on him with every step.

"Hurry!" she shouted over a vicious gale. Salt water sprayed her face, stinging her eyes.

"He's not going to make it," Tiago cried, paddling uselessly to try to slow the boat.

The rowboat continued to sail away from the beach. Away from Fetch. The cursed fox who had saved her life twice.

He was so close. Twenty more feet.

Fifteen.

Tiago was right. Fetch wasn't going to make it.

In unison, the beasts opened their cavernous mouths. The scream was coming.

Esme forgot all about her desperation to escape, to save her family and her own life. In that moment only one thing mattered.

Saving her friend.

She took a deep breath and jumped into the raging waters.

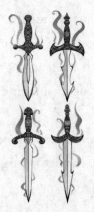

Chapter Twenty-Three

Leaping into black, stormy waters was not a smart decision. But when your spirit is sinking and your heart is breaking, you do very foolish things.

The moment Esme touched the shore, brilliant flashes of white and pink and green exploded across the beach like fireworks.

KABOOOOM!

The force hurled her into the air.

Sand poured from the sky like rain as she landed with a thud. Through the sandstorm, Esme saw the airborne fox, limbs windmilling uselessly through a cloud of green smoke before he crashed nearby.

Tiago was shouting something from the boat, his voice lost in the crashing waves, but Esme was too busy scampering over to Fetch on all fours.

"Get up!" she hollered, though her voice sounded distant, muffled, as if she was in a tunnel.

With a grin, Fetch rolled to his feet, shaking the sand out of his fur as he surveyed the damage from the explosions. All across the beach, enormous craters smoked and sputtered.

Why was the fox just standing there, smiling?

"Are they gone?" Esme stood.

With a small nod he said, "That was surprising."

Which part—the monsters? The explosions? "Can we talk about this later?"

"You didn't have to come back for me."

Esme's cheeks burned hot. "Yeah, well, you saved my life, so . . ."

The fox's eyes softened. "You still came back for me."

"Which makes us even."

"Not exactly," he said. "I've saved your life twice now, so looks like you still owe me one."

Esme smirked. "I'd rather not be in any more life-or-death situations."

"Yeah, well, we don't always get what we wish for."

"Esme!" Tiago shouted. "ÁNDALE!"

She snapped her attention to her best friend. Tiago was chest-high in the water, struggling against the waves, straining to hold the boat in place. From the looks of it, he was failing miserably, but Esme had never loved his loyalty and stubborn spirit more.

"Just tell it to stop," Fetch hollered to Tiago, who did so immediately, and the boat stopped. "I knew that," Tiago grumbled as he hoisted himself back into the now-still vessel.

Fetch hobbled along, dragging a leg behind him.

"You're hurt," Esme said, wrapping an arm around the fox's waist so he could use her as a crutch. He looped one of his front paws around her neck and chuckled. "Did you know that in this realm it's very good luck to sprain your right ankle?"

Esme laughed. "Sounds like bad luck to me."

"Maybe where you're from," Fetch said. "But now? Well, consider me your personal good luck charm."

"Okay," Esme agreed. "We're going to need it."

The sky began to lighten, shaking loose the darkness as peculiar-looking scraps floated down onto the shore.

"Fetch?"

"Yeah?"

"Please tell me that those scraps are not bone and hair and . . . Fatales leftovers?"

"Those aren't Fatales leftovers."

"You're lying."

"Yes."

She socked him in the arm, and just as they came to the water's edge, she glanced over her shoulder. An icy prickle crept across her jaw, trickling down her throat and into her chest. She could feel it—

The Fatales' dark magic was dying a slow death.

Esme didn't know which was stronger, her shock or her

relief. Maybe it was possible to have room in your heart for more than one emotion. Love and hate. Fear and courage. Hope and hopelessness.

Within moments, they were sailing far away from the forest.

Shivering, Esme stared across the gray sea, rubbing her ears, which were still ringing with pain from the Fatales' screams. She didn't want to talk about the harrowing experience they'd all just gone through. She just wanted to chart out a solid plan that would give them even a slim chance of success. With every second that went by, she pictured her sister and dad crouched in a damp corner of some dungeon with barred windows that let in only a sliver of moonlight. Were they in pain? Did they know that their memories and magic would soon be drained?

And then came the catastrophic thoughts: What if she never saw them again? What if she never got to make things right with Lenny? What if her dad never got the chance to be whole again?

What if San Bosco had already rotted away?

Fetch was right. There was agony in the waiting.

"Where do we go now?" Esme asked. "We can't just—"

"Exactly," Tiago said, but his eyes were distant, as if he was only now realizing what they were up against, how many impossibilities were stacking up, and how quickly the time was winding down.

"We can do this," Esme said softly. "We have to do this."

Tiago cast his gaze toward the black horizon. "I miss my

mom." Color flooded his cheeks.

"You're going to see her again," Esme insisted.

Tiago looked at her. "I know I seem brave and all that. And I am, I mean—" He ran a hand down his face in exasperation. "I just can't stand the thought of her being hurt."

Esme felt the tears coming. It was unlike Tiago to show this much emotion. He always defaulted to humor and a can-do attitude that Esme could lean on. But maybe the close call with death had woken something up inside him. She didn't have the heart to tell him how weak Lenny had looked, how cold she'd said it was.

"I feel the same way," Esme said.

"What if . . ." His voice was near breaking.

"Don't even think it," Esme said. "We're going to save her and my dad and Lenny."

"And San Bosco," Tiago said more to himself than to her.

She turned to Fetch. "You said you know how to find an original witch. Tell us."

The fox's eyes softened, though his furry mouth was set in a tight, determined line. "After I was cursed," he said, "I made it my mission to figure out how to find an original witch to break this curse. Last year, I came across an ancient text that described the creation of Ocho Manos. There was a map, and in the bottom corner were two words written in one of the ancient languages that took me forever to translate."

"What were they?" Esme asked.

"'Secret realm.'" Fetch's whiskers twitched. "I think it

belongs to one of the original witches."

"Secret realm?" Esme echoed.

"An alternate dimension," Fetch said. "A place beyond this world."

"I know what a realm is, but why . . . how is there one here?" Esme asked.

"Apparently, it was here long before Ocho Manos existed," Fetch said. "It was the original witches' own magic that helped create this place."

Could they really be this close to finding an original witch? A new hope sprouted deep within her.

"How long will it take to get to this secret realm?" she asked. Each hour carried the weight of her entire world. If she failed in this quest, not only would she lose her family and all the knowledge of the San Bosco witches, but she'd lose parts of herself. Her heart, her history, even her entire future, because it was nothing without the love of her family.

"A few hours," Fetch said, looking suddenly exhausted, before he told the boat, "to El Castillo de la Noche."

"Castle?" Esme asked. "I thought we were going to the hidden realm."

"We are," Fetch said. "It's hidden in El Castillo de la Noche."

"The Night Castle?" Tiago smirked. "That doesn't sound very inviting." He laid his head on the bow, his eyes glued to the fading stars above. Then, as if he was only now remembering what they had just been through, he said, "That battle was . . ."

"A close call," Fetch said, scratching at his ear.

"How'd you do it?" Tiago asked. "Do you have grenades in your coat?"

"Just magical thread."

Throwing an arm over his eyes, Tiago said, "I need some of *that* magic."

Fetch riffled through his coat, tugged something free, then handed Esme and Tiago each a shiny silver bag of caramel popcorn.

"I was sort of hoping for chicken wings," Tiago said as he sat up and took the snack. "Can't your thread conjure some of those?"

"Like all magic, the thread has limits," the fox said, "and there are spells for each spool. Like I told you, it gets really complicated. But the bottom line is, no. I cannot make food unless you want to eat string for dinner."

Tiago wiped his bloody ears with a sleeve. "I thought my eardrums were goners for sure."

Fetch opened his paw to reveal a bit of pale blue thread. Gently he blew it into the air, where it looped and floated, creating a soft glow. The light swept into Tiago's ears as the thread fluttered toward Esme and repeated the process.

"Whoa!" Tiago said, cupping his ears.

Esme felt it too. The soothing warmth that drifted into her ears, the *snip-snap-whoosh* of a flame, and then the pain was simply gone.

"Thanks," she told Fetch, wondering if he had any cures for the knots in her stomach, the fear that had coiled in her belly like a poisonous snake.

With a sigh, Fetch removed a spool of white thread, cut a length of thread with his teeth, and began to wrap it around his ankle as he chanted under his breath.

"Is that going to heal you?" Esme asked.

"I told you, it's good luck to have a sprained ankle," Fetch said as the thread began to glimmer like moonlight, casting a ghostly glow across his furry face. "But this will soak up the pain."

He propped his head on the boat's edge and folded his arms across his furry chest. She imagined what he might look like in his human form: red hair, big brown eyes, long nose, a sharp jaw.

The soft pink sky stretched endlessly as a gentle breeze swept across the sea, pushing them toward a nameless horizon.

Tiago scooted closer to Esme. "So what happened back at Ozzie's? Who saved you and why?"

Esme grinned proudly. "I spilled the curse from the cauldron all over Ozzie."

Tiago let out a pleased *woot*. Esme explained everything that had happened.

Fetch said, "That's very impressive to overcome a Fire witch like Ozzie."

Esme said, "It was luck."

"Or fast thinking," Tiago put in.

"Or sheer brilliance," Fetch added.

"What exactly were those monsters on the beach?" Esme asked, wanting to change the subject. "Some kind of banshee?

Or like cousins of La Llorona?"

"Some call them Gritaras," Fetch said. "Others Fatales. Still others call them the Sirenas. But they're all just different names for the same thing—a really wicked monster that wants to swallow your soul and then skin you to eat your bones."

A long shudder took hold of Esme. "I heard the—the victims." She would never get that sound out of her head.

"They eat *bones*?" Tiago asked, closing the snack bag with a grimace.

"Total delicacy for them," Fetch said.

Esme felt suddenly weary, and her eyes burned. All she wanted to do was sleep for a hundred years.

Silence consumed them for a few moments. Then Fetch turned his gaze to Esme, speaking quietly. "So the legend is real."

Tiago bolted upright, like he wasn't about to miss any part of this conversation. "What legend?"

"I've only heard stories—myths, really—and I didn't believe them until now, but witches of Chaos are a rare sort of power."

Esme rolled her eyes. "You mean unpredictable and dangerous."

"That too, but . . ." Fetch cocked his head. "You really don't know, do you?"

Why did Esme have a sinking feeling that she wasn't going to like whatever Fetch was about to say?

"Know what?" Tiago asked.

Fetch leaned in conspiratorially and whispered, "Anyone who makes contact with Chaos pretty much disintegrates into dust."

Esme's heart caught in her chest. "That's the dumbest thing I've ever heard."

"Yeah," Tiago chuckled, poking Esme's arm. "So much for your legend."

Fetch shook his head. "You'd have to have the intention to hurt or kill her, and *then* you would turn to dust."

"Tell him he's loco," Tiago snorted.

Esme squared her shoulders. It really did sound bananas, but she had seen it with her own eyes.

Tiago clenched his jaw. "Esme?"

"The Fatal, she tried to jam a fist into my side and . . ."

"It didn't hurt," Fetch guessed.

Tiago grunted. "You're telling me that Esme's, like . . ." His eyes flew wide, his expression shifting from confusion to surprise to recognition in the span of a breath. "That's why Lenny unspelled you. She knew your Chaos was your best protection. It's like . . . armor!"

Esme shook her head, but deep down she knew it was true. She had always felt different. Because of her secret she had walked through the world feeling separate, distant from others, and now she knew why.

"People have long feared Chaos witches for that exact reason," Fetch said. "And I presume that's why the truth was hidden beneath the idea of some legend." He made air quotes around "legend." "No one wanted even the Chaos witches to know their power."

Esme felt strangely electrified. "Why not?"

Fetch said, "Imagine a creature who couldn't be killed. Well . . ."

"I'm not a *creature*!"

"Whoa!" Tiago raised a hand in protest. "Explain, Fetch."

The fox turned to Esme. "You're not *totally* indestructible. Everyone has a weakness. Take fire, for example. Powerful. No one can stick their hand into the flames and not get burned, right?"

"Except for a powerful Fire witch," Tiago argued.

"Fine, but *water* can kill fire."

"Okay," Esme said, "so what *can* kill me?"

"No idea." Fetch shrugged. "The truth has been buried for so long, who knows which part is real and which is just myth?"

One day you will harness all that power. You'll no longer need spells to do magic. And Earth, Fire, Water, and Air will all bend to your will. But Esme's mom had never said anything about being indestructible. Was this what the witch hunter had meant when she said, *Such a shame you weren't given the truth*?

Was this the truth she meant? Or some version of it?

Fetch folded his arms across his chest and hunkered down. "We have a few hours before we reach the castle, and I'm tired. You two should get some rest, too. We can't show up even a little bit weary. Puts us at too great a risk."

"Risk for what?" Esme and Tiago said at the same time.

"Of being put to sleep forever."

Chapter Twenty-Four

The boat glided gently across the glass-smooth sea. The movement was rhythmic, even hypnotic, and before Esme knew it, she fell asleep.

She stood in a rose-scented boutique with white floors, white walls, and a green ceiling painted to look like full-canopied trees dotted with pink blooms.

All around her were tattered brown leather steamer trunks big enough for a whole person to fit inside. Many were stacked in twos and threes, while some were turned onto their sides or tossed into corners.

Each, though, was secured with a rusted padlock.

Esme's stomach gave a lurch as she moved tentatively through the space, tracing her fingers across the trunks, collecting dust as she went. There was magic in these chests—she could feel it, its desire to get out matched by her desire to get in.

She paused in front of one, then knelt down. The lock pulsed with a magic that felt wrong, foreboding.

She shouldn't do it.

But the urge was so powerful, she found her hand reaching out, tugging on the padlock.

Instantly, the chest vanished in a plume of silver smoke. Silken whispers caressed Esme's cheeks. *So close. Look closer.*

"Close to what?" she asked, but there was no answer.

Esme crept over to the next trunk. There, beneath the dust.

Peering closer, she swept her fingers across the dirt.

Carved into the leather top was a symbol. Four swirls, indicating Air magic, with a name beneath it: *Gisele.*

Could this chest hold the answers that would lead them to their families, to freeing them from Oblivion? In an excited rush, Esme swept the dust off other nearby trunks, each revealing a different symbol and name: *Lucinda*, with three wavy lines for water. *Triana*, two entangled leaves for earth. And for *Escarlata*, a single flame.

Another whisper. *Do you see?*

No, Esme thought, *I don't see.* "What are you trying to show me?"

Somewhere a lock rattled. Then another and another and another until the endless clatter of them filled the air.

In the next breath, a hush fell, followed by a resounding *click.*

Esme's eyes darted toward the sound. It had come from the trunk, the one whose lock was now open. But which sister did it belong to? She hurried over, and just as she reached the case and brushed away the grime . . .

She woke to a furry paw poking her in the ribs. "We're almost there."

Rubbing her eyes, she sat up, trying to keep the images from the dream fixed in her memory, but as the boat slipped into a silent passage, she could already feel the fragments of it breaking away.

Stone walls thick with moss and thorned vines stretched up and up on both sides, as if they could touch the sky. The scents of rust and rain swelled, and for a moment Esme felt as though she was traveling through an ancient sacred space.

"Where's the secret realm?" she asked Fetch.

The fox stood at the bow, the hem of his coat fluttering as he scanned from left to right and right to left like some kind of pirate. "Up ahead," he whispered.

"Why are you whispering?" Esme asked.

"The dead are light sleepers," Fetch replied.

"Is that a joke?" Tiago asked.

"This is the Paso de los Muertos," Fetch said quietly. "It's the only way to get to the castle. Look," he added, "we're guests here. So, please, be respectful. Act like you're in a church or a library. Or, better yet, a cemetery."

"Or else what?" Tiago said in a low voice, his eyes darting about wildly. "The dead are going to wake up and kill us?"

Fetch sighed. "Why do you always think the worst?"

"Because it's usually true," Tiago said, "and you should always be prepared for it."

"The dead have no power to kill you," Fetch said.

Esme felt relief unfurl in her chest. "That's good."

"But they can drag you into their lairs and hold you there until you *do* die," the fox added casually. "Or so I've heard."

The air grew instantly colder.

"Well, then, let's hope they stay in dreamland," Tiago said.

Plumes of white breath floated from Esme's mouth as she sat silently, reverently, remembering her own dream. What was in those trunks? She grasped at each dream fragment, trying to put the pieces together.

Look closer.

"Have you been through here before?" Tiago asked.

Fetch shook his head. "No one comes here. At least not anymore."

"What if you read the map wrong?" Tiago suggested. "Or translated the language wrong and 'secret realm' doesn't really mean 'secret realm'?"

"I didn't read it wrong," Fetch said confidently. "But there *is* one thing I can't figure out."

"Which is what?" Tiago asked.

"There was a symbol next to the words."

Esme said, "What kind of symbol?"

"Three wavy lines."

Esme froze. "For the Water witch, Lucinda."

"You got that from three lines?" Tiago asked.

Esme quickly explained her dream, then turned to Fetch. "I bet the hidden realm you saw belongs to Lucinda!"

Tiago asked Fetch, "Do you still have the map?"

The fox nodded. "We can't get distracted right now, so I'll show you when we get to the castle. And there weren't any other symbols, if that's what you're wondering. Believe me, I scoured that thing. One realm, one shot."

"If we can find Lucinda, we won't even need the other witches or realms." Esme's breath came in short, excited bursts. Lenny had said to find *an* original witch. She didn't say to find more than that, and she wasn't specific about which one. "There's another piece," she added. "I saw it in my dream. Each trunk had a symbol, like Lucinda's wavy lines. Gisele, the Air witch, had swirls. Triana had leaves. And Escarlata, a flame."

"Do you guys think . . . ," Tiago began. Then he shook his head. "Never mind."

"Say it," Esme pressed.

"Okay, it's a long shot . . . but what if the witch symbols and the map and the riddle are all somehow connected?"

Fetch stared at Tiago, his coppery eyes shining with admiration or curiosity, or maybe both. He turned to Esme. "Say the riddle again."

"The Legend of Ire is the greatest of lies," Esme recited quietly. "Easy to speak and harder to keep. If it is the truth you seek, you will not find it here or there or anywhere. For the truth can only be found inside the deception."

Tiago frowned. "No mention of a map."

"Okay, so we know the legend is a lie." Fetch rubbed a paw over his eyes. "But we don't know if that means all of it or parts of it."

"And how is a lie hard to keep?" Esme asked.

"Because it's a secret," Tiago said.

"Yes!" Fetch nodded enthusiastically. "And if the legend is a secret . . ." His voice trailed off.

"There's one line that's bugging me," Tiago threw in. "'If it is the truth you seek.'"

"We won't find it anywhere," Esme added.

Fetch's eyes widened. "Which means we shouldn't be seeking the truth!"

"We should be looking for the lie!" Esme exclaimed. "I mean the secret!"

"Great," Tiago said excitedly. "But where the heck are we supposed to find that?"

"Aren't you an Air witch?" Fetch asked Tiago. "I thought your kind was supposed to be excellent at perceiving secrets."

"Dude, I'm the guy who blew a spell and randomly morphs into animals." Tiago chuckled. "And you want me to sense some ancient secret?"

"Exactly." Fetch narrowed his eyes. "And now that you're in this realm, your magic is heightened, so use it."

"The dream voice," Esme said, still thinking about her sueño, turning it over for any other clue she might have missed. "It's different from the voice I heard in the alleyway. It's like there's one person trying to get rid of me and another trying to help me."

"But she didn't help you," Tiago said. "She told you to look closer. As if that's supposed to mean something."

"If only I hadn't woken up," Esme said. "I was just about to see what was in the trunk."

A deep laugh echoed through the passage.

Esme's blood went cold.

"Who the heck is that?" Tiago asked.

Fetch leaned closer. "More importantly, is it the nice one or the mean one?"

"It's the witch hunter," Esme said. "She's here."

Chapter Twenty-Five

The disembodied voice echoed across the passage. "Did you think you could hide?"

Esme's heart thundered in her chest. "How did she find us?" she whispered.

"So much for your sprained ankle bringing good luck," Tiago said to Fetch.

"The day's not over," Fetch argued.

Tiago frowned, then began to sniff the air. "Is it possible that I can smell her or is that . . ." He paused, stared down at his open palms.

"What's wrong?" Esme asked.

"I feel a strange breeze across my hands." His eyes met Esme's.

"Your Air magic," she whispered.

"Looks like it's time to wake the dead," the witch hunter warned.

Fetch muttered, "Empty threats. She can't wake the dead."

"How do you know?" Tiago asked.

"Because if she could, she'd already have done it."

A memory flickered. Esme whispered to Fetch, "How did you dispose of her in the alleyway?"

Bewilderment washed over his expression "I . . . didn't."

"You wrapped me in your coat," Esme insisted, her voice rising, "and the darkness went away. *She* went away."

Fetch's nostrils flared.

"You know something," Esme said.

"It's a wild guess, but it's possible she isn't fully powerful yet, if that makes sense. And so maybe she can only hover around for so long."

"That's a lot of maybes," Tiago said.

Esme's mind was floating back through time, trying to pick up clues she might have missed along the way. *She isn't fully powerful yet.*

"Oh!" Esme cried.

Fetch and Tiago turned to her, their gazes curious.

"The Legend of Ire," she whispered as they huddled closer. "It says that whoever possesses one blade will have tremendous power, but whoever possesses all four will rule the universe—"

"Like a god," Tiago murmured.

With an overly confident smirk, Fetch said, "She doesn't have all of them yet or she wouldn't be trying to stop you from getting your hands on one."

Was that what this was? A race to see who could get the most daggers? Was that why Lenny had told Esme to find an original witch?

"But if she isn't fully powerful yet," Esme whispered, "how did she get into San Bosco? How did she—"

"She had help," Tiago said.

"Help?" Esme replied too loudly. "Who would help *her*?"

"Bravo," the hunter said. "You must be so proud of your little discovery. It took you much too long. But you still do not know how many daggers I have, do you? I also have your family and friends. And soon I will have all of you."

Esme's blood boiled at the word "family." With a grunt, she threw her head back, ready to unleash her fury.

Tiago grabbed hold of her hand. His dark eyes met hers and for a blink he looked different, older. "This is what she wants," he said. "She's just trying to get you riled up, to trick you into a fight."

"How do you know what she wants?" Fetch asked Tiago.

That was also Esme's question, since even with enhanced magic, Tiago wasn't a full witch yet.

Tiago shook his head incredulously, as if even he didn't believe what he was about to say. "I . . . I can smell her secrets," he said. "They're dark and they smell like ash, smoke, maybe burning rubber, and I—I just *know* what she wants."

"Why would she want me to fight her?" Esme asked.

Fetch froze. "That's it," he whispered. "She doesn't want

you to fight. She wants you to hate. She must gain power from dark energy, like fury and hatred and other negative emotions."

The witch hunter laughed again, the wickedness of her cackle so real Esme thought she could reach out and touch it. "Your dear sister," the woman taunted, "would you like to see her? Or perhaps your father?"

Esme dug her nails into her palms, fighting the terrible urge to say yes, to beg for even a glimpse of Lenny and Dad. To beg the witch hunter to give her back her family. She *had* to see them again, to talk to them and hug them and tell them how sorry she was.

"Ignore her," Fetch said softly. "We're almost through the passage."

Esme spied the passage's opening about fifty yards ahead. Beyond it stood what looked like a gloomy black wall. That had to be the castle.

"Can't you make this thing go faster?" Tiago grumbled.

"It only has one speed," Fetch whispered. "Slow."

"I can show you your sister's suffering," the witch hunter sang. "It is no small thing to have your magic, your power, stolen—it's quite agonizing."

Fetch took hold of Esme's shoulders, forcing her to look him in the eye. "Ignore her! It's a game, do you hear me?"

But Esme was too busy analyzing the witch's words to listen. The witch hunter had said *stolen.* Was that why she had trapped all the witches in Oblivion, so she could steal their magic? But what did that have to do with the daggers? Why would she need the witches' power if she could have the strength of a god? Something was off, and Esme was going to find out what it was.

"And you, Esmerelda," the witch said almost tenderly, "*you* can help your sister. You can help them all."

Esme fought the tears burning at the rims of her eyes. Focus. Focus. "You asked me to join you once," she said.

Tiago grabbed her arm. "What are you doing?"

She shrugged free, focusing only on the hunter. "Take me instead of the witches." She hadn't given the idea any time to marinate. She was speaking from her heart, from a place of longing, to save those she loved.

"*No!*" Fetch growled.

"I do not need another Chaos witch," the hunter said. "The offer has expired."

Another Chaos witch? So that was who was helping her. But Esme didn't know anyone with Chaos magic, unless they were hiding like she was.

"Your sister is in great pain," the witch went on. Her words cut like barbed wire as Esme remembered how pale and weak Lenny had looked in the dream.

It's cold here, Es. And dark. Please . . . hurry.

"Don't listen," Fetch whispered.

"Her energy is growing," Tiago said. "It's dark."

The walls began to shake. Bits of rock tumbled into the green-black waters.

Cursing, Fetch began to riffle through his coat's endless pockets.

The passage began to narrow.

"The walls are closing in!" Esme cried.

With a scowl, Tiago danced his hands in rhythmic circles while he chanted a single word: *"Abrir. Abrir. Abrir."*

Winds gusted, fierce and biting, each gale growing in ferocity.

"It's not working!" Tiago shouted.

Fetch tossed a spool of thread into the air, but that didn't stop the walls either. They continued to inch closer and closer.

"Keep trying!" Esme yelled as she desperately searched the boat for something, *anything* they could use to stop the walls.

A dark mist, like the one from the alley, began to pour out of the rocky crevices.

Tiago thrust his arms out more forcefully, his chants growing louder, deeper, more controlled. The walls trembled. They slowed but they didn't stop.

The boat continued to glide forward.

A wide, dark opening lay before them. No, not an opening— a *mouth* with a thick black tongue and a million pointed, rotting teeth. And it was yawning wider and wider.

"Fetch!" Esme screamed. "That's NOT a castle!"

His eyes filled with terror. "It has to be!"

Esme clenched her fists. They had taken this journey to the Castillo de la Noche based on a maybe—a maybe that the cursed fox in the magical coat had read the map correctly.

The walls continued to battle the force of Tiago's magic, pressing against the little boat as a thick trail of black smoke drifted nearer, gathering above them like a storm cloud.

Fetch began to cough.

Tiago continued to dance his hands in front of him, chanting under his breath, but nothing he did slowed the darkness that had them now gasping for air. Esme's throat contracted, her lungs burning.

Her vision blurred and her knees went weak.

No. No!

This isn't how things are going to end!

In the next instant, Chaos swept through her, a wild, uncontainable thing, and she pushed her friends low into the boat before spreading her coat over them and shielding their bodies with her own.

The mist enveloped her. Esme felt the witch hunter's rage burning its way through her body. The pain was blinding, forcing a scream from Esme's mouth.

"Esme!" Tiago yelled, squirming beneath her.

The witch hunter's darkness grew more desperate, more enraged.

Even if her Chaos *was* armor, Esme couldn't hold this position much longer.

A voice, the same one from her dreams, whispered, *Let go.*

Esme squeezed her eyes closed, allowing her magic to bloom. Her Chaos expanded, coursing wildly through her blood.

A chilling awareness ignited within her. She was every magic all at once—Earth and Fire and Air and Water. It was like a storm gathering, building with heat and ice until she could no longer hold it in. Until the power exploded out of her.

The witch hunter shrieked.

Then, in a single heartbeat, everything went still.

Quiet.

Trembling with leftover magic, Esme took a deep breath, and just as the pain subsided, she looked around. "She's gone," she said shakily, getting to her feet, followed by Tiago and Fetch. "We—we did it."

"*You* did it!" Fetch reached out a paw before withdrawing it awkwardly. "Are you hurt?" he asked, scanning her up and down. His eyes narrowed. "How did you do that?"

"I have no idea," she said softly, her skin still buzzing with magic.

Tiago pulled her into a death-grip hug, laughing. "You beat the witch hunter! Man, I was so wrong."

Esme scowled. "Wrong?"

"Your magic isn't armor. You are."

Esme nodded, but Tiago was wrong—she wasn't armor.

She was a weapon.

As Tiago released her, his gaze fixed on something beyond her shoulder. His entire face drained of all color, and in the pools of his dark eyes, Esme saw pure horror.

She whirled just in time to see that they hadn't won at all.

The dark, gaping mouth moaned and then sucked them inside.

Chapter Twenty-Six

The darkness had swallowed them whole, the only sounds their erratic breathing and a persistent wind howling in the distance.

"Are we dead?" Tiago asked, his voice cracking.

"See what I mean about worst-case madness?" Fetch said just as a pale pink light illuminated the space. He held up a shimmering spool of thread like a lantern.

"Handy." Esme glanced around the chamber, relieved to see she wasn't standing on a monster's tongue. Or even the boat, which had vanished as quickly as they'd been swallowed up.

They stood in a cavernous bedroom with a four-poster bed draped in silk and cobwebs. A stained-glass window depicting a turquoise waterfall extended to the top of the pitched ceiling.

To their right was a large Cantera stone fireplace carved to look like a roaring lion's mouth. A couple of velvet chairs were set in front of it, with a small marble table between them, on which two teacups rested. Bits of ash littered the stone floor.

"This is the Night Castle." Fetch's mouth curved, hinting at a grin. "I *knew* I'd read that map right!"

"Does the castle always eat its visitors?" Tiago scowled.

"I don't think it was trying to eat us," Fetch said. "I think it was just yawning, and we got in the way."

With a harrumph, Esme said, "You never mentioned a giant mouth."

"It wasn't on the map, okay?" Fetch replied. "Besides, I've never heard of the Night Castle killing people."

"Just putting them to sleep forever." Tiago shrugged. "Same thing."

"As long as you're not tired, you'll be fine."

"Any other warnings about this place?" Esme asked.

"My grandfather is the one who told me about it," Fetch said. "I thought it was just a legend, but when I saw it on the map, I knew it had to be real and not just some tale."

"How did he know about it?" Tiago asked. "I mean, if it's so secret."

"He knew a lot about secret magic," Fetch said, his gaze falling to the floor.

Esme's pulse quickened. "Like what else?"

"Not exactly the time to go into all that," Fetch said. "And like I said, it's secret."

Esme frowned, wishing that she could open the door into Fetch's mind so she could walk around his memories.

"Listen," she said, regrouping. "The witch hunter must want all the daggers so that she can have the power of a god, right?"

"But why mess with kidnapping the San Bosco witches?" Tiago asked.

"Exactly," Fetch put in. "Why steal mere witch magic when she could be a god?"

Esme shook her head. "I think we need to find the daggers too. Maybe that's the key to Oblivion, and why Lenny told me to find an original witch. Maybe she really meant I needed to find the daggers."

"That's why the witch hunter wants to kill us!" Tiago nearly shouted. "So we don't ruin her plan to snag the blades for herself."

"And that means she hasn't found all of them," Esme said excitedly. "Or else she'd have had the power to face us in the flesh."

"Well, she did try to kill us with that dark mist," Tiago said with a shudder.

"But she didn't," Esme said. "And I think she's not showing her face because she isn't fully powerful yet."

"So it's a race to see who can get to the daggers first," Tiago said.

With slumped shoulders, the fox tugged his coat closer while the castle creaked and moaned. "Then we're on the right track looking for an original witch's secret realm."

"Only if said witch still has a dagger plunged into her heart," Tiago said.

"We have to hope she does," Esme said. "Everything depends on it."

Her eyes locked with Tiago's. He had just as much at risk as she did, and even though he hid his feelings better, she could see the worry in his eyes.

"Oh, I almost forgot," Fetch announced. "No matter what, do NOT yawn."

"Why not?" Esme asked.

"It could alert the castle to your exhaustion."

"And?" Esme asked.

"And when you're exhausted, you're in a weaker frame of mind."

"Great," Tiago said. "Now it's all I'll be able to think about."

Esme threw him a warning look. He chuckled, throwing out his hands in surrender. "I won't yawn. Promise. Hopefully." He frowned, shaking his head. "No, for sure, I won't."

Fetch's tail dipped lethargically.

"You okay?" Esme asked, thinking he seemed weaker since the battle with the Fatales. "Are you hurt?"

"I'm fine."

"You don't look fine," Tiago said.

"Do you want to waste time talking about how I look," Fetch growled, "or do you want to find Lucinda's hidden realm?"

Something was different about the fox. Esme could sense it, like a cold creeping over her skin. She took hold of his arm, forcing him to look her in the eye. "You know you can tell us anything."

"We don't have time for this," he said, pulling back.

She was about to argue, but Fetch was right. Time was winning the race, and they couldn't afford any distractions.

They left the bedroom through a carved wooden door and stepped into a windowless corridor that stretched on as far as they could see, with no end in sight.

Above them floated lit candles shaped like baby heads, like the ones they'd seen in the supply closet. Their flickering eyes seemed to follow the trio.

A cold gust swept down the hall. Esme rubbed the chill from her arms. "Does anyone still live here?"

"Yeah," Tiago said. "*Someone* had to light those creepy things."

"They're eternity candles," Fetch explained as they crept across the elegant dusty rugs, depicting woven illustrations of unicorns and dragons. "They never burn out, so they could have been lit decades ago. And no, no one lives here. Not since it was cursed."

"Cursed?" Esme whispered.

Fetch nodded. "Apparently, a guy named Palo the Valiente built the castle for his wife as a wedding gift."

"But that seems nice," Esme said.

"Until his first wife found out and hexed the place," Fetch

added. "Palo and his new wife fell asleep their first night here and never woke up. Supposedly, their bodies are still somewhere in the castle. Perfectly preserved."

"That's super gross," Tiago said as Esme came to a halt and asked the fox, "Do you think Palo knew he was building a castle over a hidden realm?"

"I doubt it," Fetch said.

"Well, *someone* knew Lucinda's realm is here," Tiago put in, "or they wouldn't have used an ancient language to point to the realm on the map."

"That's it!" Esme hollered.

Tiago startled. "What's it?"

"The water symbol is for Lucinda," Esme explained, "and we all know that brujxes can use their elemental sources for more power, right?"

Fetch and Tiago nodded, understanding dawning slowly across their faces.

"Her realm is guarded by water," Fetch whispered.

"Genius!" Tiago pumped a fist in the air. "But we just came from water and—is there a moat or something else in the castle?" he asked Fetch.

"No idea." Fetch paced. "Too bad one of you isn't of Water. You'd easily be able to locate some."

Esme remembered what had happened in the passage. The way her pain had fed her power, and how she had felt every magic all at once. But how was that possible? And what did it mean?

She gave a quick rundown to her friends, hoping one of them might have an idea, an answer that could help them now.

Rubbing his chin, Tiago said, "It has to be related to your Chaos."

Fetch stared up at the floating baby heads. His ears twitched. "I don't think it was the pain that fed your magic."

"Then what did?" Esme asked.

"I'm not an expert on Chaos," Fetch said. "No one really understands it, but it's still governed by the rules of magic, right?"

"Except that it's totally unpredictable," Tiago said.

Fetch's bushy eyebrows shot up. "Is it?"

"What do you mean?" Esme asked.

"Chaos is also the magic of surprise," the fox said, "of astonishment and amazement."

Esme liked the sound of "astonishment and amazement."

Fetch went on, "Extreme emotion will always intensify your magic."

"Like when Tiago gets freaked out and turns into an animal," Esme said.

"I don't get freaked out," Tiago argued. "And we already know all this."

"But even fear can't unleash the total power of Chaos." Fetch was talking fast now, as if he'd forget every word unless he spit them out quickly.

"Then what can?" Tiago asked.

Esme remembered what had gone through her heart when

the muertos were attacking her, trying to hurt her friends. She had felt fiercely protective, but she also knew that if she failed, she would lose her friends and family. Those she loved most in this world.

"Love," Esme whispered. "It's the only thing to control the Chaos."

Tiago and Fetch were silent for a moment. Shadows flickered across their surprised faces as they stared at Esme. The castle moaned under the force of the shrieking wind.

"Deep," Tiago finally said with an appreciative nod.

For the first time since the beginning of this quest, Esme felt as if she was onto something, as if all the pieces of the puzzle were beginning to connect. "So what now?" she asked, chewing her bottom lip. "How will that help us find water?"

As they continued down the corridor, Fetch said, "If you could somehow tap into the Water Chaos, I bet . . . I mean, maybe you could—"

"Find water?" Esme guessed.

"I'm thinking bigger," Fetch said. "Maybe you could connect to Lucinda's magic itself. That's what created her realm, right?"

"Esme's the queen of sensing magic!" Tiago shouted. "Well, except for Air. She's really bad at that one."

"Air is tricky." Esme scowled. "Invisible, and super hard to detect."

Tiago offered a smirk as if to say, *Air is the best magic*, but he didn't. "Remember in the cemetery when you had to think about a sad memory? Maybe this is the same thing. You need to focus on who you love most and, I don't know, let *that* connect you to the Water Chaos."

Fetch came to a stop again. "It's worth a shot." He folded his furry arms across his chest, waiting.

"Now?" Esme felt a nervous bolt of energy expand in her stomach.

Tiago patted her shoulder. "No time like the present."

She took a deep breath, shook out her hands, and cleared her throat.

There, in the cursed castle, beneath the eternally burning baby heads, she waited for the familiar spark of magic. For the tension in her jaw, for any tingling of her limbs. But there was nothing.

Just let the magic in, she told herself, taking deeper breaths. *Let it in.*

She waited.

The wind shrieked, battering the castle as if demanding to be let in.

"Maybe you should think about a time you felt powerful," Tiago suggested.

Esme let her mind turn to saving her friends, to the spark she'd felt when she offered to trade herself for the witches of San Bosco. There was power in such a sacrifice. Power in the love she felt for her family, and in the truth that she would do anything to get them back.

Esme's jaw tingled.

There.

She could sense the curse, its malevolence and jealousy. Its fury.

"The castle's curse," she said, opening her eyes. "It's blocking any other magic and I . . . I can't get past it." Breathlessly, she turned to Fetch. "Can I see the map?"

The fox tugged it free from a pocket. "There's no map of the castle itself, if that's what you're looking for." He handed Esme a book-sized sheet of paper, yellowed and crinkled. She held the map of Ocho Manos closer to the light, inspecting the precise drawings of strange places like Paso de los Muertos, Lago de Milagros, the Tower of Shadows—that one was a structure that looked like it was built into a rock cliff that hung over a stormy black ocean.

"See?" Fetch said, pointing to the north end of the map. "The Castillo de la Noche is right there."

Leaning in for a better look, Tiago said, "Someone should make a warning label for all those places like the Forest of the Fatales: 'Danger—one wrong move and wailing women will suck out your soul.'"

Esme thought a warning system was actually a brilliant idea, but Fetch was already shaking his head. "You're missing the point. The *unknown* is the scariest part of each place, and Ocho Manos loves to prey on fear."

"Of course it does," Tiago said.

Esme peered closer at the map. "Can you show me the symbol?"

Fetch snapped a single golden thread out of thin air and dangled it over the castle drawing, a menacing black structure that was crudely drawn with five turrets and a drawbridge that looked as though it was made of skulls.

The thread's light sparked, then three wavy lines materialized near the castle drawing, pulsing wildly.

Fetch was right. There was no way to determine exactly where in the castle Lucinda's realm was hidden.

"The realm could be anywhere," Esme whispered.

"Any chance you have a locator thread in that coat?" Tiago asked Fetch.

"That's what this thread is," the fox replied. "It reveals things that are concealed, but it doesn't have the power to locate something as big as a realm hidden by an original witch."

Remembering the night the heart spell had swept inside her, Esme floated a hand over the symbol.

She closed her eyes and pulled her sister's laugh into her memory, and the way Lenny always twisted her hair around her pinkie when she was nervous or happy. Esme imagined her dad's soft eyes and beaming smile. His kindness, like the way he would nurture a hurt bird that had fallen from its nest in the garden.

Then she did what she rarely allowed herself to do: she thought about her mother. The memories were often shadowy and incomplete, but she would never forget her mom's hands, their warmth, their softness, their gentle touch when they braided Esme's hair. She let the memories of her family fill her heart with love.

Her heart expanded one, two, three sizes.

For a moment she was no longer in the castle. She was somewhere cool, somewhere surrounded by enchantment.

She didn't dare open her eyes.

Then, suddenly, she heard the whooshing of water. A pleasant chill spread across her palms. She leaned into the feeling, the magic.

Show me. Show me.

In the next breath, she felt a sorrow so deep her eyes pricked with tears.

Water magic can hide things in plain sight, she remembered.

She gasped and looked up at her friends. "I know where the realm is hidden."

Chapter Twenty-Seven

Esme ran back in the direction of the bedroom.

The wind grew wilder, lashing itself against Castillo de la Noche. As if it knew her plans. As if it wanted to stop her.

But nothing would stop Esme. Not now.

She clung to the memory of her family, to the love still filling her heart, as she careened into the bedroom, coming to a sudden halt in front of the stained-glass window.

Fetch and Tiago were right behind her.

The fox, following Esme's gaze, suspended his light-spool in front of the window.

"The waterfall," Esme said, pointing to the illuminated glass. "This is the opening to Lucinda's realm."

Tiago crept closer. "You think it's in the ventana?"

"That's not possible," Fetch put in. "This window came

way later than the realm."

"How do you know?" Esme asked.

"Like I said, everything was built after the realm . . . so that means the castle couldn't have been here either."

Esme chewed her bottom lip, trying to control her racing heart. She stepped back and stared at the waterfall, wondering if she had been wrong. Just then the water began to shift, to flow. She gasped.

"Do you see that?" she whispered.

Fetch frowned, and Tiago scratched at his cheek and said, "Uh, see what?"

Esme reached out to touch the glass, but there was nothing unusual about it. No secret door that she could find.

"Well?" Tiago said.

Esme was still pondering. "The entrance has to be here," she whispered. *But magic isn't always predictable or obvious*, she thought. Her gaze fell to the floor beneath the window. There she spied a stone that seemed out of place. Not in size or color, but in the tiny etchings carved across it.

Three wavy lines.

Esme's jaw didn't tingle like usual. No, this was different. The Water Chaos swept over her skin like a cool breeze.

She dropped to her knees. "The waterfall just marks the spot. Look!"

It was the strangest thing to feel Water magic so clearly. It was both light and dark, wild and calm, loving and vengeful. A magic that felt as if it was everywhere all at once.

The power of it pulsed in Esme's limbs as she remembered that a very skilled Water brujx could see the future in reflections. Just like Tiago's mom had done when she left the spell that would lead them to Ocho Manos.

Fetch and Tiago squatted next to her and began tugging on the stones.

"I knew my sprained ankle would be good luck," Fetch said.

Some of the stones came up easily. Others had to be pried away. It was dull and mindless work that seemed to be taking too long.

"Why does this feel like we aren't making a dent in the floor?" Esme asked nearly thirty minutes later.

"It's a good twelve-inch hole," Fetch said. "But you're right. Not big enough to fit into."

Esme redoubled her efforts. Her fingers were nearly rubbed raw, and her back ached from hunching over.

Tiago paused and wiped his brow.

"Are you okay?" Esme asked.

He nodded resolutely, then went back to work, more slowly this time.

"Don't get tired," Fetch warned, sounding exhausted himself.

"I'm not!" Tiago growled just as a small yawn slipped out of his mouth. He froze. His eyes widened. "I—I didn't mean that."

But it was too late.

The castle walls shuddered. Flames erupted in the fireplace.

A piano sounded in the distance. Harsh whispers floated into the room.

Yes. Yes. Yes.

"What's happening?" Esme cried.

"I think he woke up the castle!" Fetch said.

Tiago's eyelids fluttered, began to close.

"Fight it!" Esme yelled, shaking him by the shoulders. Then to Fetch, "Is it bad to wake this place?"

"It's definitely not good!" he said.

"Like not good or really bad?"

"There are duendes here, and they for sure don't like visitors."

"What!" Esme cried. "Why didn't you tell us?"

"Would it have mattered?" Fetch asked.

Esme shook her head. She would have come to the castle whether the murderous elves were here or not.

The flames and the whispers and the music grew.

Stay. Stay. Stay.

"Keep him awake!" Fetch shouted.

"I'm trying!"

"I'm sorry," Tiago muttered as his head dropped and his body sagged.

"NO!" Esme yelled. "Don't you dare go to sleep."

A blast of sharp air swept into the room.

Long, thin cobwebs whooshed across the chamber. The table fell over and the empty teacups crashed to the floor, breaking apart.

Tiago's eyes rolled to the back of his head as he collapsed.

Esme caught him right before his head thunked on the stones. "Tiago!" She placed his head on her lap, nudging him, but he was out cold.

"We need to make this opening bigger." Fetch tossed a magical spool into the air, and its silver thread unraveled with sparks of light, spinning and twirling. The hole expanded but only a little.

A long groan could be heard from down the hall. The walls trembled. Dozens of tiny footsteps sounded.

"The duendes are coming!" Fetch said.

Sparkling particles rose into the air like glitter and floated toward Esme.

Water magic crept over her skin.

"I refuse to die here!" Fetch growled.

Then a familiar voice, the one that seemed to want to help Esme, whispered, *The entrance is nearly open. Wait.*

The footsteps drew closer and closer. Childlike laughter echoed across the castle.

The blue sphere Esme created pulsed and expanded the opening bigger and bigger.

It was hard to ignore an impatient and terrified fox, even harder to ignore the duendes' chilling laughter, but Esme kept her focus tight.

Wait. Wait.

The flames erupted into an explosion in the fireplace. Esme's gut clenched and unclenched as the bits of sparkling dust danced and dipped. The sphere grew and so did the entrance to the witch's realm.

Hurry.

"Now," Esme said as she began to drag Tiago across the floor.

Fetch started to lift him up. "I'll carry him."

"But your ankle—" She stopped herself from blurting, *You're not strong enough.*

With one fluid movement the fox lifted Tiago up as though he was light as a rag doll and hoisted him over his shoulder. He wavered, then regained his balance. His arms trembled.

Esme started forward to catch the extra weight. "Fetch?"

"I've got him."

The bedroom door flew open. "Stay and play," a small voice said.

"No thanks," Fetch called out, launching a spool of thread that exploded in the little monsters' faces just as Esme and the fox leaped into the Water witch's realm.

Chapter Twenty-Eight

The air was freezing cold.

Esme and Fetch trudged through a narrow stone passage as the waterfall tumbled in great splashes of foamy white to their left. The only light came from up ahead, distant and flickering like a candle.

Esme's entire being was flooded with Water magic. It was all around—on her skin, weaving through her curls, filling her lungs like air.

"It's everywhere," she said.

"Water magic?"

Esme nodded. "Lucinda isn't far. I can sense it." But she didn't feel it in her jaw like she usually did. This was different, more complete—as if she was being guided by something deep within her, something she needed to trust. And for the first time she really understood her mother's words about the butterflies: *Their internal compass never misguides them on their long journey.*

"Can you tell if she's in a good mood or not?" Fetch asked, repositioning Tiago. "Because we need her to be accommodating."

Esme hadn't given much thought to the witch's mood. What if Lucinda was a wicked beast? Surely being trapped in a hidden dimension for so long had to have made her sort of unhinged. And Water witches *were* known for their mercurial natures.

"Do you think she can wake Tiago?" Esme asked.

"I hope so."

They came to a crevice just wide enough for the trio to slip through sideways, skimming against the rocks. When they emerged, they found themselves standing beneath a gray sky. Esme blinked, unsure how to take it all in as she stared in awe at a vast stone landscape, carved with dozens of water channels, all leading to an iridescent lake. Black birds circled overhead, cawing as their large wings cast shadows that seemed to wriggle and writhe in the waters.

As Esme scanned the horizon, her gaze landed on the only human structure in sight: a white cottage with a turquoise roof, perched on a stony hillside. Swirls of smoke rose from the chimney.

"Looks like someone's home," Fetch said.

Just then the air shimmered gold and brown, and Tiago

changed into a sparrow. Fetch nearly dropped the sleeping little bird before catching him in his paw.

"I didn't think magic could work if you're under a sleeping spell," Fetch said.

"Yeah, well, magic is feisty and unpredictable," Esme muttered. "And you said it was magnified in Ocho Manos, so maybe this realm is having some kind of effect on Tiago's Air." She took her best friend from Fetch, cradling him in her palm.

"Excellent point."

As they ascended the rocky hill, Fetch said, "We should go over the plan."

Esme stepped over a crevice as Fetch hobbled across the rough terrain slowly.

"We're going to talk to Lucinda," she said. "Scope out whether she can help us."

"Get to Oblivion."

"So we can save our families and the witches."

"And then you'll ask her about the witch hunter, and how to defeat them."

Esme nodded. "And how to get to the other daggers before the witch hunter does."

"Right," Fetch said, rubbing his furry paws together. "Plus, you'll ask Lucinda to wake Tiago."

"Uh-huh."

Fetch paused. He looked over at Esme with those big dark eyes. "And then . . ."

She knew what he was asking, and she only hoped she could make it happen. She owed him that much. With a pat on his shoulder, she said, "We'll ask her to break your curse."

"Yeah," Fetch said, but it sounded more like a relieved exhale. His ears drooped listlessly and he swayed on his feet. "I just need . . ."

"Maybe we should rest first," Esme suggested.

"No, we have to keep going."

"But you look . . ." The word "awful" was wiggling up her throat and across her tongue. She tried to swallow it whole, but the blasted thing erupted from her mouth as "Super bad!"

"It's the curse," Fetch managed. "I'm getting weaker the closer . . . I get to the end."

"Don't say that!" Esme cried. "We are going to get through this, and Lucinda is going to break your curse, and someday we'll be laughing about all this like it was just a bad dream."

Fetch cocked a single eyebrow. "That sounds like a lot of wishful thinking."

"Or hope."

The witch hunter's words surged in Esme's memory. *Hope is the great executioner.*

"That's never gotten me very far," Fetch said.

Esme thought Fetch must have gone through some really bad things to be so cynical. And yet here he was, traveling with strangers, clinging to a single hope that Lucinda could help him. And if she couldn't? Then what? Was Esme ready to leave the fox behind, to watch his heart stop? Would there be anyone in Ocho Manos who would miss him?

The thought made her stomach roil. "Do you really not have any family left?" she asked.

Fetch went silent, and Esme was sure he was going to ignore the question again, but a moment later, he said, "I told you. . . ."

"I know, but there has to be someone who cares, some friend or . . ." Esme couldn't shake the feeling that he was hiding something.

Fetch's nostrils flared. "I have—*had* a younger sister."

"What?"

"She was taken by the winter queen to serve her." Fetch looked away, ran a paw over his face with a shudder that broke Esme's heart. "I'm not sure if she's still alive or—it was a long time ago. She was only five."

Esme touched the fox's arm. She didn't know what to say.

"I tried to find her, to rescue her and . . ."

"That's when you were cursed," Esme said, wishing she couldn't believe someone could be so cruel—but this quest had taught her otherwise.

"I was told that she was dead," Fetch went on, "and that I would be too if I ever tried to break the curse."

"So it was the winter queen who cursed you?" Esme asked.

Fetch cast his gaze at her. "Can we not talk about it?"

Esme wanted to press for more, but she understood that memories and words, when mixed just right, could be like poison.

She gave a barely-there nod. "Lucinda's going to help you."

Fetch's tail fluttered in the breeze. "Only one way to find out."

The fox and the witch stepped onto the rocky, uneven ground. Glittering fish glided through the water channels as the massive black birds continued to soar above.

Caw. Caw. Caw.

"Why does it feel like we're walking on a treadmill?" Esme asked.

"We are most definitely not getting any closer."

"Maybe there's like a secret password or spell to get us to Lucinda's house," she said, just as they slammed into some kind of invisible wall.

Both were thrown off their feet, Tiago's little body bouncing across the rocks. Esme scooped him up just as the air went still. The birds froze mid-flight. The water and the fish ceased moving.

Then—a spark of rose-colored light. A blurred world coming into focus. Not the rocky, gloomy place with too-thin air, but rather what appeared to be an enormous framed painting floating before her, depicting a deep blue chamber with sparkling formations suspended from a vaulted ceiling.

Esme reached out to touch it.

A woman's voice said, "I've been expecting you."

Chapter Twenty-Nine

A fine mist swept across the terrain, wrapping itself around Esme.

She tried to peer through the fog, but it was so thick. And it was bleeding color—blue, pink, purple, like streaks of paint on a windowpane.

Mystified, Esme held Tiago closer and extended her free hand. The liquid colors dripped into her palm, vanishing on contact.

"Fetch?"

There was no answer.

The paint swirled all around her now, a vortex of rainbow energy that pulsed with a warm, peculiar magic—the kind that belonged to no one.

A magic that runs wild.

In the next breath, the haze cleared, and Esme found herself *inside* the blue chamber. *Inside* the painting. Her entire being hummed with Water magic.

Dazzling jellyfish structures as big as hot-air balloons floated above. Instead of tentacles, shimmering ribbons hung from each. The sack-like bodies were adorned with what looked like millions of diamonds, emeralds, and sapphires, their reflections dancing across the glass floor, where schools of vibrant fish—striped, spotted, big, and small—drifted through clear water.

For a brief moment, Esme forgot herself, her problems, her fears, totally hypnotized as she studied what had to be another optical illusion, one that made the fish look as if their scales were made of precious stones.

They were . . . beautiful.

The fish rushed to the glass surface, staring at Esme with lidless eyes, opening and closing their mouths as though trying to tell her something.

Fetch stumbled into this world headfirst, with his furry legs nearly tripping over his coat. His eyes locked with Esme's, and for the briefest of moments, his body slumped before he righted himself.

"What is this place?" he asked.

"The magic here is . . ." She fumbled with the words, shaking her head, trying to absorb the strange formations that swayed gently above. "I think we stepped into an actual painting!"

"Why would she live inside a painting?" Fetch asked, more to himself than Esme.

"I've heard of stranger things."

Fetch smirked. "Stranger than living in a hidden realm that's actually inside a painting with giant bedazzled jellyfish?"

"Do you not remember that creepy witch Ozzie?" Esme asked. "Or the thieving giant? Or the night castle?" Her gaze fell to the swarming fish beneath their feet.

"Depends on what you're used to."

"How could she be expecting us?" Esme asked, holding Tiago gently in her hand. "And where is she?"

"Water witches *are* adept at seeing the future."

"Yeah, but she'd have to know what to look for, and how in the world could she see across dimensions?" She leaned closer and whispered out of the side of her mouth, "And imagine how old she must be. How can she still be alive?"

"Magical creatures age strangely," Fetch said.

"Are you sure you're okay?" Esme asked. Worry expanded in her chest, making it harder to breathe.

"I'll be fine," Fetch muttered. "We just need to find Lucinda and . . ." His eyes drifted to the dazzling installments above their heads. "Do you think those stones are real?"

"Of course they're real," came a voice behind them.

Esme and Fetch swiveled to find a slight woman standing before them. Blue-black hair fell over her shoulders in silky heaps, reaching the waist of her silver beaded skirt. Her enormous eyes were the color of a moonlit sea, but if Esme peered closely, she thought she could see the reflections of crescent moons there.

Esme stood dumbfounded, trapped between awe and a little bit of fear. "Are you Lucinda?"

"You are Esmerelda Santos," the woman said, ignoring the question. She turned her gaze to the bird-Tiago. "He is of Air, descendant of my sister Gisele—and there is a quite unfortunate spell lingering in his blood."

"How—how'd you—" Esme stammered, holding Tiago closer.

"I am of Water." Lucinda's voice was smooth, almost musical. "I can see beyond the obvious."

"So you *are* her," Esme said, hardly believing they'd made it this far. Just a couple of days ago all she'd had was a heart filled with hope that she was strong enough to save her family. And now here she was, standing before an original witch, just like Lenny had asked. All the pieces were coming together, and soon, Esme prayed, she would be reunited with her family.

"If by 'her,' you are referring to Lucinda, original witch, then yes, I am her." The brujx's gaze fell to Fetch. "Oh."

"Oh?" Esme screwed up her face. "What's that supposed to mean?"

"It means exactly as it chooses," Lucinda said. "Infer what you will." She crept closer to the fox. Fetch didn't move an inch.

"Such darkness," Lucinda whispered, an expression of

sympathy crossing her luminous face. Fetch still said nothing. "Well," she said. "You must rest and eat and then we shall talk. There is much to discuss."

"She's right," Fetch said with a slight tremble in his voice. "We should rest."

"But—" Esme began, only to be silenced by Lucinda's gaze.

"There is much to discuss," the witch said, "but conversation will be futile if you are not revitalized. You have just crossed over to a powerful realm where no other humans have ever stepped foot."

Lucinda went on. "I did try to make the journey somewhat easier, but you know how magic hates the obvious. Like a door, for example."

No, I did not know that, Esme thought as Fetch adjusted his coat unnecessarily. She made a mental addition to her running list of notes on all things magic.

"So you made the painting the doorway," Fetch said. "Interesting."

"There was no entrance before that," Lucinda said. "And it is the last one I will ever create."

"We really don't need to sleep or to eat," Esme insisted, even though her bones were screaming for rest. "Fetch only has a few hours . . . maybe. And we don't even know yet if you can help us or if we came to the right place."

Lucinda took a deep breath. "Do you think it was an accident that the fox came across the map?"

"You know about the map?" Fetch's eyes widened.

"I created it," Lucinda said, "And I used an ancient language, knowing that you had the right brand of magic to decode it."

The fox's whiskers twitched as Esme's stomach churned with a mix of nausea and exhilaration.

"You sent Fetch to help us?" Esme asked. "You saw him before today?"

"'Saw' implies the use of one's eyes," Lucinda said. "I felt his troubles, his fears, and I knew that he could prove useful."

Esme knew those troubles rested on the loss of his little sister. Was she still alive? Would he ever see her again?

"You used me?" Fetch looked woozy.

"Of course I did, and if I hadn't, none of you would be here. Now," Lucinda said, "you must rest. And do not worry. You will not be here long, and it will be well worth the time you spend."

Esme cast her gaze to Tiago, his wings tucked tightly against his small body. No way would she let him sleep forever. He'd never forgive her if he missed out on the quest. Missed out on his life.

Lucinda added, "I can sense that your magic is quite spent. And you will need all of it for what's ahead."

"Can you define 'ahead'?" Fetch asked. "You *are* a Water witch, so perhaps you can tell us how this ends."

One corner of Lucinda's mouth curved ever so slightly. "There are too many variables at play."

"But we're running out of time," Esme cried. "And

Fetch—his heart is going to give out unless you break his curse." Esme was surprised by how much she had come to care about the fox in such a short amount of time. In some ways, she felt like she had always known him.

"There can be no more discussion until you sleep," Lucinda said.

Three jellyfish pods began to lower slowly from the ceiling. Esme could see now that each was wrapped in silk and velvet, and the stones sewn into the fabric were even more brilliant close up.

"You want us to sleep in those?" Esme asked as ribbons of fabric unraveled and spilled onto the floor, revealing small entrances to each.

"Once inside," Lucinda said, "you will want nothing more than to fall into the world of dreams. These pods are quite potent. They will most definitely regenerate you."

Fetch eyed the structures with suspicion. "We're going to sleep inside magical jellyfish? How do we know this isn't a trap?"

Lucinda sighed. "The tide is rising, and if you stay here, then you will drown in less than a minute. The choice is yours."

"The tide comes into this room?" Esme asked, glancing around.

"Looks are deceiving, child."

"Like that cottage we saw," Fetch said. "It was a painting, too, wasn't it?"

"Yes and no and not exactly."

The floor began to shudder beneath their feet. The fish zigzagged wildly, anxiously.

"What about Tiago?" Esme asked. "He's already asleep."

Lucinda gently scooped Tiago into her hand, carried him to the nearest bejeweled pod, and set him inside. "Let's see what happens."

Esme shared a glance with Fetch, then stepped into her own jellyfish compartment, a closet-like space with a narrow bed filled with pink satin pillows. Her first thought was *This is like a genie's bottle*, and her second never came because the moment she was inside, she was asleep, floating in a dream-world where she felt loved and protected.

She stood at the edge of a desolate valley, dwarfed by the black volcanic walls rising above it on both sides. The light was dim and gray.

A child, no older than six, appeared next to her. A girl with golden locks and dark eyes, wearing overalls and a hoodie, and carrying a silver lunch pail.

"Who are you?" Esme asked.

"I'm a water spirit, here to escort you."

Esme nodded and said, "What is this place?"

"Not my favorite," the girl said. "But this isn't my dream."

Esme stared out across the lifeless basin. "Everything looks so dead."

"It's the Valley of Fantasmas Perdidos."

"Lost ghosts?" Esme said.

The girl nodded. "All lost in their own way."

"And they live here?"

"They don't live at all," the girl said, swinging her pail. "They linger here. Some are easy to talk to, others still think they're alive, but the worst are the ones that are filled with anger and resentment that their lives were cut short. Watch out for those on your journey."

"Wait. I have to go in there? Aren't you coming with me?"

The girl shook her head.

"You said you were my escort."

"Back to the land of the living," the water spirit said, "not through the lost dead."

"Why do I have to go in there?" Esme asked. This was her dream, so shouldn't she have some control over it?

The girl looked up at her. "Because someone wants to talk to you."

Chapter Thirty

Esme wasn't exactly keen on ghosts.

Not that she'd ever met one, but that water spirit kid didn't make them sound too appealing or friendly.

And what did she mean, someone wanted to talk to Esme? Like some kind of wise spirit? Or maybe a messenger from the other side?

Or maybe my mom?

A spark of hope ignited inside her heart, then quickly fizzled. She didn't want to think that her mom was some lost ghost stuck in this dreadful place.

As Esme placed one foot in front of the other, the world grew darker. The footpath was littered with deadwood, ashes, and picked-over bones. Stars sped across the sky like a time-lapse video.

Shadowy, faceless figures rose from the ashes to her left and right as murmurs and groans floated all around her.

If this is where the dead go, she thought, *I am so never going to die.*

The witch hunter's voice broke through the darkness: *Such a foolish, foolish girl. To come all this way for naught.*

Esme felt a surge of confusion.

How was the witch hunter so powerful that she could find Esme in her dreams? Had she gotten her hands on a dagger—or more than one?

She'd read about certain witches who had the ability to infiltrate dreams, but it had been outlawed forever ago because of privacy and consent issues. No one wanted some stranger stalking their dreams. Esme's dad had called it a lost art. Esme wasn't so sure.

More like a creepy stalker art, she thought.

With each step she grew colder. She rubbed the chill from her arms, thinking maybe she should wake up now. But then she felt a fine threading of fingers through her hair, gentle and soft, the way her mom used to do it.

Chaos magic began to spread across her chest and rise up her throat like a gasp of air needing to be spent.

After a quick breath, she coughed. Flecks of iridescent dust flew from her mouth.

The shadowy figures began to fill in, gray and pale. Gaunt creatures with veiny skin who looked as if they'd never had a meal.

Esme gulped down her terror, reminding herself that no one had ever been murdered in their sueños. Or at least she had never heard of such a thing. Hopefully that also meant the witch hunter couldn't send some of her darkness to try and swallow Esme up again.

White petals fell from her hair onto her shoulders, then tumbled to the charred ground like snowflakes. The ghosts halted. They stared with their vacant, hungry eyes, recoiling as if the flowers could hurt them.

Esme clenched her fists at her side. This was just a dream. None of it was real. Not the water spirit, not the witch hunter, and not the lost fantasmas.

Petals continued to pool around her feet, bringing her to a halt. They rose in heaps around her ankles, around her legs, then up to her waist.

Suddenly Esme's flowers exploded into a billow of white. The sweet scent of roses infiltrated the stale air, and when the cloud cleared, she found herself in her mom's moonlit garden.

But the jardín wasn't dead like it was back in the real world.

It pulsed with life, with magnificent blooms and lush green vines.

Esme's heart thrashed wildly.

"Mom?" Esme's voice was small, unsure. Filled with longing.

Patina Santos materialized before Esme's eyes. Young and beautiful, just the way Esme remembered her.

"Is it really you?" Esme's voice quivered.

Her mother took a step closer, reaching out her arms.

She fell into them. Her mother was so real, so solid.

"Do you live here?" Esme asked tearfully. "Are you lost too?"

Patina continued to stroke her hair gently. "I am not lost. But the only way for you to speak to me was to first go *through* the lost. We don't have much time," Patina said, pulling free. She looked into her daughter's eyes. "I'm here to warn you."

Esme blinked. A single tear rolled down her cheek. She didn't care about warnings and dream languages. All she cared about was her mom. "I want to stay here with you."

"All is not as it seems," Patina said. "You have to give up this quest."

Anger knotted in Esme's heart. "The witch hunter has Dad and Lenny," she cried, trying to make her mom understand. "And all the other witches are gone too. They're stuck in Oblivion and I have to save them, and San Bosco is going to wither away and you said that me and Tiago had a great destiny and maybe this is it and . . ." She knew she was blubbering but she didn't care. Years' worth of sorrow poured out of her, along with a whisper. "I'll never give up."

She expected her mom to say something like, *Oh, I had no idea*, or *Of course you have to save them*. But she didn't. Instead, Patina's face tensed and she said, "If you continue with this quest, you could die."

"I don't care! I want you back," Esme blurted. "I want you to come home." It was a childish wish, but it felt good to say it. To hope it.

"And I want you to be safe."

"I will be once I get to Oblivion and save—"

"Only the witch hunter can take you to Oblivion," Patina argued. "Don't you see? The one thing you want, you cannot have without the hunter's consent, and she'll never agree to it."

That changed everything. But Esme refused to believe in nevers and impossibles. "Do you really want me to give up on Dad and Lenny?"

"There are powerful forces at play here, Esme."

No. She'd never ever give in. She had to see her sister and father again. She had to make sure magic had a home in San Bosco.

"I'll find a way. With or without your help."

"I was worried you might say that." Patina drew herself up. "The witch hunter is in the Place of Almas Angustiadas."

Esme knew about the Place of Agonized Souls, where tormented witches left their very souls, to grieve, to discard unwanted memories and unload whatever pain they were carrying. But it was also a place of such anguish that many of the souls never made it back to their owners and were instead sucked into a dark abyss forever, neither alive nor dead.

"How do you know?"

"Those souls . . . many are so lost and already very close to death," her mother said. "The distance between life and death is shorter than you think."

"Do you know who the witch hunter is?"

"I can't see her face, Esme. I can only feel her energy—

a darkness growing and growing, touching all realms."

All realms? That sounded really bad. Esme had started this quest thinking only San Bosco had been affected, but now she saw that it was so much bigger. "Okay, so how do I get to the Place of Agonized Souls?" she asked.

"No, Esme. You cannot go unless you leave your soul there, and what would be the point of that? You would be powerless without magic, and if you stayed too long, your soul would be lost forever."

Esme felt like a kite drifting aimlessly across the sky without a string. "Then why did you tell me where she is?"

"Because you need to know that the witch hunter is growing in strength," Patina said. "She's been using the suffering in the Place of Agonized Souls to multiply her powers. At least until she can get all four daggers. Once she does, she will be unstoppable."

"Mom, there has to be a way!" But even if Esme managed to find the witch hunter, how would she ever talk her into freeing Lenny and Dad and the others?

"The only way is to find the remaining Daggers of Ire before the witch does."

The witch hunter had at least one Dagger, which meant that Esme was already far behind in a race she didn't even know she was running. But the witch hunter knew. And she had a head start.

"You must use them to defeat her," Patina added. "Only then will her hold on the witches in Oblivion evaporate."

Esme felt sick. Finding her family and saving them sounded so much simpler than defeating a powerful witch.

Her mind whirled in every direction, searching for answers, for any crumb of hope. "I'm in Lucinda's realm," she said. "Maybe she'll give me her dagger. I mean, if she still has it." Was this the real reason Lenny had told her to find an original witch? So she could get her hands on a dagger? But why the cryptic note? And what did the riddle even mean?

Patina drew closer. "You have to remember that there are many versions of the truth, depending on who is doing the telling. Do you understand?"

Esme had so many questions, so many things she still wanted to say, but the edges of this world were blurring, dissolving, and she knew the dream was coming to an end. She couldn't let that happen without saying, "I love you, Mom."

Patina smiled. "I will always love you, Esmerelda." And then her mother was gone.

Silence fell over the garden.

The water spirit reappeared. She took Esme by the hand and began to lead her through the garden.

"I don't want to leave." Esme felt untethered. Like all she had left to hold on to were memories, but that wasn't enough. She wanted her mom.

"The living aren't meant to stay with the dead," the water spirit said.

The world was vanishing, bleeding down the edges.

Just before it disappeared altogether, Esme extended her

hand and snatched a rose from the vine.

When she stirred awake, the memory of her mom began to pale.

Esme sat up, wondering if the dream had been just some fantasy. And then she remembered the rose she had taken. If it was real, surely the flower had returned from the dreamworld with her.

She lifted her pillow to find nothing. In a state of frenzy, she fumbled with the other pillows, tossing and scanning and probing with no success.

So it *was* just a dream, she thought miserably.

Tiago's voice carried from outside the pod. He was awake! Esme jumped up, tripping over her own feet as she fell to the floor with a *whomp*.

Perched on her hands and knees, she froze, staring.

There, peeking out from under the bed, was the rose.

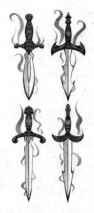

Chapter Thirty-One

The pod lurched. Up and up and up.

Frantically Esme pulled back the silks draped across each wall, searching for the exit.

"Hello!" she shouted.

She could no longer hear her friends' voices.

"Tiago!"

The jellyfish pod came to an abrupt halt, knocking Esme back.

She clung to the rose as two bits of fabric rippled, then parted like a theater curtain.

A wedge of sunlight seeped into the space, forcing Esme to shield her eyes.

"Are you feeling refreshed?" Lucinda asked, standing at the entrance, blocking any view of the outside world.

Esme had to admit that she was. She felt as though she'd slept eons and then some. "Where am I?" she asked. "And where are my friends?"

"They will join you shortly."

"They're okay?"

A faint smile tugged at the corner of Lucinda's mouth. "It is no accident that they are with you on this journey. You will need them greatly."

Esme was about to ask if Lucinda had broken Fetch's curse, but she was silenced the moment Lucinda's gaze fell to the rose in Esme's hands. "I see."

"I brought it from my dream," Esme admitted. "That means it was real, right?" She didn't know why, but she needed someone to tell her she hadn't imagined it, that the sueño wasn't just some kind of wish fulfillment.

Lucinda backed up a few inches, never taking her eyes from the bloom.

The flower rose on a soft breeze, whirled like a vortex, and then—*pop!*—vanished into a trail of dust.

"Hey!" Esme cried.

"Dreams are not meant to cross into this world," Lucinda said. "Come."

Esme followed the Water witch out of the pod, nearly tripping over a mound of fabric as she spilled into the sunlight. She had expected to see the blue chamber or a kitchen, maybe even an elegant dining room, but not this.

She stood on a thick lawn overlooking a lush world of

greens and blues. For as far as she could see there were open fields, shimmering lakes, and winding footpaths. Her gaze came to rest on a stone mansion bordered by an impossibly tall hedge dotted with tiny blue flowers.

"It's beautiful, isn't it?" Lucinda finally asked.

Esme didn't think that word was enough to describe not just what she could see but what she *felt*—gone was her sense of nervousness, replaced with a feeling of comfort, calm, peace.

"Did you build all this?" she asked, falling into step beside the witch, wondering how she could ever work up the nerve to ask Lucinda for her dagger.

"I did, but it isn't always this beautiful."

"What do you mean?"

"My world never stays the same," Lucinda said. "Sometimes I like to change the house to a castle, sometimes a cabin. I change the lakes too, and depending on my mood, I often live by the sea. Anywhere that I am inspired to create with my watercolors. But there are days," she said wistfully, "when only a bruised sky will do, when the trees are merely skeletons of their former glory."

Esme couldn't imagine having the ability to change her world with the stroke of a brush. They followed a path to the right. "But why wouldn't you want it beautiful all the time?"

Lucinda hesitated, then smiled softly and said, "I paint according to my mood."

Esme wanted to know more, but the sound of laughter drew her attention. As she and Lucinda rounded the bend, a sparkling pond dotted with lily pads came into view. Bright blue fish leaped out of the water, arcing through the air.

Were they whistling?

Esme was about to ask when she stopped in her tracks. There, near the edge of the pond, was the water spirit from her dream. The girl was sitting on a big wool blanket with a boy who looked the same age and had the same golden hair.

The girl was real? Esme's pulse quickened. Maybe she could ask her more questions about the Valley of Lost Ghosts or maybe the girl could take her back for another visit. She started to run toward her.

"Oh!" Noticing Esme, the girl waved, jumped to her feet, and came over with a pail in her hand.

"It's you." Esme stopped in her tracks.

The girl handed her lunch pail to Esme. "I hope you like bologna sandwiches. It's all I know how to make."

Esme's heart thundered and she felt suddenly woozy. "You—you were really there."

"Do you mean in your dream? Of course I was there." She stood taller. "And see, you made it back here. I'm really good at my job."

"But I'm better," the boy announced, coming over.

The girl rolled her eyes.

"I wanted to escort you," he went on, "but Lucinda wouldn't let me. She said it had to be my sister, which really stinks because there's not a lot to do around here and searching dreams in other realms gets boring and—"

Lucinda cleared her throat, silencing the boy.

"Searching dreams in other realms?" Esme repeated, not sure she'd heard him right.

"That will be all," Lucinda said to the water spirits.

The boy glanced up at Esme. He poked a thumb into his chest. "*I* made the cookies."

And then he and his sister morphed into a couple of water bubbles that floated through the air and into the pond with a *pop*.

"Do they always do that?" Esme asked.

"They can take any water form." Lucinda gestured toward the blanket where the two had been sitting. "Now, we have exactly forty-seven minutes, so let us begin."

Esme was bursting with questions, but she knew that she had to start at the beginning. Before she could possibly ask Lucinda for the dagger, she had to make her understand why she needed it.

"It all started with the witch hunter," Esme said. "Or maybe the magic panels. Or was it the glowing rain? The daggers? No," she decided. "It was the grimorio."

Lucinda said, "Eat, and then you will know exactly where to begin."

Suddenly famished, Esme reached into the little silver pail to find a sandwich with the bread crusts neatly cut off, and a stack of pink heart cookies with blue icing, each wrapped in transparent paper that read: *never ending*.

Esme didn't give it a second thought until she ate a cookie

only to find it replaced in the stack a blink later.

For the next twenty minutes, she unfolded the tale, beginning with the night of the motorcycle races. Never once did she leave out a single fact. It was as if she were a book being read, and when she was done, when the story brought her through the dream and to this moment, she took a much-needed breath. "I have so many questions—like, who's the witch hunter? Why did she throw all the witches into Oblivion? We don't even know how many daggers she has or whose she has or how she got them! And now she's sucking power out of the Place of Agonized Souls."

"What did you just say? About the Place of Agonized Souls?"

"That's what my mom told me." Esme waited for Lucinda to say something, but the water brujx said nothing, only stared across the glistening lake.

"And I'm pretty sure the witch hunter doesn't have all the daggers," Esme said, remembering how the hunter had tried to convince her to give up her quest with her threats and warnings. "Or she wouldn't be trying to stop me."

Lucinda snapped her gaze to Esme. "She's spoken to you? What did she say?"

"Mostly she told me to give up. Oh, and she sent some wicked smoke too." These were facts, but they didn't explain the why of it all. Why was the witch so afraid of Esme's quest? And who was she? Could she really be someone Esme knew?

Lucinda said, "I saw glimpses of you in the water. It's why I called you all this way, why I tried to communicate with you through the rain back in San Bosco."

Esme remembered the glowing torrent the night they broke into the museum—the same night her family vanished. The same storm that followed her to Ocho Manos, warning her to stay away. "That was you? Did you also make the crack in the sky?" she asked, remembering how, on the night of the races, the sky had split open and darkness had escaped.

Lucinda narrowed her eyes. "That wasn't me, but I know who it was."

"The witch hunter?" The gears in Esme's mind began to turn. "That's how they got into San Bosco, after the panel was busted."

"Sometimes what appears obvious is really just a diversion."

"So it *isn't* how the witch hunter got into my world and took all the witches?"

Lucinda looked suddenly exhausted, her face worn and drained of color. "Only time will tell."

Esme pressed her hands into her face and took a deep breath, examining each nugget of truth. "Were you the one who told me that I was going to die and all was lost?" she asked, remembering the voice in the graveyard and in Ocho Manos.

"I did no such thing," Lucinda said.

So the wicked messages *had* been from the witch hunter. But then Esme remembered the dream voice. "You told me to find Ozzie. You said that Ozzie would give but also take, which was super true, but I could have used a warning about how wicked she is."

"Ozzie?" Lucinda shook her head, looking perplexed. "That wasn't me either."

"What about in the Paso de los Muertos? You told me to let go—" She stopped cold. Lucinda was staring at her, bewildered. "If it wasn't you," Esme said, "then who was it?"

"I don't know, but I can only communicate beyond this realm through water."

Esme took a deep breath and then another. "My mom—in the dream, she said I could trust you, and that I need to find the daggers if I'm ever going to beat the witch hunter and free my family. And maybe it's too much to ask, but . . . can I have yours?"

If Lucinda was shocked, she didn't show it. She stood and went to the water's edge, then knelt before drifting her fingers through the pond, which sent wide, shimmering ripples across its surface. Though she was gone only a few seconds, Esme held her breath, waiting, wondering, feeling the weight of forever.

When Lucinda returned, she sat back down and waved a hand through the air.

Instantly the sun vanished under the cover of a massive gray cloud. The air turned cold. The pond iced over. The trees shivered and the grass turned brown.

"What just happened?" Esme asked.

"I am about to show you something that is far too dreadful

to be seen in the light of the sun, a story that you must see for yourself. But please understand that this is only one part of the story."

Her words rang with the memory of Patina's words: *There are many versions of the truth, depending on who is doing the telling.*

A swirl of blue mist arose from Lucinda's chest, dancing and whirling. Esme watched with wonder as the mist took a form.

The form of a dagger, plunged into the Water witch's heart.

Esme gasped. The blade looked identical to the one that had been buried in Lenny's stomach. Gold scrolls etched into a black handle. The memory of it made Esme feel sick.

"My sister had one like this stuck in her stomach," she said.

"It could not have been a true Dagger of Ire. Perhaps a memory."

"Memory?"

"Is your sister of Water?"

Esme nodded.

"Water witches are quite good at replicating an object or person they've seen, but the object never takes a real form."

Esme remembered how her hand had moved right through the ghostly blade.

"It's time." Lucinda inched closer. "Take the dagger."

A painful knot tightened in Esme's throat. She clenched and unclenched her fists. "What will happen to you? I mean, it's not going to kill you, is it?"

Lucinda said, "No. But I will lose my magic."

"What? Why would you be willing to give that up?"

"Because if I don't, you have no hope of defeating the witch hunter."

Esme swallowed. She extended a trembling hand, wondering why Lucinda was so invested in Esme finding the witch hunter. "Why are you helping me?"

"All will be revealed soon enough."

Except that *soon* felt very far away.

Curls of mist twisted between Esme's fingers.

She took hold of the dagger.

Then, with a tug, she pulled it from Lucinda's heart.

Chapter Thirty-Two

Esme felt as if she had been swept out of the stratosphere. As if her entire being was floating somewhere between here and now, then and there, to a place that didn't—*couldn't*—exist outside any logic.

And yet here she was, standing on the bank of Río Místico.

She glanced down at her hands, her body, her legs. She was nothing more than a flickering blur, as though she was made of a million particles of dust that could vanish any moment.

"The full moon loomed," a lyrical voice echoed across the water. It took Esme only half a blink to realize that the voice belonged to her. But how? Esme had seen and experienced lots of weird things, but this was reaching beyond her comfort zone into bizarre.

"A giant fish eye floating in the black summer sky," her

other self went on, "watching closely as four young and beautiful sisters rushed toward the river for a peaceful midnight swim. But they soon found they weren't alone."

The voice vanished as the scene zoomed into view.

There was a young man asleep on the banks, just like the legend told.

She watched, unseen, as three of the sisters gathered around him. Esme recognized a younger Lucinda—long, dark hair swept into a low braid that hung over her shoulder. A stark contrast to the sister with silvery hair and striking blue eyes— that must be Gisele, the Air witch.

Esme studied the third sister, who had soft brown locks and faint freckles dotted across her full coppery cheeks. Triana, the Earth witch.

Escarlata was nowhere near them. She was singing as she floated peacefully in the moonlit water, her long red hair pooling around her face like a flame.

Esme shifted her attention back to the others just as Lucinda and Gisele kissed the sleeping man's face.

He immediately awakened at the touch.

The sisters recoiled, at first giggling and then . . .

"Do you know who I am?" the man growled, so forcefully the trees quivered.

Lucinda, Gisele, and Triana shook their heads, looking suddenly afraid.

"I am Nocturno, the god of night and burden," he bellowed. "And you have stolen that which does not belong to you!"

"We didn't know," Gisele cried.

Triana, looking the most composed, said, "Truly, we're sorry."

"The deed is done," the god insisted. "For the stolen kisses hold a spark of my powers, powers that are now infiltrating your blood." He hesitated. His mouth fanned into a smile. "And they will kill you soon enough."

A trail of iron-gray mist curled around the sisters. Lucinda and Gisele immediately collapsed, grasping at their throats.

"Stop!" Triana shouted, falling to her knees next to her sisters. The mist swept into her gaping mouth, silencing her.

Escarlata raced onto the scene, eyes filled with terror. "Let them go!"

The god's eyes bore into Escarlata. For a long moment, the god and the girl stared at one another, waiting, daring the other to speak first.

"The gods were never meant to mingle with humans," he whispered, "and now it is too late. Now . . . they must suffer forever. But you—I will allow you to choose freedom or to share their destiny."

Esme blinked. Why would the god offer this to Escarlata and not the others?

Trembling, Escarlata swept a tear from her cheek. "They are my sisters," she said, hardening her expression. "I will always choose them."

The god scowled. "So be it."

In a flash, he materialized four daggers, and with a single

fluid movement, he plunged one into Lucinda's heart and another into Gisele's. Triana threw herself on top of her sisters just as the god flung a blade into her chest.

Escarlata attacked the god with teeth and fists.

He took hold of her arms, pinning her in place, searching her eyes. Her gaze was cold and hollow.

"As you wish," he whispered, and drove a dagger into her heart too.

Escarlata's fury could be felt in the earth, in the sky, even in the river itself.

The daggers pulsated with a force so powerful Esme could feel it in every breath.

Magic.

It was then that Esme understood.

The legend was a lie. It wasn't the god's ire that had created magic.

It was Escarlata's.

Chapter Thirty-Three

The riverbank was engulfed by a black cloud.

In a whoosh, Esme was swept back into Lucinda's world, feeling different than when she had left. As if her mind and heart were balls of clay, reshaped in a way that she would never see the world in the same way again.

And not because of the truth she had learned, or the sorrow she felt, or the loss that continued to carve a hole in her heart.

She was different because she had not only seen with her own eyes the birth of magic, she'd *felt* it like a bolt of lightning.

For the first time her Chaos didn't feel like a storm brewing inside her. It was more of a bright sunbeam wrapping itself around her body.

"Do you see now?" Lucinda asked as Esme took deep, even

breaths, still gripping the smoking dagger. "The blades are more than weapons. They are conduits of truth."

"Untold stories," Esme breathed. She stared down at the divine blade. Gray smoke weaved between her fingers and swirled around the gold scrolls etched into the black handle. "The Legend of Ire is the greatest of lies," she said, repeating the riddle. "Easy to speak and harder to keep. If it is the truth you seek, you will not find it here or there or anywhere. For the truth can only be found inside the deception," she whispered. "The daggers . . . they're the lie."

Silence stretched between the two witches.

"Escarlata was the one who created magic," Esme said. "It wasn't the god at all."

"Her fury was the genesis of the magic," Lucinda said, "but when it latched onto my and my sisters' fear and love and betrayal, a perfect storm was created."

A storm of magic made by all four sisters, Esme thought.

Lucinda went on, "When that untethered emotion touched even a speck of the god's power, well . . ." Her voice trailed off as she turned her gaze to the darkening sky.

"The god of night and burden," Esme whispered, remembering his name. "Nocturno."

Lucinda nodded.

Esme had read about the gods. She knew their triumphs and tragedies, but they were just myths. Or at least that was what she had always thought. "He's . . . real."

"They all are."

Esme wasn't ready to process that, plus she had a million other questions. "But why did there have to be a lie at all?" she asked. "Why not just tell your truth?"

"We agreed not to blame each other, and no one wanted Escarlata to endure that dark legacy. I guess it was easier for people to think the ire came from the god than from a witch."

Esme scrunched her toes tight inside her tennis shoes, thinking, processing, searching. "I don't get why he offered Escarlata freedom and not the rest of you."

"Like I said, there are several versions of the story. This is my memory. My sisters have their own. All of them matter. And each blade will reveal a different truth."

Esme tried to shake off the confusion coursing through her. She needed to put her flustered thoughts in the right order, but an avalanche of whys was already tumbling from her mouth. "Why did you suddenly vanish one night? Why did you make this realm? Why didn't you take the daggers out before now? Why didn't you stay with your sisters? And how am I supposed to use this to defeat the witch hunter?"

Lucinda spoke slowly, deliberately. "As the days and months passed," she said, "our powers grew. They became the magic of Water, Earth, Air, and Fire, each element choosing one of us. We found peace after many years, but soon others learned the infinite power of the daggers. They realized that to acquire one was to possess great magic, but to acquire all would be to possess—"

"The power of a god," Esme finished.

"That's when we knew that we had to vanish, to create safe realms where no one could find us, and that meant . . ." She drew in a long breath. "That meant we couldn't be together ever again."

"But why couldn't you all just hide in one realm?"

"When the dagas are in close proximity," Lucinda explained, "they emit even greater power and are easier to track. One day I saw our futures in a lake. I saw the day a faceless witch would steal one, setting all this in motion. So I convinced my hermanas to hide."

They had sacrificed one another to protect the magic of a god from falling into the wrong hands. And now it seemed that it was all for nothing.

Esme felt a sharp pain in her heart. She couldn't imagine her life without her sister, without Lenny's laugh and hugs and love.

"Hold up," Esme said, backtracking across her memory. "You didn't answer why you never just took the daggers out yourselves. You could have hidden them or . . ."

Lucinda's gaze dropped to the dagger still in Esme's grip. "Many times we tried, but we didn't have the power."

"Then how did I . . ."

"Only a witch of Chaos, one with every element in her blood, has the power to remove the blades."

The understanding gathered like a storm. "That means the witch hunter has to be of Chaos too." The idea of it turned Esme's stomach. "I mean, if she has a dagger, right?"

The sky began to bleed gray, trickling like paint into the pond, the trees, the horizon.

Lucinda nodded. "Tell me," she said, "what did you feel in the vision of the night that magic was created?"

"I could feel the magic coming to life." Chaos pulsed gently in Esme's chest, her limbs, her throat. The sensation was warm and buzzy. She had always thought her magic was something separate from herself, something wild and uncontainable. Now she saw that her Chaos was as much a part of her as the sangre flowing through her veins. She told Lucinda about that Fatales' attack, how she had protected her friends, how she had been like armor. "Is that the power of Chaos?"

Lucinda opened her mouth, then closed it again. "To understand Chaos, you have to know where it came from."

"Darkness," Esme said, repeating what she had always been taught. "Greed. Hate. Fear."

Lucinda shook her head. "It came many years after that dreadful night at the riverbank. A rare form of magic born unto itself. And like all species, magic must evolve too. It must survive." She glanced at Esme. "Your magic did not come from the dark. It was created from the love between me and my sisters, a blend of each of our powers."

Tears welled in Esme's eyes.

"What is it?" Lucinda asked.

"It's just—if people tell you something about yourself long enough, then you start to believe it too. Even if it's all lies."

Lucinda crept closer. "You can harness that power,

Esmerelda. You can call on all four magics."

Esme felt a wall go up inside her. Yet she knew Lucinda was right. Esme had already felt Air, Water, Fire, and Earth all at once in the Paso de los Muertos, when the mysterious voice had told her to *let go*.

Lucinda gestured to the vanishing sky. "Call on the wind."

"Like a spell?" Esme was pretty sure she didn't know that one.

"You do not need spells. Only your mind."

One day you will harness all that power. You'll no longer need spells to do magic. And Earth, Fire, Water, and Air will all bend to your will.

With a deep breath, Esme closed her eyes. She willed her magic to rise, higher and higher, watching in her mind's eye as it spread across her chest in a swell of blue and white. She imagined it floating out of her in a wave of light, touching the air, spinning it into a gale.

A cold wind gusted, blowing Esme's hair into her face. She opened her eyes. Three tiny flames flickered in the air before her, and a stream of water shot out of the lake like a geyser. "Uhhh . . ."

Lucinda smiled. "Well, *that* is quite impressive."

It wasn't impressive at all. "You said to call the wind," Esme argued. "Not little flames and water."

"It will take practice." The witch swept a hand through the air, bringing the magic to a halt. "Of course, it is easier to command magic when there is no fear, no immediate danger present."

Like when vicious hags are trying to suck your soul out of your body, Esme thought. "Fetch told me that I have a weakness, too, that I'm not . . . unkillable," she said.

"He's right."

Esme had sort of been hoping he was absolutely, positively, dead wrong.

"An accident could end you," Lucinda explained nonchalantly. "Or another creature, one with the same magnitude of magic and strength as yours, could kill you too."

"Like another Chaos witch." *Like the witch hunter.*

"Indeed. And for the record, we never called it Chaos," Lucinda said. "Others gave it that name because they didn't understand, and people will always try to destroy that which they are most afraid of. So they decided the magic was wicked, taboo. Even shameful."

Not Chaos. Esme felt her insides turn over. She was about to ask what the magic was called when the blade grew warm in her grasp. Swirls of silver mist curled around her wrist. She stuffed it into her coat pocket.

"There is one more thing," Lucinda said. "Whoever possesses a dagger has access not only to its power but also its truth."

"Its story."

"Yes."

Which meant the witch hunter had already seen at least one truth, but whose? And what had the dagger revealed to her?

"Do you know who's the one behind all this?" Esme thought

it would be better if she knew who she was dealing with versus some faceless witch.

Lucinda walked to the water's edge. Esme followed, watching as she knelt and peered into the pond. "Touch the blade to the water," she told Esme.

Esme fumbled with the dagger before she plunged it into the pond, wishing it would sink to the bottom.

Instantly, four violet waves rippled across the water. A small, shimmering sphere formed in the center. It floated up, hovered for a moment, then sailed toward the shore.

Esme watched with fascination as the magic sparked and spun, expanding taller and wider than a door. It was like looking into a giant iridescent soap bubble.

A sharp wind gusted.

And then, with a violent crash, the sphere exploded, showering Esme and Lucinda with its magic.

Esme jumped back, wiping the water from her eyes. She turned her gaze to Lucinda.

The witch's expression dulled. Her eyes darkened.

The lead sky continued to melt into the forest and the lake, pooling into a puddle of dismal gray. "Another dagger has been found and . . . removed. I can sense it."

The witch is growing in power.

"What?!" Esme's heart clenched tight.

A shadowy gate appeared before her. It swung open, revealing only a bleak grayness. "This is my last act of magic," Lucinda said, her voice suddenly brisk and distant. "One that will lead you to a bridge between realms. You must find it and cross it. But beware, travel in the between is perilous. Do not waste a moment. Do you understand?"

"What's on the other side of the bridge?" Esme asked.

"Hurry!" Lucinda cried as she began to fade. "The gate to Triana's realm is closing."

"You saw something else in the water!"

Lucinda's gaze met hers. "I refuse to believe it."

"Tell me."

And just as she and her world faded altogether, just as Esme was shoved into the gloom, she heard the brujx's last words: "The witch behind all this is one of my sisters."

Chapter Thirty-Four

Esme stood in a dense fog.

She couldn't see her hand in front of her face, never mind a whole bridge.

The witch behind all this is one of my sisters.

The words were too cold, too harsh, too impossible to accept. How could sisters who had stood by one another, had protected one another, and had been through all they had together—how could any of them be capable of such evil? And why?

Esme's entire body trembled with the mystery of it all as she placed one foot in front of the other, trying to pick her way through the thick mist.

We never called it Chaos.

Born of love. Not darkness.

Esme removed the Dagger of Ire from her pocket and stared at its beauty—a blade made by a god. She couldn't begin to imagine the power within just this one dagger, and now the witch hunter had two. Esme knew she wouldn't stop until she had the third, and this one too.

The mist curled around her wrist like before, looping up her arm slowly. The magic within her, the one she'd always called Chaos, swelled as if answering the blade.

Just then her jaw tightened as she sensed an unfamiliar magic nearby. It felt like a spring storm, like the fluttering of wings. So much like . . .

Tiago?

No way. She'd never been able to sense Air magic before. But she was sure now, not only was it Air, it was a very particular brand—warm, funny, loyal.

Powerful.

The magic was so powerful, it had to be that of a *full* witch. Esme stumbled back, stunned and delighted as her friend's magic washed over her. "Tiago!"

There was a chilled silence, and for a blink Esme thought maybe her senses were wrong. Then . . .

"Esme?" Tiago shouted back.

A wave of utter relief swept through her. "Where are you?"

"Over here!"

"That doesn't help!" Esme whirled in all directions. "I can't see a thing."

There was a grunt. "Are you in that cloud?"

"I'm in *a* cloud." *I think.*

A single word rushed through the fog. "Evaporarse." His voice sounded so close, almost as if he was standing right next to her.

The mist evaporated instantly.

Esme found herself in a world made of ice.

She stood on a solid lake that led to a semicircular arch of cascading falls, frozen over into a wall of blue ice that looked more sky than water. All around her were jagged black peaks, impossible climbs—and not a single bridge that would lead her to Triana's realm.

Esme was so caught up in the moment, so filled with wonder, that she neglected Lucinda's warning: *Travel in the between is perilous. Do not waste a moment.*

"Oof!"

She spun toward the sound. Over to her right, Tiago was inching down from a narrow crag. Carefully, painstakingly trying to navigate the icy hill.

But where was Fetch?

Tiago waved and smiled, then he slipped right onto his bottom, sliding the rest of the way until he landed at Esme's feet with a dramatic spin.

"I did that on purpose," he said, standing up with a pained grimace.

"You're awake!"

"I do *not* recommend a sleeping curse," he said. "Trippy dreams."

Esme didn't know where to begin. "You—your magic—it cleared the mist."

"Es, I *am* of Air."

"But you made it seem easy. Like *super* easy." How had he gone from botching spells to being a real brujo so quickly?

"Not easy," he said with a frown. "More like . . . natural."

Esme crept closer, nearly pressing her face up to his. "Tiago! HOW?"

His frown deepened as he stepped back. "Lu said that magic can be activated when someone faces death, and then she showed me some things, okay?" His face broke into a smile. "Imagine, I got tips from one of the most powerful witches to ever live. Oh, and adiós, rodents and animals—that dumb spell is long gone too."

"So no more cute rats with pink noses and long tails?"

"Har har."

Esme hesitated, then in a softer voice, she asked, "Do you feel different?"

Tiago was silent, as if unsure how to answer. "Strong enough to save my mom and the others," he said with a solid conviction that buoyed Esme's hope.

She socked him in the arm. "Well, we're going to need all your magic." She glanced around. "Where's Fetch?"

"Took another doorway," Tiago said, rubbing his lower back. "Something about odd numbers or whatever. Anyhow, he's here. I heard him up that hill." His eyes dropped to the dagger in Esme's grasp. "Whoa. Is that what I think it is?"

"A Dagger of Ire."

"Lu gave it to you?" His eyes grew three sizes. "Explain."

Esme was about to when she heard a loud, "OW!"

She looked up. Fetch was rubbing his forehead as he exited a cavern in the mountain above.

Everything felt charged, as though little bolts of electricity were igniting all along Esme's skin. "He . . . he's still a fox."

Fetch slid down the mountain, windmilling his arms awkwardly yet managing to stay on his feet. At the last second, he maneuvered wrong and—*BAM!*—crashed into Esme.

The two fell to the ground, tangled up, fighting for a foothold on the ice.

"Watch where you point that thing!" Fetch growled.

Esme rolled her eyes as she finally righted herself and the two got to their feet.

"She didn't break the curse," Esme said.

"You have a Dagger of Ire in your hand," Fetch said. "But you want to know about the curse?"

"I asked first."

"Technically, you didn't ask," Tiago said.

Esme glared at him, then at Fetch. Without thinking, she pressed a hand to his chest. She held her breath, lowered her ear to his heart. Slowly, sadly, she looked up. He still had no heartbeat.

"She said that if I break the curse, then I will never use magic again," Fetch managed, "that my threads will be useless and . . ." He snorted. "Wouldn't you know there would be some dumb loophole?"

"But you'll die if you *don't* break it!" Esme cried.

Fetch pulled his coat collar closer to his furry neck. "She was able to remove the death sentence, at least."

"That's great!" Esme nearly leaped into the air. But then she saw the sorrow in Fetch's eyes, and her own heart deflated.

The fox reached into his coat pocket and removed a silver-dollar shell. "She told me that if I break this in half, then my magic will be even more powerful, but I'll stay a fox. Or I can bury it and I'll return to normal but . . . it would be a life without magic."

Esme raised a hand to her mouth as Tiago shifted his feet and said, "But maybe that wouldn't be, like, so bad."

Fetch swallowed. "No one would survive in my realm without magic, remember?"

Esme could see his sorrow so clearly she was sure her heart would break. "You could come home with us," she suggested. "I mean, after all this is done."

Fetch smiled. His whiskers twitched. "I'm not meant for your world."

The choice was the worst kind—cruel, impossible, with no happy ending either way. Fetch just wanted to be human again, but the price was too high.

He wasn't meant for her world, that was true, but not because he was a fox. Because he needed to go back to Ocho Manos. He needed to find out the truth about his sister.

"That's a terrible choice," Tiago said.

Fetch nodded. "Both have possibilities, yet both are impossible, and I . . ." He turned his gaze away before looking back at Esme and Tiago. "I don't want to be a fox forever, but what if my sister is alive?" His voice cracked. "What if I need magic to find her?"

"You don't have to decide now," Esme said gently.

Fetch's eyes drooped as he sighed, and after a moment, he switched gears.

"So tell us," he said. "How do you have one of the most powerful objects in the universe?"

Esme recounted everything she had learned, from the now-solved riddle to the witch hunter's quasi-identity.

"The witch hunter is an original witch?" Tiago asked.

Esme nodded.

"Well, that narrows it down to Gisele, Triana, or Escarlata," Fetch said. Then he echoed the riddle's words. "The truth inside the deception. Brilliant."

"Except that it's only one truth," Esme said.

"And the fact that the *sisters* created the magic?" Tiago looked as if he'd been knocked back with a right hook. "And one of them is the witch hunter, who now has two daggers? Man, I did not see that coming. Is Lucinda sure about the daggers?"

"She said she could sense it," Esme said.

"I don't suppose she said which sister?" Fetch said.

Esme shook her head.

"Well, we've only got three choices," Tiago put in.

Then, as if remembering that they were standing on a lake of ice, Fetch glanced around. "Anyone know where we are?"

"We have to find a bridge and cross it," Esme said.

"To where?" Tiago asked.

"Triana's realm."

Fetch's eyes narrowed. "How do we know *she* isn't the witch hunter?"

"We don't," Esme said. "But the only way to defeat the witch hunter is to get another dagger."

"So we hope Triana still has her dagger," Fetch said. "And isn't the evil one."

"And how do you know all this?" Tiago asked Esme.

"I had a dream about my mom, and it was real," she said, wishing she still had the rose as proof. "She told me the witch hunter is in the Place of Almas Angustiadas. She's been feeding on the souls to multiply her powers, and now her darkness has grown so much that it's touching all realms."

Fetch's jaw tensed. "If that's true, she'll have the power to infiltrate any realm, to absorb its magic. Or even destroy it."

"Great," Tiago muttered as a cold ache throbbed in Esme's throat. She closed her mind to the awful possibilities Fetch talked about. It wouldn't get that far. They'd succeed. They'd defeat the witch hunter.

Tiago drew closer. "You . . . saw your mom?"

Esme dipped her head in a small nod as she studied her best friend. So many emotions crossed his face at once—disbelief, fear, shock, sadness—everything Esme had felt ever since they'd left home.

Then he coughed out a sound that was half grunt, half chuckle. "There has to be another way."

"There isn't."

"Es! That's just stupid and reckless. How can you—we—go up against one of the original witches?! And how are you going to find her? I mean, if she's in the Place of Agonized Souls chomping on all that pain and suffering?"

"We're wasting time arguing," Esme said.

Fetch removed his watch from his pocket and glanced at it. "Well, it appears you are now down to roughly two days."

"Two days!" Tiago said.

Esme wanted to throw up. There was too little time, too many variables, too much she didn't know. Not to mention one big impossibility: going up against an original witch. But she couldn't get distracted. "Look," she said, "we just need to find the bridge and get out of this between and—"

Fetch went stone still. "Did you say *between*?"

Instantly Esme remembered Lucinda's warning. How could she have gotten so lost in their conversation that she had forgotten?

"Am I missing something?" Tiago asked.

"There's no survival between realms," Fetch replied. "It's like a dead zone—super-dangerous travel, which means either (a) Lucinda wants to kill you, or (b) she's sending you through a back door where no magic can track you. But either way, the clock's ticking."

"I'm so sick of ticking clocks," Tiago grumbled. "How long do we have?"

Fetch looked down at his pocket watch. "About six point five minutes."

"Are you sure the point isn't a zero?" Tiago asked hopefully.

"Definitely not a zero."

"And if we don't find the bridge in that time?" Esme asked.

Fetch looked at her. "Are you really going to ask me that?"

"No gracias to dying in some frozen-over dead zone," Tiago said. "So which way? Because I don't see a bridge."

Esme bit her bottom lip, thinking. But no answers came to mind. She closed her eyes.

"Uh, this is no time to sleep," Fetch said.

"I'm trying to sense something," Esme said. She let her Chaos come to the surface, channeling the energy outward as she searched for another source of magic. At first she felt only a small pulse, a shiver of something. Then came the cold and darkness.

"Well?" Tiago said.

Opening her eyes, she said, "There's magic coming from"— she glanced down—"under the ice."

Something between a hiss and a gurgle erupted from the frozen lake.

Beneath the blue ice, a shadowy figure swept past so lightning fast that all Esme caught was a long body and shocking white hair.

"What the holy heck was that?" Tiago asked.

Fetch grimaced. "Our executioner."

Chapter Thirty-Five

"I think the bridge is under the lake," Esme said. White puffs of air floated from her numb mouth.

Tiago grunted. "You mean down there with the executioner?"

"This is a pretty big lake," Fetch said. "Do you have any idea *where*?"

Esme glanced around, clinging to the leftover bits of cold, dark magic. She pointed toward the falls. "Over there."

But no one moved. They all stood there, dazed, as if waiting for the others to take the first step.

Tiago rubbed his hands together. "Well, I guess we better get a move on then." He marched straight toward the dark unknown.

Esme and Fetch took off without another word, charging

across the lake. They had finally caught up to Tiago when . . .

Craccccckkkk!

Esme halted mid-stride, her arms frozen in front of her like a weirdly posed mannequin. She watched in horror as the fissure split dangerously across the ice.

Tiago and Fetch stopped so fast they nearly tripped over themselves.

Esme scanned the area, looking desperately for an escape, when Fetch began to open his coat, no doubt to transport them across the lake.

But he was stopped cold when they heard a brittle voice. "Oh, come now," it said. "Do you really want to leave so soon?"

They all glanced down.

The beast stared up with three lidless black eyes—they were endless, as though an entire world was inside each of them. The monster sneered, whipping countless octopus-like arms through the water. With each stroke, the thing grew, its torso and arms seeming to expand longer and longer.

Before she had time to blink, Esme was wrapped in the fox's coat, and just as they lifted off, just as they were about to fly away, the monster released a snarl and thrust an arm through the ice. A storm of shards exploded, raining down so hard, the trio broke apart.

There was a groan behind her. She spun toward Fetch. A splinter of ice was poking out of the side of his furry neck. Blood . . . there was so much blood.

Esme lunged for him just as the beast's claws reached up

and out, dragging him under.

"NO!" she screamed.

Tiago spun his hands in the air, chanting. A brutally cold gust swept across the lake, but it was too late for his magic.

Too late for him.

In a dizzying flash he was hauled beneath the water too.

There was a moment, a gap of sickening silence, when everything turned in slow motion. When Esme's heart split open. When her mind dulled. When her Chaos thudded.

Gripping the dagger, Esme drew in a deep breath and jumped into the freezing, bloody waters.

The pain was immediate, like a million knives stabbing her all at once.

She forced her limbs to move as she scanned the water. But it was so dark, so empty.

The dagger began to glow blue like it had at Lucinda's, enough to illuminate the space and show Esme that Tiago, Fetch, and the monster were nowhere to be seen.

But there, in the watery depths, was the murky, unmistakable form of a dilapidated sunken bridge. It had to be the one Lucinda had told her about! All Esme had to do was swim across, get to Triana's realm, and avoid this watery grave.

But she couldn't, wouldn't leave her friends to die here.

With renewed determination, she held the divine blade up, searching the depths. Trying to ignore her lungs, which were screaming for air. She couldn't hold her breath much longer. A terrible despair filled her just as a veil of darkness wrapped itself around her body.

She kicked, swimming wildly, trying to escape.

Out of the blackness emerged the three-eyed beast.

Its silvery hair hung limply around its face, flesh peeling off in chunks and before Esme could blink, its impossibly long arms shot out at the speed of light, seizing her, digging its claws into her legs.

But there was no pain.

And just like her encounter with the Fatal, the water beast's hand wasn't solid, but a thick chain of mist.

The monster froze, bared its teeth. Its endless black eyes grew wider as it drove its vaporous claws into Esme a second time.

With each thrust, Esme's magic pulsated more powerfully beneath her skin, right below the surface, rising and expanding as Esme drove the Dagger of Ire straight into the creature's chest.

Chapter Thirty-Six

The wail was deafening. Louder even than the explosion of light that seared the beast, dragging it into the deep.

Esme made her way to the surface. She sucked in lungful after lungful of air, cold and burning.

There was a tug on her leg.

Water rushed into her mouth as she was dragged back under. With sudden terror, she realized that the chains of mist were still wrapped around her legs, pulling her deeper and deeper.

She tried to pry herself free. It was no use. The more she struggled, the thicker and stronger the chains grew.

With each inch she descended, she felt a rush of power. Her magic, but not quite. It was as if it was splitting in two, or three, or four. As if it was making room—

Her Water magic surged.

Waves of energy blasted through the lake, swells of magic that shattered the icy surface. Then the water parted all around her, rising into colossal fountains.

No longer buoyed by the water, Esme was in free fall, tumbling a good ten feet to the sandy bottom, where she rolled to a painful stop.

Getting to her feet, she saw Tiago first, tied to the edge of the bridge with some kind of wire. Fetch was on the other side, his head lolling back.

Please don't be dead. Please don't be dead.

Hoping her magic would keep the water back, Esme staggered over to her friends. She grabbed hold of Tiago first, shaking him. "Wake up!"

There was no response.

They'd been without air for how long? A minute? Two? Was it possible to come back from that? Hot tears streamed down her face. She pressed her hand to Tiago's neck, searching for a pulse.

He stirred. One eye opened. Then another. "Took you long enough," he choked out, wheezing like an old man using his last breath.

Fueled by anger and relief, Esme unraveled the wire holding him.

"We have to hurry!" she said, scrambling over to Fetch on hands and knees.

"Es . . ."

"He's out cold!" she cried as she freed him and laid him down gently, hoping he was alive. But without a pulse, how could she know for sure?

She began CPR, hoping she was doing it right. She'd only ever performed the moves on a dummy.

Compress. Compress. Compress. Over and over and over. The rushing sound of the magically restrained water made it all so much harder—to hear, to concentrate, to hope.

But Tiago's voice somehow broke through all the chaos.

"He doesn't have a heart, Es," he said softly. "Remember?"

Tiago was wrong. The fox *did* have a heart. It just didn't beat.

And no way would Esme give up. Not on Fetch, who had saved her life so many times, who could have walked away after Lucinda's. He didn't need to come on this leg of the journey, and yet here he was.

Lifeless. Half-cursed.

Esme pressed her hands into his chest over and over, breathing into his mouth, willing him to wake up.

He has a heart. He has a heart.

The ground shook.

Tiago shouted, "The water's coming back down!"

Esme spun and thrust out her hands, releasing every ounce of Water magic she could muster. Her strength wavered as exhaustion overtook her.

Her arms shook with the force of the energy pouring out of her. She knew it was only a matter of seconds before they all drowned.

She heard a breath. Keeping her hands in position, she twisted to see Tiago blowing air into Fetch's mouth. She *felt* the power of his magic going into Fetch's lungs.

Fetch spasmed, then coughed up a lungful of water. He glanced up at the incoming doom. "So it wasn't a nightmare," he mumbled.

Tiago helped him to his feet. "Can you use your coat to get across the bridge?"

Fetch tried, but his magic was too spent.

In the span of seconds, the brujxes and the fox were run-hobbling across the weathered planks. With each step they drew closer and closer to what they hoped was the entrance to Triana's realm.

"It's just a wall of ice," Tiago shouted.

He was right. The massive wall reached higher than Esme could see. It was frozen over, cracked in places, opaque and thick without a door in sight.

"The bridge goes nowhere!" Esme cried.

The giant fountains of water began to fall from the sky, slowly at first and then with the force of a world-ending flood.

Waters raged, filling the space, rapidly swallowing up the end of the bridge behind them.

They only had about twenty feet until *smack*.

"It's a false wall," Fetch said so weakly Esme wasn't sure she'd heard him right over the thunderous waters. He tossed a spool of thread directly at the ice. It was sucked inside. "We've got to have momentum or we won't make it." He staggered back, nearly collapsing. "You two go first."

"We go together!" Esme shouted, using all her strength to slow the water down, buying them time, seconds maybe.

"You'll never get enough speed if you're hauling me too!" Fetch growled.

"No one's getting left behind." Tiago cupped his hands around his mouth and blew out a long breath. There was a hiss and a distant howl.

A blast of air zoomed in from all directions, so powerful Esme thought it could lift them up and away. Or maybe hold the water back. For a moment she felt a tiny pinch of hope until the wind dwindled to a pathetic little breeze.

Until the waters engulfed the basin, rushing toward them with a ferocity that would break them apart.

Esme threw her hands out again, desperately reaching for her magic, but there was nothing left.

"We need more power!" Fetch yelled. He removed the silver-dollar shell from his pocket.

"No!" Esme shouted.

"Fetch," Tiago screamed. "Don't do it!"

He gave them a quiver of a smile.

And then the fox snapped the shell in two.

Chapter Thirty-Seven

There was a burst of light, followed by the sound of waves crashing. Then an eerie quiet settled over them, and Esme felt the warmth of Fetch's coat wrapped snugly around her as they sped through the air, which smelled faintly of honeysuckle and freshly tilled earth.

Esme's heart hammered against her chest, twisting itself into a knot of fury and disbelief as she replayed the image of Fetch snapping the silver-dollar shell in half as if it was nothing. In a rush of anger, she pushed the fox away, and as she did, she fell a few feet before drop-rolling across a moonlit landscape of dried-up leaves. With a huff, she plucked a dead leaf from her hair and got to her feet. She stood in a small dead garden. Its endlessly high walls were choked with weeds, thorny vines, and withered plants.

Tiago and Fetch stood too, grunting and groaning, but then their gazes fell to Esme and hers to Fetch. No one said a thing.

It was as if none of them wanted to be the one to admit the truth. Fetch had sealed his fate when he broke the silver-dollar shell. Now he would be a cursed fox forever.

Esme forced herself to look at him. With a frown, she opened her mouth, closed it again. But no matter how she tried, she couldn't find the right words.

Fetch scanned her face, then hardened his gaze. "Would you rather be dead?"

"I'd rather . . ." Esme faltered. She'd rather what? That he'd had a better choice? That he could have his wish to be human and keep his magic too? That Oblivion didn't exist? That there was no witch hunter?

She cleared her throat. It did no good to talk about what was done and couldn't be undone. "You're not . . . bleeding anymore," she said, noticing his neck wound was gone.

His paw snapped up to his neck. "I guess it's true," he said quietly.

"What is?" Tiago asked.

"Any injury you suffer in the between," Fetch replied, "it doesn't last if you make it out, which no one ever does because, well . . ." He took a deep, shuddering breath.

Tiago raked a hand through his hair and looked at the ground. "I'm sorry. I . . . I thought I could save us, but my magic just wouldn't come."

For the first time since the beginning of this awful quest, Esme looked at Tiago, really looked at him. He seemed changed—older, maybe tougher, and probably not so impetuous that he would rush into danger without asking a single question anymore.

"We all tried," Esme said. "And together we—we survived."

A lock of hair fell over Tiago's right eye. He looked at Fetch. "Thanks, man. You saved us."

Fetch gave the smallest of nods. "I didn't do it just for you. I think . . . I'd rather live a life of magic."

"Because you can't survive Ocho Manos without it?" Esme guessed.

Stuffing his paws into his coat pockets, Fetch said, "It's like air. Once you possess it, it's impossible to give up."

If Esme ever understood the fox, it was in this very moment—the longing in his eyes, the desperation in his voice leaning toward something that came with too high a price tag.

She thought about her family, about the price they were paying—the price they would continue to pay unless she could save them. She had kept the awful idea of failure at bay, but now, seeing Fetch lose a part of himself forever, it drove home that her family's magic could be lost too, along with their memories. Oblivion would suck them dry and spit them out as empty, unrecognizable vessels. Esme didn't think her heart could take it, not after seeing what grief had done to her dad.

"Maybe you can still find a way someday"—Esme's voice quivered—"to break the curse."

"Maybe." His ears lay flat and his tail drooped. He didn't believe it. She wasn't sure she did either.

"Hey, Es?" Tiago said, staring at her quizzically. "Your hair . . ."

"What about . . ." She ran a hand over it. Her hair had grown past her shoulders. Down to the middle of her back. White blooms sprouted between her locks. Her heart swelled at the sight of them, the part of her that she thought she had given away. "How did this happen?" she asked, pleased.

"You're in the Earth witch's realm," Fetch said, studying her with a look of fascination. "Its magic must have had an effect on your hair."

Esme swept her dark hair over one shoulder and examined its shimmering tips. She could sense the power of her Earth magic pulsating in each lock. A small, tender smile spread across her mouth just as Tiago said, "Guys?"

He was gazing up at the night sky. "Does that moon look like it's growing? Or is it falling?"

Instantly, the full moon zoomed closer, like a giant spotlight falling from the sky. It brightened, flooding the dead garden with so much light that Esme had to shield her eyes.

"Are they all here?" asked a young voice.

"Two witches and a fox," said another voice, deeper than the first. "Just like she said."

She?

"Hello?" Esme said, doing her best to sound friendly. "Can you turn off the light?"

"You're burning a hole through my eyes," Tiago added grumpily.

"That's the point," the deeper voice said. "We have to scan your magic. Confirm your identity. We're all good here, Buster."

There was the grinding of gears and then a soft *click*.

Esme rubbed her eyes, then opened them to find two massive owls perched on the vine-choked hedge. One was gray with fat black streaks, and the other was chocolate brown, its feathers mottled with orange.

"Those birds are huge," Esme whispered to her friends.

"Aren't owls carnivorous?" Tiago asked.

"Definitely meat eaters," Fetch said.

"We can hear you," the gray owl with the deep voice said.

"We do love a good chunk of raw meat," Buster said. "But I prefer to skewer mine, eat it slowly." He spread his wings, the span of a truck for sure, and his size multiplied another two feet.

The gray owl rolled his eyes. "Stop showing off."

"Just making sure they know who they're dealing with, Leonard." Buster cast his wide golden eyes on the trio, craning his neck closer. "We guard this realm and its inhabitants."

Esme took a deep breath to settle her nerves as she tried to sense Triana's Earth magic, to make sure they'd made it to the right place. But there was nothing more than a dark, bitter expanse of . . . sickness and doom.

"Is this . . . Triana's realm?" Esme asked.

Leonard gave a single curt nod. "She said you were coming."

"How could she have known?" Fetch asked.

"She's an original witch." Buster cocked his fluffy head to one side. "You think you would have made it within a mile of this place if she hadn't approved your arrival?"

Leonard soared down and landed on the ground, towering over them at close to eight feet tall. "We're here to escort you to her."

Buster eyed them hungrily. "Ready?"

Esme stepped back, trying to look unintimidated but it was hard when a giant owl with ginormous razor-like talons was staring down at you as though he couldn't wait to stick you on that skewer.

Glancing up at Leonard, Fetch said, "Then let's get going."

The owl sighed and narrowed its gaze. "I expected more patience from a fox."

Fetch's jaw clenched tight. "And this isn't the kind of place I was *expecting* an Earth witch to create."

"Good point," Tiago muttered out of the side of his mouth.

Buster said, "I don't care what you were expecting. There is a reason for all this."

"Escort," Tiago said with a hopeful grin, or maybe he was just trying to change the subject. "As in fly us?"

"As if." Buster tucked his wings tight to his body while Leonard rose into the air and said, "We do *not* transport witches or cursed woodland creatures. You'll walk."

Esme's heart folded in on itself. Was that what Fetch would

forever be, a cursed creature?

The owls flew over to the edge of the shrubbery, where they extended their massive wings, the tips barely touching. There was a spark of light and then the dead hedges parted like drapes.

Just as Esme made her way through the exit, she gasped, coming to a hard stop. The moonlit world was an endless vision of brown rolling hills that butted up to a frail forest populated with deformed, skeletal trees. For as far as she could see, there were withered bushes, crumbling boulders, decaying vines.

It was as if the hand of death had swept through here uninvited.

"It used to be beautiful," Leonard said.

"What—what happened?" Esme asked as they made their way across the terrain. Dead leaves rolled past. Swirls of dust lifted into the sky.

"Triana is not well," Buster said glumly.

"She's sick?" Fetch blurted. His voice held the same surprise that Esme felt.

But the owls said nothing, merely soared above. Their wings cast long, dark shadows across the cracked earth below.

"It's why I can't sense her magic," Esme whispered to her friends. "It's too weak. But how? Why?"

She wrapped her fingers around the hilt of the blade in her pocket. The dagger thrummed with energy. She felt a pull, like two magnets being drawn to each other.

When the dagas are in close proximity, they emit even greater power and are easier to track.

"She still has the dagger," Esme said, speaking in low tones, explaining what Lucinda had told her.

"So the witch hunter hasn't been here yet," Tiago guessed. "That's good, right?"

Esme nodded, holding tight to a hope so fragile, so brittle that she was sure one wrong move would shatter this entire mission. All she needed was some luck, Triana's dagger, and . . .

She thought about Lenny and Dad, and her heart gave a lurch. She missed them so much she ached, but more than that, she couldn't stand the thought that they were suffering.

And she only had a measly forty-something hours to save them.

They climbed a ridge overlooking a valley that might have once been farmland. Thick, lifeless vines crawled across the parched ground, twisted and gnarled. A few black mice scurried between. Esme's heart sank. The rodents looked so skinny, so . . .

Fetch tugged on her sleeve and pointed to the horizon.

In the distance, waves of glowing green and pink and lavender lights bent and swayed, similar to the aurora borealis, but unlike the great northern lights, black, veinlike streaks pulsated closer to the ground.

The air crackled with an energy that gripped Esme. Beyond the weak Earth magic, there was another magic here, one more powerful that she couldn't identify.

"Wow," Tiago said. His eyes were fixed on the shimmering lights.

"Don't look at that," Leonard warned, flinging a giant wing up to block Tiago's view.

"Why not?" Fetch asked.

"It'll burn your eyes out of your head," Buster said snidely before he chuckled.

Esme couldn't tell if he was kidding or not, but better not to take the chance. She quickly averted her gaze. "Those dark lines," she said to the owls, "they look like—like they're trying to break through."

They reminded Esme of the crack in the sky the night of the races.

Leonard's eyes narrowed and his sharp talons flexed. "We better check the sentry, Buster." Then to Esme and her friends, "Follow this path to the house. That's where you'll find her. And be quick about it."

In an instant the two owls spread their massive wings and flew in a dizzying circle before they vanished into the night.

The afterglow of their departure illuminated a white cottage with a turquoise roof that hadn't been there a moment ago.

The cream-colored drapes were closed, and a soft light glowed behind them.

Tiago stopped short. His eyes went wide. "Es, do you see what I see?"

She nodded. The cottage was identical to the one in

Lucinda's painting. Had she been here before?

Just as they reached the house, the door swung open, creaking on its hinges.

A shadowed figure leaned against the doorjamb, and a woman's tired voice said, "Come. There isn't much time."

Chapter Thirty-Eight

Esme knew that voice—it was the one from her dream with the trunks and symbols, the one from the Paso de los Muertos.

The one who had led her to Ozzie.

Her hopes lifting, she stepped into the small room.

The woman had her back to the group. Long brown hair woven with tiny blue flowers cascaded over her shoulders. She gathered a green shawl around her as she hobbled to a worn wooden chair near the fireplace, where embers smoldered.

"Welcome," the woman said as she turned to them, easing herself into the chair. Her face was pale and gaunt, but there was beauty behind the frailty, as if there was only a thin layer between then and now, healthy and sick, beautiful and strained.

Esme saw no dagger plunged into Triana's heart. Were they too late?

The room was cold, barely furnished with a table made of twigs, a tattered brown sofa, and a wooden ladder that leaned crookedly against the stone wall. Copper pots and dried bunches of yellow flowers hung from rough-hewn timbers.

Esme could feel the magnetic pull of the dagger in her pocket, trying to drive her closer to the woman. "Triana?" she asked.

The woman looked up. Her green eyes were dull, but there was something familiar in her expression that was so like Lucinda.

"The fox and the other witch must go," Triana said, coughing a few times before adding, "I must speak to you alone, Esmerelda."

Tiago nodded. "We'll wait outside."

"You're safer indoors." Triana waved a hand through the air and a shimmering emerald veil appeared, separating Esme from the others and enclosing her in the tiny space with the witch.

"I can sense Lucinda's dagger," Triana said gently. Her eyes crinkled at the edges in an almost-smile. "I miss her so much."

"She misses you too." Esme sat on the couch. "You're the one who tried to help me in the passage, who told me to find Ozzie in my dream."

Triana nodded. "You and I are connected by Earth magic." Her eyes alighted on Esme's hair as if she was noticing it for the first time. "Such beauty," she said. "Such power."

A warm feeling washed over Esme. She had never considered

herself beautiful or powerful, but now, with the Earth magic weaving between the stands of her hair, she felt both. "Why are you sick?" she asked Triana.

"Keeping the borders of my realm safe," Triana said, "has taken more of a toll than I imagined."

"The black streaks in the sky," Esme guessed.

Triana nodded, closing her eyes briefly. "Before we go any further, I must know that you are worthy."

"Worthy?" Panic struck Esme like a kick to the ribs. "How am I supposed to show that?"

"By simply answering a question. If you had to give up one magic, which would it be? Air? Earth? Fire? Or perhaps Water?"

Esme stared at her, dumbfounded. Was there a wrong answer? Or better yet, a right one? Lenny was so good at riddles. If only she were here to tell Esme which element to pick. For the first time, thinking about Lenny didn't terrify Esme. Instead, love flooded her heart and she wished—oh how she wished—that it was enough to bring her sister home.

Did Triana feel that way about Lucinda, Gisele, and Escarlata?

The question made Esme wonder if all sisters shared a singular bond that could never be broken.

"Well?" Triana asked.

Esme looked up at the witch. "I'd choose none."

There was a fleeting spark of surprise in Triana's eyes. "That isn't an answer."

Esme folded her arms across her body. "The elements are bonded . . . like sisters. Tied together by a powerful magic that should never be broken. So the question," she said, "has no answer."

For a moment everything stood still, and Triana stared blankly, saying nothing. Then she raised her hands. A bright light illuminated the space, forcing Esme to shield her eyes. A second later, the light vanished.

"What was that?" Esme asked.

Triana didn't answer the question. She merely said, "You know the value of love and of magic."

Esme felt the tight ball of panic unfold in her stomach. She could feel her Earth magic buzzing, as if her flowers were reaching toward Triana. She plucked a bloom from her hair and handed it to the brujx. The witch stared at it lovingly as it grew bigger in the center of her palm. In the next instant, the color rose in her cheeks.

"They're healing you," Esme said.

Triana shook her head. "If only that were true. Your flowers can only offer me temporary health." Sure enough, before the last word left her mouth, her cheeks paled once again. "I used the last of this realm's magic to awaken yours."

Esme frowned, unsure she'd heard Triana right. "What do you mean?"

"You will need your Earth magic to defeat her."

Her.

Esme was about to ask which sister was the villain when

a swirl of mist materialized near Triana's chest, forming into a dagger that was thrust deep into the witch's heart. "Go ahead," she said. "There is no time to waste."

Esme swallowed, and as she rose to her feet, she felt the magnetic pull again, driving her forward, urging her hand toward the dagger. Her gaze met Triana's, and just as she was about to take the blade, the witch wrapped her hand around Esme's with surprising force, and together they pulled the dagger free.

Esme was lost in a cold abyss. A terrible pressure built in her body, in her mind, in her heart, threatening to break her into a million pieces.

Then, just when she couldn't take the agony another second, the darkness vanished, and she found herself standing on the moonlit bank of Río Místico again.

Triana stood next to her.

"Why . . . how are you here?" Esme asked.

Triana shivered. "I never wanted to see this place again," she said. "But I had to come with you, to make sure you saw the hidden parts of the story beyond this riverbank."

Just as it had with Lucinda, the scene played out before them: the stolen kiss, the god's ire, Escarlata's pleading, the daggers being driven into each witch's heart.

Esme knitted her brows together. So far this was no different from Lucinda's version of the truth. When she said so, Triana closed her eyes, inhaled a deep breath, and murmured,

"Watch. My sin is coming."

Sin?

Without realizing it, Esme stepped closer to the scene, near enough to see the young Triana break away from her shell-shocked sisters. Near enough to follow the witch into the trees above the river Místico, where the god stood.

Young Triana drew closer to the god of night.

He narrowed his gaze. "Come to beg for your life?"

"I'm not here to beg," Triana said haughtily. "I'm here to—you said that the blades will kill us soon enough."

The god glared at her. "And?"

"You gods like sacrifices, don't you?" she asked.

He tilted his head to the side. She had his interest.

"I'll—I'll sacrifice my life," Triana said, "if you'll just let my sisters live."

The god threw his head back and laughed. "You, the one who planted the first kiss. You come to me to negotiate?"

Triana stood her ground, but Esme could see her clenched fists trembling at her sides. "Yes."

"I admire your tenacity, but the deed is done."

Trails of tears streaked Triana's face. She wrapped her hands around the dagger in her chest, trying to pull it free, but it was no use. She looked up at him and whispered, "You would let *her* die?"

His face went slack. His eyes filled with a flicker of surprise before they hardened. A stretch of silence lingered between the god and Triana. He stepped closer. "I will offer *all* of you eternal life, but you must make a forever promise to me."

"Anything."

"You have created a great and surprising power tonight, and such power comes at a cost, one you must be willing to pay."

Triana pressed her lips together, nodding, looking less sure of herself.

"You will live," the god said. "Your powers will grow, and as they do, the darkness of my night and burden will too." A smoky haze surrounded him. "And there will come a day," he said, lowering his voice, "when the dark shall possess one of you and drive you to great evil."

"The dark?"

"A force that feeds on grief and anger and misery."

Triana hesitated. "I . . . I can't do that, not unless it's me who becomes . . ."

"Then you are not serious about saving your sisters."

Triana chewed her bottom lip, her expression pained. "Who will the darkness possess?"

"The not knowing is the risk you must take," he said with a thin smile. "Do you accept my terms?"

Esme wanted to yell at the witch, wanted to tell young Triana to run away, but the witch was already telling the god, "I accept."

The second the deal was struck, Triana fell to her knees. The stars streaked across the sky and the yellow moon quivered. And in the next blink, Esme found herself back in Triana's realm.

Triana sat slumped by the dying fire. She turned to Esme. "Do you see now? This is my fault. I made a secret promise. I lied to my sisters."

"But you were trying to save them. They'd be dead without you." Esme wasn't sure she wouldn't have done the same thing to save Lenny.

"I never even asked them, because I thought saving their lives was more important than . . ." Her voice broke into a quiet sob. "And now I see the burden we must all share."

Triana's dagger in Esme's hand pulsated. She could feel its power growing, searching. "Who's the witch hunter?" she asked. "Who turned to evil?"

"Those are two different people."

A tremor of shock rolled through Esme. "I don't understand."

"The one who turned to evil is Escarlata."

Esme took a shaky breath. "Then who's the hunter?"

A wave of confusion swept across Triana's face. "I—I thought you knew."

"Knew what?" Esme felt suddenly panicked. "Who is it?"

A soft whisper fell from Triana's lips. "Your father."

Chapter Thirty-Nine

The world fell out from under Esme. She was nothing more than a speck of dust being blown around by a punishing storm. Triana was wrong. There had been a mistake. Her dad was *not* the witch hunter. He was too gentle, too kind.

"That's a lie!" she cried.

"I wish it were not."

"Dad would never hurt Lenny or the other witches! There must be a mistake."

"If you search your heart, you'll realize that what I'm telling you is fact."

Esme balked. "No way. Lucinda said that only a witch of Chaos could remove the daggers!" As soon as the words left her mouth, she froze. The dawning was slow at first, an unwillingness to accept the truth, followed by a rush of pain.

"He is of Chaos, Esme."

Esme couldn't move. She felt suddenly spent, as though she didn't have the energy for a single breath. Why had her mom and dad never told her? Without realizing it, she collapsed onto the sofa, her mind a hurricane of emotion and memory. But it didn't matter that her heart was breaking; she still had to save her sister and the others, even if it was her own father who had locked them up.

She sat up, clenching Triana's dagger in her fist. "How did he do it?"

"This realm has eaten too much time already. You must go now."

"Eaten?" Esme's nerves snapped to attention. "We just got here."

"Time is a cruel master, child."

"How much time?"

"You have lost a day. This realm will fall into a deep sleep in a matter of minutes," Triana said. "And if any of you remain here, you will sleep too. You must go now."

Esme felt as if she was spinning and spinning in the dark abyss of space—*a day, a day, a day.*

In a single breath, the fireplace vanished, the walls fading so thin that Esme could see the dead world outside waning, coming in and out of focus. It was as if someone was erasing this place one stroke at a time.

"Tell me how to leave," Esme demanded.

Triana looked down at the dagger in Esme's hand. "You

hold two of the most powerful objects in the universe. Together, they will take you to the destination you choose. All you have to do is ask."

Triana flickered once more. And then she was gone, along with the emerald veil.

Fetch and Tiago stood there, staring at the dagger in her hand.

"You got it," Tiago whispered, a look of shock on his face.

Fetch glanced down at his pocket watch. "We have precisely seventy-nine seconds to vacate this realm. And I truly hope the witch told you how to do that."

"I'm voting for an exit without a monster this time," Tiago put in. "Es? What's wrong?"

"I'll tell you when we get out of here." She bit her lip, trying to think of what to do next. If she went to the Place of Agonized Souls, she could lose her soul. And there was no guarantee her dad was even there or that he hadn't already taken the Dagger of Air to Escarlata.

How was it even possible that he could do something so awful?

"Fifty seconds now," Fetch said.

"Es, what's the exit plan?" Tiago asked.

It is no accident that they are with you on this journey.

But what if Tiago knew my dad had trapped his family in Oblivion? Esme felt the hot sting of shame as she turned to the fox. "Can you use your coat to get yourself back to Ocho Manos?" she asked, remembering what he had said about its magic—that it would always take him home.

"I can."

"Then you should go home."

Esme felt a sudden emptiness at the thought of saying goodbye to Fetch, but she couldn't ask him to face off with one of the most powerful witches in history—made even more powerful by the daggers—to save a bunch of strangers.

Fetch dropped his head and then did the most peculiar thing. He bowed.

Esme stiffened. Was this his way of saying goodbye?

"How can you leave—" Tiago began.

"In my world, when you bow it is for one reason only," Fetch said.

Tiago and Esme stared at the fox.

"It is a way to pledge yourself and your loyal service to someone for as long as they need you," he said softly. "Do you accept?"

Esme's heart swelled as Fetch rose to his full height, gazing at her, waiting for her answer, but all she could manage was a simple nod.

Chapter Forty

Fetch said, "Well then, it's all settled, and we now have twenty-five seconds to go."

Esme removed the Dagger of Water from her pocket. She stared at both blades now in her grasp.

Both vibrated and warmed. Ribbons of mist curled up her arms. She could feel the magnetic field the daggers created, the force of their strength.

The cottage walls were thin as tracing paper, giving Esme a view of the shimmering horizon just as it was swallowed by the blackness.

The ground began to tremble. A distant wind howled. The dead trees bent and swayed. Birds and insects sang their last songs, the creatures' sadness like a thread unraveling Esme from the inside out.

"Fifteen seconds," Fetch said.

"You guys each put a hand on my shoulder and hold on."

Fetch and Tiago did as she asked.

"Where are we going?" Tiago asked.

Esme took a deep breath, then let it out, hoping that she was right. And that if there was any part of Siempre that was still her dad, then maybe he'd go to the one place where he stood a chance of fighting the darkness.

"Home," she said. Then she pressed the twin blades together.

The daggers fused together in a flash of green and blue. If there had been power in each knife before, it was nothing compared to what she felt in the now-single blade—raw, formidable, unwavering. Earth and Water.

The trio was swept up into a powerful vortex of energy. It felt like the time Esme had bungee jumped off a bridge—the drop in her stomach, the feeling of free-falling, the rush of air.

And then she was standing in the moonlit shadows of the mesquite tree in her front yard. She felt as if she had stepped into a worn memory, as if this place existed only in her mind and heart. And yet here she was.

But now her house looked dilapidated, as if one gust of wind could send the whole thing crumbling. Cobwebs hung from the top of the door, nearly covering it. The night was still, quiet, as if everyone had already left San Bosco and the town was now nothing more than a distant memory.

"Where are we?" Fetch asked.

"This is my house," Esme whispered.

"It's so . . ." Tiago glanced around at the washed-out world. "Gray."

Esme pressed her lips together to stop from crying. Then she remembered a terrible fact. "Fetch, did we just lose more time by going from Triana's realm back to our world?"

The fox gave a small, regretful nod.

"How much time?" Tiago asked.

"Likely eight hours," Fetch said.

"That only gives us less than a day," Esme said, hoping it would be enough time, hoping she hadn't made a mistake and wasted hours by coming here.

"Why are we here?" Fetch asked.

How could Esme begin to explain? "I—I'm hoping my dad maybe came here and . . ." She remembered his words that night she had stolen the dead thief's lock of hair. *Things are going to be better than you could imagine.*

But how was carrying out Escarlata's evil plans going to accomplish that?

Still, there was hope in those words. Esme just prayed she wasn't too late, that he hadn't already delivered Gisele's dagger to Escarlata and removed hers.

"Your dad?" Tiago frowned. "He's in Oblivion."

Esme shook her head. "He—he—" She was stopped short by a light flicking on in the study.

She bolted into the house, with the fox and Tiago right behind her.

The second she stepped into the foyer, she knew her father was here. She could feel his Chaos. At no point since this whole quest began had she ever once considered that it would end this way. She had never imagined a moment when she would have to face off with her own father, a man who felt lost to her now.

Her heart pounded so hard that little black dots danced in her vision.

Flecks of dust floated through the air. A beam of moonlight spilled through a hole in the roof.

"Es," Tiago whispered, "what's going on?"

"My dad's in there," she said. "I'll explain later, but right now, can you guys guard the study doors?" She knew she had to give them a task if she had any hope of going into that room alone.

Fetch nodded, reaching into his coat for a spool of green thread.

"What does that do?" Tiago asked.

"It'll block anyone else from going in," Fetch said. "Well, once I lay it across the threshold."

"Like Escarlata?" Tiago guessed.

"It's not *that* powerful."

Esme stared at the closed doors. If she was lucky, she could get through to her dad, convince him to give her the Dagger of Air. And then she'd wait for the witch. Because Esme knew she'd come.

She reached into her pocket and wrapped her fingers around the fused blades, as if they could give her the courage she needed. With a deep inhale, she inched one of the doors open. It creaked on its hinges, but her dad didn't turn. He was standing near the dusty bookcase with his back to her, staring at something on the shelf.

She stepped inside and closed the door behind her, watching as his fingers danced across the book spines. Was he looking for something? In that single moment, the world retreated, and all Esme felt was angry. Angry that she had to be here, that she had to face a father she had thought was suffering in Oblivion—a father she had vowed more than once to save. Everything up to this point had had a purpose, some kind of meaning, and now? Nothing made sense. It was as if reality had collapsed all around her.

"Dad?" she managed.

At the sound of her voice, he straightened but still didn't turn.

"It's me. Esme," she said quietly, hot tears threatening. She wanted to yell at him, to ask him *why, why, why!* But it was like approaching a wild animal. One wrong move and the stillness could unravel.

Slowly, he faced her. His eyes were entirely black, their darkness filling up his sockets so there wasn't a speck of white. His face was gaunt, unshaven.

He was a stranger to her.

Esme stopped breathing.

A slow smile curled his lips. "We knew you'd come, you little fool," Siempre said.

We? Her heart pounded so hard she was sure it would

explode out of her chest.

He held up a single dagger. Air.

The witch's voice swept into the room like a sharp wind. "Take the daggers from her now."

Esme knew that voice—it was the one that had followed her, taunting and threatening her. So it had been Escarlata communicating with her all this time.

"I'll never give them to you!" Esme shouted. When would the Fire brujx finally show her face?

Her dad growled, a horrid, hollow-sounding thing. "You have never understood the rules of magic, or its secrets. Give me the blades or I will take them from you."

"Dad, please." Esme inched back. "I know this isn't you. I know that evil witch did this to you. You—you have to fight her."

Escarlata's laugh echoed across the bookshelves, making them shake. A framed family photo fell onto the floor, the glass shattering. Esme remembered the day it was taken— they had all gone on a drive out to the country. Her dad had set up the camera's timer but hadn't quite made it back to the group, so he was half-turned, laughing. It had been only a month before her mom died, before everything changed.

But why was it here? He had put away all the pictures of her mom after she died.

Her dad's gaze dropped to the photo. There was a flicker of recognition. The blackness of his eyes receded and for a blink he looked like himself.

"Escarlata's using you," Esme cried. "And Lenny—she's

in Oblivion. She's going to lose all her magic and memories, Dad. We might never see her again!"

He stepped toward her.

"I saw Mom in a dream!"

The words seemed to harden something inside him as the darkness flooded his eyes again. He held up his blade. "Give me the daggers or die."

Tears spilled down Esme's cheeks. All the fury she had felt moments ago was gone, replaced with a terrible grief.

With a trembling hand, she reached into her pocket and removed the united daggers. The powers of Water and Earth surged through the blade and into her hand. She had Water and Earth and her dad had Air—but had he already pulled Escarlata's fire blade?

"If you give him the daggers," Escarlata said coldly, her disembodied voice hovering in the small space, "I will release him and your family."

"You're a liar!" Esme shouted. Escarlata had gone to impossible lengths to get this far, so there had to be a reason she needed all of San Bosco's witches out of the way. But what was it?

"Very well," Escarlata sighed.

At that, Esme's father fell to his knees. His face contorted, then his eyes returned to normal, softening at the edges. "Esme?"

"Dad?"

He stared at her, then at the shattered photo on the ground. "Esme, you must run. Now!"

"Dad, give me your dagger. Together we can beat her!"

He clenched the blade, shaking his head. "I don't want to hurt you. Please forgive me. Please. I was just trying to make things better." He grabbed at his throat, as if struggling to breathe.

"Stop!" Esme screamed. She wanted nothing more than to run to her dad, to help him, to drag him away, but it was too dangerous to get that close while he was under the witch's control.

"Give him the daggers!" Escarlata commanded.

Esme's Chaos stirred. Escarlata wouldn't let Siempre die. She still needed him to deliver the Dagger of Air. But why didn't she come and get it herself?

The air grew unbearably hot as the gears in Esme's mind clicked into place. The witch must be trapped in the Place of Agonized Souls. The place where tormented witches gave up their souls, their unwanted memories. Where they discarded their sorrows. But if left there too long, they lost their almas forever.

That's why she needs all the daggers. It's the only way to free herself.

Just then her dad lunged, throwing Esme to the floor. He hovered over her, his Dagger of Air aimed at her heart.

"Dad?" she whimpered. The blooms in her hair shivered. Petals dropped to the floor all around them, enveloping them in magic.

Siempre recoiled as if one touch of Esme's magic would

ruin him. Still he just kept lowering the blade closer to her heart.

"Fight it," Esme pleaded as she struggled against him.

His face tightened, twisted beyond recognition.

A gust of wind swept through the room, blowing Esme's blooms into a tailspin.

Siempre brought the knife down.

Esme threw up her own dagger, clanging its blade with his. The sound was like a million clashes of thunder.

The force threw him back and he collided into the bookshelves, somehow managing to keep his grip on the blade.

Fetch and Tiago burst into the room just as flames erupted, smoke and heat and rage filling the air. The door slammed behind them. Esme reached for Water magic, but the flames were so high, so hot.

"Bring me the blade!" Escarlata's voice echoed through the study.

Her dad stood and stumbled closer just as the flames spun into a sphere near the door. There was nothing but darkness inside it.

Wails and groans sounded from inside, each louder and more painful than the last.

A gravitational force wrenched Esme closer to the darkness. She struggled, gripping the bookcase with all her might. Siempre clung to a chair, but his efforts were useless. The flaming void ripped him free. Esme watched in horror as her father fell onto his back, slid across the floor, and was sucked into the black hole.

"No!" Esme ran toward the darkness, toward her dad.

"Esme!" Tiago grabbed hold of her.

But Tiago was no match for the Chaos that had erupted inside her. She broke free just as Fetch tossed a spool at the gateway. "I'll hold it open as long as I can," he shouted. "But be quick!"

Esme raced into the Place of Agonized Souls.

Chapter Forty-One

Esme found herself in a dark stone tunnel. In the next blink, gray light glinted across the walls.

"Dad?"

There was no answer.

She walked quickly, remembering her mom's warning.

You would be powerless without magic, and if you stayed too long your soul would be lost forever.

The flickering lights began to take shape, dreamlike images playing across the walls like a movie.

Esme didn't slow her pace, not until the moving images came into sharper focus. Then she came to a grinding halt.

These were memories. *Her* worst memories.

Her eyes fixed on her ten-year-old self dropping a single daisy onto her mother's grave. She saw her aimless father closing the door to his library, telling her to stay out. And then Lenny lying in the street with a dagger in her stomach.

Memories were a part of you forever. They weren't something you could just unload somewhere because they were too heavy to carry. But that was exactly what Esme wished she could do, and now she understood why so many witches came here, why they risked their very souls just to feel a moment of happiness.

Clutching the dagger, she inched forward, trying to ignore the shredding she felt inside, as though pieces of herself were being ripped away.

She quickly glanced over her shoulder. In the distance she could see a pinprick of light from her dad's study. Fetch couldn't hold the entrance open forever. But how much time did she have? She had no idea.

"Face me!" Esme shouted to Escarlata.

For a moment there was only Esme and her awful memories, until a barely-there light pulsed up ahead and Escarlata appeared in the tunnel before her, ruby-red lips, red hair swept over her shoulder, and skin as luminescent as moonlight. If she wasn't so evil, she might be beautiful.

"I knew you'd come to save him," Escarlata said. "So pathetic and predictable."

Had this been Escarlata's plan all along? To lure Esme here?

Escarlata drew closer. Her black dress floated around her bare feet. She glanced at the wall, where Esme's memories continued to play on repeat.

The sounds of each memory echoed through the tunnel

louder and louder, as if Escarlata had turned up the volume.

"Such suffering," the witch said, turning her gaze back to Esme. "Don't you wish to forget these moments? To leave them here?"

Esme trembled, struggling to breathe evenly. No matter how bad those memories were, they were an important part of her story, an important part of her. But she wouldn't give the witch the satisfaction of telling her so.

"Let my dad go!"

Escarlata narrowed her dark eyes. "You would want a hollow, deranged man for a father?"

"He wasn't always that way," Esme insisted, feeling braver with each word. "You did this to him."

"His weakness did this to him."

Esme felt a tug deep inside her chest, and she worried that pieces of her soul were breaking free. Her eyes shifted to Escarlata's right hand. She was holding the Dagger of Air. Escarlata followed her gaze. "I couldn't have done any of this without him."

Just then Siempre emerged from the shadows.

"Dad!" Esme burst forward. Escarlata raised her empty hand, her dark magic pinning Esme in place.

Siempre's eyes were hollow, his gaze vacant. Esme could sense his Chaos, tangled and burning. Could feel the struggle inside him. "Fight it, Dad!"

"Remove my dagger," Escarlata commanded him, never taking her gaze from Esme.

The Dagger of Fire materialized. Swirls of black smoke engulfed the pulsating blade still plunged into Escarlata's chest.

"Don't do it, Dad," Esme begged. But his hands were already on the hilt, and just as he was about to rip it free, Esme cried, "I'll give you the Daggers of Earth and Water if you let him go!"

"You're going to give them to me anyway," Escarlata said with a sinister smile. "Only another minute to go, but not to worry, the ripping away of a soul isn't too painful. It's the after that is truly agonizing."

Escarlata placed her hand on top of Siempre's, urging him to remove the blade as only a Chaos witch had the power to do. "Do it," she growled. "Now!"

His entire body shook. Esme could see the struggle as he battled Escarlata's mind control. A battle he was losing.

A surge of violent wind tore through the tunnel.

Tiago burst from the darkness and grabbed Siempre, tearing him away from the witch.

Escarlata screamed.

Esme lunged, colliding with her.

"No!" Siempre shouted.

The Fire witch seized Esme, her grip tearing into her sides like sharp claws. The agony darkened her vision until all that was left was the witch's anguish—her grief, sorrow, and fury consuming Esme from the inside out.

Escarlata watched with a twisted expression as Esme fell to

her knees. The witch reached out for the now-merged Daggers of Water and Earth. And just as she placed her hands on the hilt, Esme dragged out the words, "Take us to Río Místico."

Esme rolled onto the river's moonlit bank alone.

She jumped to her feet, still holding the dagger as she searched desperately for the witch she had now set free from the Place of Agonized Souls. But it had been her only choice, her only hope. She had to force Escarlata to see the truth.

"You think you've won?" came Escarlata's voice from everywhere all at once.

Esme spun, scanning the river, the trees, the brush. The air was cool and crisp with the familiar scent of mesquite.

"I am more powerful than you can imagine," Escarlata roared.

"Then show your face!" Esme demanded. Her voice echoed across the landscape, and for half a second she thought that maybe Escarlata would flee, that she'd go back for Siempre so he could remove her dagger and Esme's plan would disintegrate into dust.

The air shifted and Escarlata materialized before her. "You think you're so clever, bringing me here. And for what? Do you really think you can beat me?"

Esme tugged the Daggers of Water and Earth apart, wielding one in each hand. Her Chaos continued flowing, warming the blades. "I won't let you take my family or the other witches."

"I already have." Fiery chains grew from Escarlata's hands.

Esme jumped back, swiping at the chains with the daggers and slicing them in two. But the flames magnified and expanded with each swipe, faster and faster until the manacles wrapped around Esme's wrists, clutching her tightly.

Groans and whispers floated from the chains.

Escarlata's strength was incredible, power she had stolen from the Place of Agonized Souls, one that came from a darkness that grew from so much grief, just like the god had warned Triana.

There will come a day when the dark shall possess one of you and drive you to great evil.

Escarlata sighed. "I thought you might be a truer adversary, but you're as weak as your father."

Esme dropped to her knees. Beneath the cool, moist dirt she could sense the trees' roots twisting and shifting at her touch. Her Earth magic pulsated deep in her bones. The flowers in her hair fluttered. A whisper rustled from the blooms: *Make her see.*

Esme looked up. The witch's red lips parted in a wicked smile. "Let the darkness in, Chaos witch."

The Dagger of Earth surged with a power that wanted to be spent.

Make her see.

"Just tell me why you did it," Esme said. Why did Escarlata want the power of a god, anyway? What did she plan to do with it? Rule the world? To what end? It didn't make any sense.

"That is the dullest part of the story," Escarlata said, still two arms' lengths away. "I would think you would be more interested in the how. The grimorio was the connection. Your father searched those pages for a spell to bring your mother back from the dead. Sad, isn't it?"

Esme's heart collapsed. She bit back tears.

"People will commit such atrocities when they are desperate," Escarlata went on. "I fed his hope, telling him that if he helped me, I would breathe life back into your mother." Her eyes glittered at the memory. "That was all it took for him to fall under my spell."

"You tricked him!"

"I merely used his agony to my advantage."

"Like your own agony."

Escarlata stopped cold. Her eyes narrowed.

"Your fury and pain—they created magic," Esme said. "I saw it all."

"Enough!"

"I saw your sisters try to save—"

"Do not speak of those traitors!" Fire erupted in the witch's palms, the flames rising higher and higher.

Using the two daggers' magic, Esme thrust her wrists wide, breaking the fiery chains. "I won't let you hurt my sister and the other witches."

Escarlata laughed. "Their magic is nearly drained, feeding into my own," she said with a sigh. "Would you like to see?"

Before Esme could reply, an image materialized before her. A large black cage with a form slumped inside it.

The figure raised its head slowly.

"Lenny!" Esme shouted. She tried to run to her sister, but her legs were planted firmly, as if they'd been glued to the earth.

Lenny's long red hair was now short and gray. Her limbs were skeleton thin, and her eyes were hollow, empty.

Ice moved through Esme's veins. She was looking at a ghost. Again, she tried to lunge for her sister, but the vision vanished into a trail of smoke.

She spun toward Escarlata, her anger coming to an unstoppable boil.

Escarlata smiled. "You want to kill me. Don't you?"

A burning rage consumed Esme. Yes, she wanted to end Escarlata. But kill? Could she ever do something so terrible?

"I can feel your desire to strike me down," Escarlata said. "But before you even try, you must know that if you *were* to kill me, then your father would die as well."

Esme went still as stone. "What are you talking about?"

"He made a vow of service to me, and his life is therefore tethered to my own. If I die, he dies."

"No! That's a lie!"

"Are you willing to take that risk?"

Esme's fury rose like a storm. The river waters foamed. Wind tore through the trees. The earth rumbled and quavered as though it might split open any second.

"Chaos," Escarlata seethed. "Such a waste. Now, where were we?"

Esme knew she had to understand Escarlata in order to have a chance of defeating her. She needed to see her truth. And she had one shot to do it.

In a single swift move, Esme leaped for the witch and ripped the Dagger of Fire from Escarlata's heart.

CHAPTER FORTY-TWO

In an instant, Esme found herself in another vision on the riverbank.

But something was off. Unlike her other visits here, there were no sisters, no god, no familiar scene playing out.

Had she made a mistake?

Just then two figures emerged from the trees. Escarlata—younger and more beautiful than she was now—and the god of night and burden.

Esme's breath hitched in her throat.

The two held hands as they walked down the moonlit embankment to the river's edge.

"I want it to always be like this," Escarlata said blissfully.

"Then it shall be," the god said, holding her close. "But only if you remember what I told you."

Escarlata sighed. "That I can never kiss you."

Escarlata loved the god? Triana's words flashed across her memory—when she had confronted the god, she'd asked, *You would let* her *die?*

And now Esme understood why. Triana had known about their relationship. But she must not have known the rules.

"If any human were to do so," the god said, "then my rage would rise like a storm. I would return to my godly form, and we couldn't be together."

Escarlata leaned her head on the god's shoulder. "Then let this be enough."

Esme felt a terrible sadness filling her. No wonder Escarlata had been so angry. Her sisters had broken both the rule and the bond they hadn't known existed. And still Escarlata had chosen them over him.

Esme would have done the same. She'd risk anything to save Lenny, to protect her. Patina had once told the girls that a bond between sisters was an unbreakable cosmic thread, one that connected your hearts, your histories, your futures. It was bigger than even magic.

Esme could still remember the way Lenny had laughed, then tickled her fiercely. "I guess you're stuck with me forever."

The vision faded, and Esme found herself facing the witch once again.

"You—you loved him," Esme said softly.

"How dare you!" Escarlata wrenched the Dagger of Fire from Esme's hands.

"You chose your sisters. . . ." And if Escarlata had known that kind of love, then surely her heart couldn't be all evil, could it?

Make her see.

Esme extended the Daggers of Earth and Water, knowing Escarlata would take them. Hoping they would transport her to the river, too, so she could see the truth.

Confusion washed over the witch's face, soon masked by greed and triumph as she snatched the blades with a wave of magic. The daggers spun above her open palms.

Winds howled. Thunder boomed as lightning slashed the black sky.

"Now that I have Nocturno's power," Escarlata bellowed, "I can finally destroy him for what he did!"

Something was wrong. Escarlata wasn't vanishing back to the riverbank like her sisters had.

"You need to touch the daggers," Esme cried. "To see the truth!"

"I know the only truth that matters."

Esme reached for her Chaos. She stirred the air with it, bringing forth a gusting wind that distracted Escarlata for a nanosecond, long enough for Esme to lunge at the witch and force the knives into her hands.

The world came to a sudden standstill and then the witch vanished.

Esme fell to her knees, catching her breath. This had to work. If it didn't, Esme was all out of ideas. There was no plan B, no imaginative comeback, no way back to her family.

A moment later, Escarlata reappeared, her face twisted with anguish. "It's trickery," she seethed. "All lies!"

"It's the truth," came a familiar voice. Lucinda materialized, along with Triana and Gisele. Their faces looked worn, their eyes more hollow than before. It was as if all the hope had been drained from them. Esme sucked in a sharp breath as she watched the ghostly figures float closer.

Escarlata's expression went from rage to confusion to sorrow in less than a blink.

"Fight the darkness, sister," Triana said.

"We love you," Gisele added.

Escarlata backed away, shaking her head. "Get away from me!"

"If you destroy the god of night and burden," Lucinda said softly, "what will you gain?"

"Revenge!" Escarlata's voice was deep and raspy, not her own. Her eyes blazed with red flames, and smoke rose from her body as her skin began to peel away to reveal gray scales.

"Malvada," Triana breathed. "It's the dark he told me about—the price we would pay. And now it's possessed her entirely."

"Malvada?" Esme whispered.

"The darkest of magics, born of a god's hatred and vengeance, and of utter hopelessness," Lucinda said.

Escarlata's chest heaved as she glared at her sisters. Then she growled, "And now you shall all perish."

She raised all four daggers, bringing them together with a thunderous clash.

"Escarlata!" Gisele screamed as blackness spilled from the blades, consuming the river, racing toward the sisters with a vengeance.

The darkness morphed into a twisted, eyeless face with a wide, cavernous mouth.

In the next instant Escarlata's sisters were swallowed by the dark.

Chapter Forty-Three

Esme's Chaos churned, storming from her in a burst of light.

The monster stretched open its endless mouth, consuming her magic as if it was nothing.

Esme felt the weight of the pain and agony and grief that had created the Malvada. She stumbled, choking on the darkness.

The air filled with a thick smoke, burning her eyes and nose and skin.

Escarlata's limp form lay a short distance away. The blades were strewn across the ground.

Esme dived for them, coming up short and crawling the last inches.

The Malvada gripped her ankles.

She spun onto her back to see the darkness wrapping itself

up her leg, twisting itself around her body, climbing toward her throat. Pulsing and reaching like it wanted inside her. Esme kicked wildly, refusing to give the monster a body to possess.

The darkness clutched her throat, squeezing tighter and tighter, forcing her to open her mouth.

No!

She clenched her jaw. Her vision dimmed. Her body felt like it might float up and away.

That was when something erupted inside Esme. A hot sensation coursed through her veins, growing and building until her Earth magic exploded out of her in a blast of power. The Malvada screamed, falling back.

The ground shook violently, rupturing in a storm of dirt, forming a narrow chasm that momentarily separated her from the monster.

There was a breath of a moment as the Malvada and the Chaos witch stared into one another's eyes, each daring the other to make the first move.

The beast surged forward, wild-eyed. The force of it knocked Esme off her feet and to the ground with a hard *thump*.

The air was knocked out of her, leaving her gasping.

She turned just in time to see the monstruo soaring toward the daggers, its shrieks reverberating through Esme's bones.

No!

Esme no longer felt the exhaustion in her body. She felt only the memory of her mother, of her hands through her hair, of her words on her skin: *Someday you will harness all that power.*

Esme hadn't come this far to fail.

She jumped up and thrust out her hands. Hot winds and rain ripped across the landscape. A million jolts of electricity moved through her, shaking her body with the power of Chaos.

The monster gnashed its teeth, barreling ahead with ferocious determination.

It was inches from the daggers.

Esme pounded a fist into the earth. Instantly, the ground erupted, throwing the blades into the air. They spun over the monster's head, whipping across the winds and through the rain.

The Malvada reached a long, skinny limb up and up.

Esme vaulted herself into the air—reaching, stretching, hoping.

She caught one, two daggers. The others fell to the ground as Esme landed with a stumble several feet away.

She could feel the heat of the Malvada, the weight of its darkness drawing nearer and nearer.

With one last heave, Esme threw herself onto all four daggers and spun onto her back.

The Malvada flew at her, bigger, faster than before, its mouth a gaping black hole of terror.

Esme united the blades with a clash.

And just as the beast reached her, Esme drove the dagger into the Malvada's heart.

A million screams rose up.

The Malvada writhed and twisted, and then it broke apart into a million bits of ash that floated up and away into the night sky.

Esme dropped the dagger and fell to her knees, trying to catch her breath.

"Esme?"

She looked up.

Gisele, Lucinda, and Triana were near the tree line. All three were covered in soot.

"Is it gone?" Esme croaked.

Triana nodded as the sisters rushed to Escarlata, who was stirring awake, getting to her feet. She clung to her sisters, crying. "I'm so sorry. I'm so sorry."

After a moment, they separated and Escarlata turned to Esme.

"They didn't betray you," Esme whispered.

Triana crept closer. "It's my fault. I chose this path for us all when I agreed to the god's terms to save our lives."

"And I kept your secret," Lucinda said to Escarlata. "I never told a soul that it was your fury that created the magic."

Gisele said, "I was the one to dare my sisters to kiss the god. The one who looked for him for years, calling on him in every dark hour to convince him to set us free of the daggers. But . . ."

"You never found him," Escarlata uttered. "I thought . . . I thought you were trying to save yourself."

"That's because you couldn't see past the darkness," Lucinda put in.

Escarlata shook her head. "I went to the Place of Agonized Souls so that I could get rid of the memories, but instead I . . . found solace in the pain and suffering. I found power in the grief and before I knew it, it consumed me. It convinced me that you had all betrayed me." Tears filled her eyes. "How can you ever forgive me?"

"We already have," Gisele said gently.

Esme felt warm tears prick her eyes. She was happy to see the sisters reunite, but it only reminded her of her own longing to hug Lenny. She was almost afraid to ask. "What about my family?"

Escarlata smiled softly. "They are already free."

Esme's tears fell now, from all the hope she had held on to so tightly that she could finally let go. "How?"

"When you killed the Malvada," Escarlata said, collecting the fused daggers from the ground, "it released its hold on them too, including your father. Now that its curse is no longer a part of him, you will find him quite healed."

Esme wanted to run home that very second, but she still had to know. "What about the magic that was drained from the witches?"

Escarlata hesitated. "I'm sorry, Esme, but some have lost their magic forever. They were too weak and the darkness was too powerful."

Esme's insides went cold. "You have to fix it!"

Escarlata shook her head. "I don't have the power to do that."

"You can use the daggers. They have the powers of a god!"

"It wouldn't work," Triana said. "And it could have unintended consequences—dark consequences."

Esme felt nauseous.

Escarlata said, "I know it is too much to ask, but someday I hope you can forgive me."

Esme thought of her dad. She had seen firsthand the way pain and grief could drive someone to a terrible dark place that swallowed them up. There was more power in love than in hate. "I . . . I do forgive you," she said.

"You saved us," Lucinda said to Esme. "And we will be forever grateful."

"What will happen to you now?" Esme asked.

Escarlata raised the daggers. "This time we will create a single realm where we can live together happily and in peace."

"But what about the daggers?" Esme asked. "People will still come for them."

Triana said, "I have an idea. I'm not sure it will work, but . . ."

Everyone turned to her.

With a sly smile she said, "Give me a bit more time before I share."

As the sisters began to walk away, Escarlata joined them.

Triana looked over her shoulder at Esme. "Your Earth magic is powerful. Use it wisely."

And then they vanished into the trees.

Chapter Forty-Four

Esme ran all the way home, across the bridge, through the stone tunnel, skirting the edges of town for fear of being seen, of having to explain, of being asked questions about why she and Tiago hadn't been trapped in Oblivion.

What had everyone been told? What did they know?

Some have lost their magic.

The idea made her sick.

As Esme rounded the corner of her block, she skidded to a halt.

Color. There was so much color. It was in the hydrangeas and oak and jacaranda trees. The houses were restored, maybe even fresher than before.

Her heart expanded as she raced through the shadowed streets. The sky was already lightening, turning a pale grayish pink as she ran into her not-dilapidated house.

There was a creak, a groan, the sounds of a house waiting for someone to come home. And then shuffling in her dad's study.

Esme hurried to the study, slip-sliding as she threw open both doors.

Fetch turned from the pristine bookcase to face her. It was as if no dark force had ever touched this room. "You've got some great books here," he said.

She stopped short, catching her breath. "Is my family home yet?"

He shook his head.

"And Tiago?"

"He said he had to get home. He received a message that his mom was safe." Fetch smiled gently. "That means you succeeded."

Esme ran toward her friend and wrapped him in a tight hug.

The fox coughed. "You're wrinkling my coat."

"I don't care," Esme said, squeezing even tighter.

A small laugh bubbled out of him, and his paws went around her waist for a brief moment before he pulled back and said, "Are you going to tell me what happened?"

Esme wiped a tear she hadn't felt leak out. She collapsed onto the leather sofa and told him the entire tale, from the second she'd gone into the Place of Agonized Souls to her return home.

Fetch nodded every so often, stroking his chin. And when

she was done, he simply said, "Astounding. So the Malvada was created by all the grief and agony . . ."

"And Escarlata's own pain."

Fetch said, "The monster, it's gone?"

Esme nodded and got to her feet. "We couldn't have done any of it without you and your magical coats! You saved me so many times," she blubbered, "and you held the portal open and . . ." She took a shaky breath. "You didn't break your curse. It's not fair!"

Fetch stuffed his paws into his coat pockets. "Nothing is ever fair, Esme."

Like losing your sister.

"You're going to look for her, aren't you?" she asked.

"If I do, I'll be killed."

Esme took a deep breath. "But you'll risk it."

Fetch bowed his head and went silent for a few beats before looking up at Esme.

"Like you did."

Esme said, "Can you tell me her name?"

"Names have no meaning, remember?"

Esme tucked a curl behind her ear. "They do to the people who love them."

Fetch hesitated, then softly he said, "Violet. Her name's Violet."

"I hope you find Violet."

Fetch gestured to Esme's coat. "You can keep it."

"Really?"

"To remember me."

She'd never forget the cursed fox, who once upon a time didn't have a heartbeat.

A thick lump formed in her throat, and she could barely get the words out. "I don't want you to go."

Fetch gave a small smile and glanced at his pocket watch. "Walk me out?"

Esme and Fetch strolled into the front yard, where the sun was peeking over the horizon. They stood beneath the mesquite tree. Somewhere in the distance, a dog barked.

"I'm glad everything worked out for you," he said. "You deserve it."

"Will I see you again?"

The fox's shoulders slumped, and his eyes softened. "The gates of Ocho Manos will always be open to you." His voice held a hint of sadness, yet he also seemed content. As if he knew he'd see Esme again.

Esme took his soft paw and squeezed tight. She had so much to say but couldn't find the right words. "You pledged yourself to me," she said, "and now, well, we don't have anything like a bow in this world, but . . . if you ever need anything—"

His mouth curved into a crooked smile. "Are you pledging yourself to me?"

"I just mean if you need help with—" Esme stopped short. "Yes."

Fetch plucked a flower from her hair. "If I'm ever in a dire situation where the world is going to end, I will definitely call."

He turned to go. Esme grabbed his arm and spun him back around. Then she reached up and kissed his cheek. "I'll never forget you."

His dark eyes shimmered a brilliant gold. "I know."

He turned and walked down the road, into the pink morning light. The fox's coat fluttered once, twice.

And then he was gone.

Chapter Forty-Five

After Fetch left, Esme went back inside the house.

The waiting was agony, but so was Esme's exhaustion. Before she knew it, she had collapsed onto the sofa, where she fell fast asleep.

And she dreamed.

She stood on the bank of Río Místico. The sun was high, its light dancing across the water's surface like glitter.

"Hello, Esme," Triana said as she emerged from the trees. "I've come to tell you my solution for the daggers."

She reached into her dress pocket and removed a small gray river stone, plain and smooth.

"What is it?" Esme asked, confused, as she took the rock from the witch.

"The daggers, hidden in plain sight." Triana beamed proudly.

"Cool. But . . . why didn't you do this before?"

"Only the power of love and forgiveness and truth allowed us to do this. It is no easy thing to change the magic of a god into another form."

Esme nodded, staring at the stone. "What am I supposed to do with it?"

"Take it to the river and bury it using your magic," Triana said. "The earth will hide and protect it as long as you never break the spell."

"But what if someone else does?"

"No one will have the power except for you. That's why we are asking you to do it. We trust you." Triana smiled. "Will you agree?"

"Of course, but Lucinda said dream things weren't meant for this world."

"This is no dream thing, and besides, the daggers originally came the real world." Triana gazed across the river and exhaled. "Our realm is so beautiful. Buster and Leonard are quite happy there."

Esme was glad to know that the giant owls weren't in a forever sleep in a dying realm. "Tell them hi for me."

Triana nodded and said, "Good luck, Esme."

Esme woke with a start.

She glanced down. And there in her hand was the most powerful stone in the universe.

Chapter Forty-Six

With a yawn, Esme began to straighten the pillows on the sofa. She was just about to hunt down some food in the kitchen when familiar voices carried from the garden.

Lenny!

Esme raced outside to find Lenny and Dad sitting at the long wooden table, talking. The roses were in full bloom, fragrant and colorful.

Everything happened so fast, Esme didn't know who reached for who first, who hugged the tightest, who cried the hardest.

When they finally broke apart, Lenny's gaze fell to Esme's hand.

"I lost your ring," Esme admitted. "Traded it away. I had to . . ."

Lenny hugged Esme again. The scent of strawberry shampoo lingered in her hair. "I know you must have had a good reason."

Esme clung to her sister, grateful she wasn't angry.

When they broke apart, Esme studied her dad. She exhaled in relief as she noticed the color in his cheeks, the brightness of his eyes.

"He told me everything," Lenny said, not letting go of Esme's hand.

Siempre shook his head. "I will never forgive myself."

"You have to, Dad," Esme said. "You were under a spell." The darkness that had poured into this world was how Escarlata had possessed him, how he had unknowingly invited her in.

"But I put us all in such danger. My . . . Chaos."

"Why didn't you ever tell me?" Esme asked. "That *my* Chaos came from you?"

"Your mom and I thought we were protecting you. If the Witch Council had found out . . ."

Lenny rolled her eyes. "Well, they're all for your magic now, Esme."

"How do you know?" Esme asked.

Lenny's eyes flicked to Siempre's, then back to Esme. "Because it's what saved them. *You* saved them."

Esme still couldn't understand how so much had happened so quickly. When she asked about the logic of it, Lenny smiled. "You've been out for two days."

"Two days! No! I just went to sleep."

Siempre said, "Your magic needed time to restore itself."

Which reminded Esme. "Do you have your Water magic, Lenny?"

Lenny nodded.

Esme released a long breath. She had so many questions, she didn't know where to begin. "Did you write the note with the riddle?"

"No. I found it under the desk in Dad's office."

Siempre said, "I wrote it and put it there the night I left. The part of me that was fighting the spell was hoping one of you would find the note and begin to put the clues together."

Lenny tucked a lock of red hair behind her ear. "I was puzzling over it when I heard someone in the house. It was so dark. The next thing I knew, a shadowed figure came at me. He blew ashes into my face." She shuddered. "I couldn't see a thing, but I used my Water magic to reveal that it was Aguilar. I could tell he wasn't himself."

"Escarlata spelled him too," Esme guessed.

"I did," Siempre said, lowering his gaze. "I think a part of me couldn't bear to send Lenny to Oblivion, and I stupidly thought if someone else did it I could wash my hands of the deed."

"I warned Aguilar to get out," Lenny went on, "but I felt a terrible pain in my stomach and knew I'd been cursed. I held on for as long as I could, Esme. I used every spell I knew, trying to wait for you, so that I could warn you." A faint smile appeared on her trembling lips. "I hid the note, thinking you were never going to come, but then I saw you in the street and I knew that I had to unspell your magic if you were going to have any chance of surviving and finding us."

"But the dagger," Esme said. "It couldn't have been an original and yet it looked so real."

"I was trying to show you what to look for."

"But how did you know?"

"It was the one word I understood in the note." She looked at Siempre. "And earlier that night Dad had told me to find the daggers. I thought he was just being weird, but—"

"There were brief moments," Siempre put in, "when I tried to break through the spell." He took Esme's hand and gave it a squeeze.

Esme suddenly felt exhausted, as though she'd been run over by an eighteen-wheeler. "There is one more thing." Siempre stood and began to pace. "Some of the witches," he began, "well, their magic was entirely drained from Oblivion and . . . it was my fault and—"

"Escarlata told me," Esme said. "It's really awful."

"But now no one is without their powers," Lenny said.

Esme wasn't sure she'd heard her sister right. "What?"

Lenny's eyes flicked to their dad's.

"I used my Chaos," Siempre admitted, "to give them back their magic."

Esme's stomach tilted. "How?"

"Only a Chaos witch could do it," Lenny said.

"Each element courses in our blood," Siempre added. "Mine could someday lead me back to the dark, and I never want to hurt you again."

Esme jumped up and threw her arms around her father's neck. He held her tight as Lenny wrapped them both up in a hug. Esme understood his need to make amends, to sacrifice something in order to feel whole.

And maybe now they could all feel whole. Together.

Chapter Forty-Seven

"I don't see why I have to wear this dumb suit," Tiago said, straightening his blue-and-gold tie.

He and Esme stood outside the giant wooden gates of Malu's house. Music filled the air. "Because it's a big party, and you know how strict Malu is."

Esme pressed her hands to the green dress she'd put on over her swimsuit. Her stomach fluttered nervously.

A week had passed and this would be the first time she'd face the town's witches since everything had happened. The council wanted to celebrate and said that they had a surprise for her and Tiago, which to be honest didn't sound so great. The last time they'd gotten a "surprise" from the council, it was a box of almonds that tasted like glue.

Esme opened the gates to an oasis of perfectly trimmed

grass and palm trees. A waterfall spilled into the gold-bottomed pool, which glistened in the waning sun. Everyone stood around drinking and laughing and talking.

A stage had been set up nearby, where a band played a jazzy tune.

"There they are!" Malu said, sauntering over in a floral jumpsuit and wide-brimmed hat. The band stopped playing.

Everyone turned. Lenny and Efrain waved at Esme from the corner where they were hanging out with Siempre.

Malu took Esme and Tiago each by the hand, leading them up to the stage.

She leaned into the microphone. "Our young heroes," she said.

The crowd erupted in applause.

Esme's cheeks warmed.

"This is the worst," Tiago said out of the side of his mouth.

Malu began a lengthy speech about magic and gratitude and risk as she relived all the horrid details of Oblivion. Esme only half paid attention. Her mind wandered to what she had to do after the fiesta.

She gripped the stone in her pocket, rubbing its soft edges.

"And tonight," Malu said, finally taking a breath, "Chaos magic will have a new name."

Esme snapped her attention to the witch.

"No longer something to be feared," Malu said, tugging her hat back.

Esme held her breath.

"But something to be celebrated, honored," Malu went on. "From here on out, all Chaos witches will be known as Lumbras. Witches of Light."

Esme's heart swelled as the crowd applauded.

"And as a symbol of our thanks," Malu said, "we have a gift for each of you." She reached behind the drummer for two shoeboxes and handed one to Tiago and one to Esme.

"You first," Tiago said.

Esme fought the urge to roll her eyes. She lifted the lid. Inside was a small spell book titled *A Beginner's Guide to Brujería*.

"A reminder of your roots," Malu said, beaming. "And it's signed by the entire council."

"Thanks," Esme said, not having the heart to tell Malu that she didn't need spells.

"Yeah, thanks," Tiago said, peering into his box to find a thinner book titled *Air Spells 101*. His frozen smile was enough to send Esme into a fit of laughter, but she somehow held it together.

"One last thing before you scamper off," Malu said. "Tell us. Did you truly hold the Daggers of Ire?"

Esme cleared her throat, hoping she didn't look as guilty as she felt. "Yes."

People began to shout questions.

What did they look like?

What did they feel like?

Tell us about the original witches.

"Enough!" Siempre shouted to the crowd. "The council has the entire written report." His scowl was quickly replaced by a winning smile. "I thought this was a celebration, not an inquisition."

Malu harrumphed. "It is, but there is one odd thing in the report." She turned to Esme, her eyes glittering greedily. "You said that the daggers were destroyed."

Esme felt the sudden weight of the stone in her pocket. "That's right."

"Blown to smithereens," Tiago added confidently.

"Such a shame," Malu murmured. Then she forced a wide smile, showing off her horsey teeth. "Let us get back to the celebration!"

An hour later, after the sun had set, Esme and Tiago slipped out, climbing over the back wall so no one would see them leave.

They ran all the way to the river.

Esme kicked off her shoes and plopped down. Tiago sat next to her, tugging off his jacket and tie before taking off his shoes and socks. "*A Beginner's Guide*? So boring."

"I'm sure she thought she was helping."

"Yeah, right. Malu hates the idea of anyone having more power than she does." He fanned open his book. "Mine's for Air witches, but look—not a single invisibility spell."

"That's because it's illegal."

Tiago grunted.

A beam of moonlight shone across the water's surface.

"Are you sure you know what to do?" Tiago asked.

"Not exactly."

"Oh, okay. No pressure that you're burying the most powerful object in the universe that's been made to look like a rock. Cool."

"Tiago."

"Okay. Okay. How can I help?"

"Just . . . don't talk."

Esme stared at the rock in her palm. Then she lifted her finger and twirled it in a circular motion. The sand shifted, and soon a hole opened in the earth, wider and wider, deeper and deeper.

She turned to Tiago. "Swear that you'll never tell anyone about the stone, never reveal its location."

"I swear."

"Even if it means death."

"You're so dramatic."

"Say it."

He rolled his eyes. "Fine, even if it means death."

She dropped the stone inside the deep hole. The earth closed up with a hush.

"Is that it?" Tiago asked.

Esme nodded. "I think so."

Tiago stood and stripped down to his swimming trunks. He took a deep breath, closed his eyes, and clenched his fists.

"What are you doing?"

"Breaking the law." He smiled and said, "Invisibilis."

Straightaway, Tiago faded to nothing more than a fuzzy outline of himself.

"Oh my god! You learned invisibility!"

"Not exactly," he said. "It only lasts a minute, but I'm getting closer."

He stepped back and then, with a running start, he cannonballed into the river. "Woot!"

Esme laughed, tugged off her dress, and dove into the cool water.

A splash hit her in the face from nowhere. Esme floated a hand over the water, spinning it into a wave that rose higher and higher.

"Don't even think about it!" Tiago shouted.

Esme flung the water at him.

Tiago materialized a few yards ahead of her, shaking water from his hair, laughing. "Race you to that tree." He took off, with Esme right behind him.

As she sped through the waters, she felt free, as if everything was right in the world. She was safe. Her family was safe.

And, finally, the daggers were safe too.

Epilogue

Like all sinister stories, this one ends with a dash of foreboding and a dusting of nightmare.

For while the witches celebrated, and while Esme and Tiago raced across the river without a care, a broken darkness was simmering, searching for a home. It reached into the farthest corners of this world, never quite finding what it was looking for. Until—

It discovered Ocho Manos.

A banished realm where *forbidden* magic runs wild.

Where a certain fox, cursed and alone, was leaning over his worktable.

The Malvada watched from the corner, sensing the fox's dark curse as he stitched a coat with magical threads, dreaming of a new life and of finding out the truth about his sister.

Dreams are for the weak, the Malvada thought eagerly, perhaps a bit too loudly, for in that moment the fox sensed something. He lifted his eyes to see nothing there.

And yet he could sense he was not alone.

The Malvada drew closer, grinning. . . .

Your new life isn't going to be what you expect, little fox.

It is going to be so much worse.

Acknowledgments

The idea for this book came to me when I imagined a girl who grew flowers in her hair. Next came a stubborn, loyal boy, and a mysterious fox who possessed a special brand of magic as well as a mountain of secrets. And so, *The Daggers of Ire* was born.

But no book is born without the talent, determination, and absolute dedication of so many people.

I'd like to thank my agent, Holly Root, who possesses not only wicked talent, but a rare brand of magic all her own.

To my editor, Kristin Rens: A million thanks for seeing the power of this story, for championing it so fiercely, and for being sheer brilliance from start to finish.

To the entire HarperCollins/Balzer + Bray team: Joel Tippie in design, Erika West and Mary Magrisso in copyediting and managing editorial, Sean Cavanagh and Vanessa Nuttry in production, Sabrina Abballe in marketing, Sammy Brown in publicity, Christian Vega in editorial, Kerry Moynagh and team in sales, and Patty Rosati, Mimi Rankin, and team in school and library marketing. I am so grateful to each of you for all the energy and imagination you've brought to this book.

An enormous thank-you to Brittani Hilles, publicist extraordinaire, whose single-minded determination is unparalleled. I'm so grateful to have you on my team! And speaking of the team, it began with one: Sarah Simpson-Weiss. I truly couldn't do what I do without your oversight, organization, and true care. Thank you!

And of course, no book would come to life without my amazing friends and early readers: Janet, Loretta, Alex, and Rosh. You're all brujas!

I also want to thank my family. Without you, I wouldn't be who I am. It's your light and love that always carries me through. To my mom for reading everything I write and loving it no matter what version it is. And to Joe for always being willing to go on another adventure, no questions asked. I love that about you.

And finally, to Alex, Bella, and Jules. You are the inspiration for everything I create. More than anything I hope that each story I write leaves you a rich legacy of love and magic.